MW01092506

The Frogman
Of
Cedar Creek

Jim Willi

The Frogman of Cedar Creek
Jim Willi
Copyright 2020

Published by
Newsdoc Publishing

Acknowledgements

I'd like to thank the many people who have offered en-couragement, ideas and suggestions on my first novel. This book wouldn't have been published without the guidance and expertise of Dee Dees. The cover artwork is from the very talented Amanda Potter.

1

The noisy, lightning-filled thunderstorms have passed on to the east, and a fiery sunset has tucked itself into the western horizon across Cedar Creek Lake. The quarter moon sends a sliver of sparkling light onto the gently rolling water.

It's a Tuesday night so the lake, about an hour east of Dallas, is a peaceful place. A solitary figure sits in his battered fiberglass boat, about fifty yards offshore, surrounded by darkness except for the spotlight shining off a nearby dock into the water below.

For the last ten minutes, he's been casting and working his Rattle-Trap, hoping to entice a big hybrid striped bass into latching on to the shiny, silver and blue lure. He casts again, and it plunks into the water, floats toward the bottom, and then the fisherman reels it back in at a pretty good pace.

The lure, with its six razor-sharp hooks makes noise as it flashes through the hazy water, its chrome finish designed to catch the eye of a big, hungry bass.

With a sudden thud, a hybrid bass grabs the shiny lure and heads in the other direction. With practiced skill, the fisherman whips the rod upward, setting the hooks into the soft flesh around the fish's mouth, and prepares for the short, exciting fight to follow.

In the heat of battle, the fisherman never notices a slight ripple in the murky water just behind his bobbing runabout. He isn't the only one on this side of the lake tonight. Air bubbles are popping the surface a few feet behind the boat.

The fisherman is focused on his prey. He had fought these mini battles many times before, so he patiently plays the fish. He has to wear him out because these hybrid bass are big and strong and really get spooked when they get close enough to see the boat. The sighting makes them dart away again, fighting with all their might against the hooks and the line that is keeping them from escaping with their lives. Finally, the fish tires, and the fisherman yanks him into the boat.

Suddenly someone grabs the fisherman by the back of his gray flannel shirt and lifts him expertly out of the boat and soundlessly carries him under the water, all in one quick motion. In a flash he disappears into the dark, chilly water. The intruder holds the fisherman's arms to his side and wraps his legs around the startled man's legs. There is no struggle. The fisherman is in a vice grip so tight it's as if he were encased in cement.

After a few minutes, the fisherman's lungs fill with water, and he sinks to the bottom, in only about fifteen feet of water. The killer remains underwater, and quietly, calmly swims away into the darkness with just a few bubbles to mark his exit.

2

More than half the residents of Cedar Creek Lake are "weekenders." They make their big bucks in Dallas during the week, and escape to the lake on the weekend. Since this is a Tuesday night, most every lake house along the shoreline is dark and deserted.

The only sound is the bass flopping around inside the boat, struggling to breathe. The fisherman has already taken his last breath.

The wind picked up during the night as the cold front came through the lake area, just as the Dallas TV weathermen had promised. Rainy winds, whipping along at 20 miles an hour, pushed the dead fisherman's runabout out toward the middle of the lake, about a mile from where he had been murdered.

A fishing guide on a morning excursion with his client, discovered the drifting boat and called the Coast Guard Auxiliary on his cell phone. The guide tied the battered runabout to his sleek black bass boat and waited for the Coast Guard volunteer to arrive. When his client asked what happened, the guide explained that with the strong winds overnight the boat most likely broke free from a nearby dock and drifted out into the lake.

Tommy Smith was nearly 70 years old with a shock of thick white hair, and the weathered face of a lifelong boater and fisherman. He

3

was one of a handful of fulltime lake residents who volunteered to help boaters in distress through the Coast Guard Auxiliary. Tommy pulled up to the guide's bass boat about fifteen minutes after getting the call. The Coast Guard Auxiliary flag fluttered in the light breeze, as the ancient, but carefully cared for, 24-foot Chris Craft wooden speedboat neared.

The deep-throated chugging, of the Chris Craft's powerful inboard engine, echoed across the lake as the volunteer expertly guided the wooden beauty with the deep, glossy shine next to the bass boat. The guide shouted a "hey" and held Tommy's boat next to his own bass boat.

"Hey, Billy, how's it going?" Tommy asked the well-known fishing guide.

"Well, we got a couple of nice sized sand bass in the live well, but this is the biggest catch of the day," the guide chuckled, as he hooked the rope up to Tommy's boat. His client was getting itchy to resume their search for big bass.

Tommy recognized the battered boat that the guide had found floating out here in the middle of the lake. He had helped the owner just a few weeks ago when he ran out of gas, at night, just as a storm moved in. The guy had been lucky that Tommy was nearby when it happened, trying to get back to his own lakeside home before the waves really kicked up.

The guide asked, "Tommy, you know who belongs to this old scow?"

"Don't rightly recall the feller's name," answered Tommy, "But I do remember that the feller was half-drunk and damned obnoxious, didn't even say thank you when I helped him out a little while ago." It briefly crossed Tommy's mind that maybe the crazy bastard had had one too many and had tumbled out of the boat.

"Yah suppose it just drifted away from the dock in the storm last night," Billy surmised to the Coast Guard volunteer.

Tommy replied, "Sure hope so, otherwise we might have a drowning on our hands. But I reckon it just broke loose during the night. If I had a dollar for every time that happened over the last 15 years, I'd be in Vegas yankin' on them one-armed bandits, instead of wastin' my time pickin' up floating trash all over this lake."

Tommy slowly towed the empty boat to Wesley's Marina, just across the channel from Tommy's lake home. He used the boat registration, which had expired a year ago, to get the name of the owner. His name was Claude Young and he lived on the other side of the lake.

Tommy looked up Claude Young's phone number and gave it a call. No one answered. That wasn't unusual, maybe he was a weekender, or maybe he worked during the day.

3

When Crystal, the bartender, showed up to open Wesley's Marina Bar and Grill at eleven that morning, she saw Tommy down by the pier. She stopped down to say hello.

Tommy appreciated that. Crystal Disborn, a short, but shapely brunette was looking mighty fine in her white short shorts and green halter-top with the marina logo on it. Tommy told her the story about the drifting boat, and his attempt to reach its owner, a guy named Claude Young.

Crystal furrowed her brow a bit, and then replied, "I know that guy. He doesn't have a job. He spends his afternoons drinking beer, and his nights fishing."

She told Tommy that Claude should be stopping by around noon for lunch, and to start his daily elbow bending at the bar. Tommy had a lemonade and waited.

He related to Crystal how he'd rescued the guy from the lake as a storm moved in a week or so ago. "Seemed like he'd had enough to drink that day," Tommy told her, "He was an ornery cuss fer sure."

Crystal chuckled at that one. "You should be sitting here with him after he's been tippin' the Budweiser for a few hours," she said, "He'll start an argument in a New York minute. He can really piss off some of the regulars with his crazy theories and arguments."

Tommy asked her if she'd seem him recently. "Oh yeah," Crystal nodded her pretty head, "He was here all afternoon yesterday. Had to kick his butt out the door so I could lock up."

"Was he drunk?"

"Nah, no more than usual," Crystal said, "He can hold his beer, that's for sure. Ole Clyde told me he was heading out to get some big bass. Said they'd be hittin' good because a front was coming in."

Crystal filled Tommy's glass with some more of the delicious homemade lemonade, and they waited until about two o'clock. A dozen or so customers drifted in for lunch or a cold brew. Claude Young never showed up.

At about that same time, a few miles away, on the other side of the lake, Jim Plinkton, longtime president of the Lakeside Homeowner's Association drove by the members-only boat launch. Plinkton, who'd retired to the lake about twenty years ago, knew everybody in his community, and everyone seemed to know him. He was the kind of neighbor everyone wished for. Jim helped everybody with their projects at the drop of a hat. He was nearing 80, but he had the energy of a 50-year-old. He was a wiry, bald man who could still shimmy up a ladder in a few seconds. The old-timer spent his days picking up errant limbs and twigs in his yard that had been sent to the ground by strong winds from the many thunderstorms that struck from the west and rolled across the lake.

Plinkton shook his head in disgust as he drove into the boat launch area. The gate, which every member knew was supposed to be kept locked, stood wide open. He recognized Claude Young's car parked inside.

"Damn drunk," Jim mumbled to himself. He thought it was unusual that Young would be out fishing in the morning. Jim was well aware of Claude's schedule of drinking by day and fishing by night. He locked the gate and left.

When Plinkton got home, there was a message on his answering machine from the Gun Barrel City Police Department. The Coast Guard Auxiliary had found Claude Young's boat floating out in the middle of the lake. Did he know where Claude worked?

That message caused Plinkton to be concerned about the old drunk. He called the police, reporting that Young's car was parked at the boat launch – with no sign of Young anywhere. Plinkton related Claude's normal drinking and fishing schedule to the policeman on the other end of the phone line. As he talked, the thought crossed Plinkton's mind. Had Young fallen out of his boat and drowned?

The Henderson County Sheriff's office water patrol, along with the Coast Guard Auxiliary dragged the lake for three days. It was a primitive practice. They used big hooks and a thick rope trailing behind their boats, trolling the lake bottom for a human catch.

They concentrated on the area near the middle of the lake where the fishing guide had found the empty boat. The water was nearly thirty feet deep. They found nothing, and reluctantly called off the search. The sheriff's office tried to find relatives of Claude Young. They found none. He was truly a loner.

From interviews with Young's neighbors, Crystal, and some of the Marina customers the police pieced together information about the missing man's life. On the night he disappeared, he'd spent the afternoon at Wesley's Marina, drinking beer, and getting into arguments, at times, with some of the regulars. At closing time, around seven o'clock, Crystal had to practically push him out the door so she could go home.

After a quick pit stop on the way out the door, he'd slumped into his battered, rusting car and driven away. He'd had enough to drink, probably about dozen beers over the course of five or six hours, but Crystal didn't think he was drunk. She told the police, "That old goat can hold his beers."

Claude had apparently driven around the lake, and then wound his way through the maze of roads that surround his side of the lake, where a neighbor spotted him pulling into his gravel driveway, around 7:30 that night. The neighbor filled the police in on Young's life.

He was a 58-year-old retired Army officer who led a lonely existence. The neighbor related that she had never seen anyone visit Claude. His wife left him many hundreds of beers ago, and he lived alone in a rundown, singlewide trailer that was dented and dirty, tucked under a few scrubby Post Oak trees, about a mile from the lake. It was a dump. The neighbor said it was the best Claude could afford on his Army pension. When Claude first moved to Cedar Creek Lake, four years ago, he tried to get a place on the waterfront, but those places, even the ones with older trailer homes like Claude's, were beyond his means if they fronted the shoreline.

4

The Cedar Creek Lake Reservoir in East Texas stretches about 17 miles from the north to the south end and widens to a mile or so in stretches. The Army Corps Of Engineers flooded a valley in 1965 by building a dam on one end to create the lake. It is a pretty setting, with lots of trees and lake houses dotting the shoreline. The reservoir was built to send water to the city of Fort Worth, nearly 90 miles away.

The lake is about an hour drive from Dallas, so it is a convenient weekend getaway. Those Dallasites had driven up the price of lakeside property over the years, relegating many of the fulltime locals, like Claude, to less expensive lots without a lake view, since it was the best they could afford.

The neighbor said that Claude sleeps all morning, and drinks beer all afternoon at Wesley's Marina, or in Gun Barrel City at Jake's Pub. His routine seldom changed, including his nightly tour of the lake searching for hybrid striped bass, and what locals call sand bass.

The Texas sun is relentless from late April until early October. That's why many anglers prefer night fishing. It's cooler and the fish are hungry and more active.

The neighbor told police that on Tuesday night, she'd seen Claude back his car up to his boat trailer, and hook it up for, what she guessed was his normal quick trip to the nearby boat launch.

The police found a resident who lived next to the boat launch who had seen Claude back his trailer into the shallow water and float the boat to the pier where he tied it off. Then Claude had driven his car onto a grassy parking spot a few yards away and headed out on the lake. The boat launch neighbor thought that he'd disappeared into the darkness of the deserted lake about eight o'clock that night. The car was still parked in that spot when Plinkton spotted it the next morning.

The fifth day after the boat was discovered, a Monday, a fisherman was trolling for sand bass about a hundred yards out from the members-only boat launch when his fishing pole nearly snapped in half. The fisherman quickly reversed his pontoon boat's motor and worked to get the snag free. After several minutes without any luck, he yanked on the pole, and it came free.

He reeled in the hook and found a large piece of cloth attached. It looked like part of a flannel shirt. He had heard about the missing fisherman and wondered if it could be him down below in the water, water too murky to see anything below the surface. The man called the sheriff from his cell phone.

Police converged on the waterfront near the boat launch and dragged that area. A sheriff's boat soon pulled out the waterlogged body of Claude Young.

5

Dwayne Murphy, the intrepid, some would describe him as "the pain in the ass," reporter for the *Cedar Creek Gazette,* heard the call on his police scanner. They'd apparently found the missing fisherman. Murphy headed to the boat launch.

The *Gazette* was a low circulation weekly newspaper located in Gun Barrel City, a city of about 6,000 people that bordered the lake. Construction of the lake in the mid-60's had caused the sleepy city to grow.

Only 60 people lived there in 1970, about five years after the lake was built, when they voted to incorporate as a city. The city fathers pushed incorporation so it would be legal, under Texas law, to sell beer to all the tourists flocking to the lake on summer weekends.

The unusual name came from Gun Barrel Lane, which has now become State Highway 198. It was a straight shot, like a gun barrel, between two other larger towns in the area.

Now, Gun Barrel City was hopping. There was even a big Lowe's store opening up. It was an event that was listed as the top local story of the year in the *Gazette's* annual year-end edition.

Dwayne Murphy, an average looking guy with a crooked nose, caused by his smart mouth and someone's wicked punch, a crew cut, long brown sideburns, and a slight build, had grown up in Seven Points, a small town with just one stop light, and about a 15-

hundred residents, across the lake from Gun Barrel City. He was quite a character.

Murphy was single, 39 years old, a non-stop talker, and convinced that he was God's gift to journalism. Unfortunately, no one else saw it that way.

For 15 years Murphy had been toiling for the *Gazette*, trying desperately during that entire time to get a job with the two big city papers to the west – the *Dallas Morning News*, and the *Fort Worth Star-Telegram*. He could have papered a 4,000 square foot home with the rejection letters from the two newspapers. But he forged on, undaunted.

Murphy, a likable enough goofball, spends his time hanging out with all the local cops, lawyers, and courthouse workers, always on the prowl for that big, juicy story that will earn him a spot at one of the big city behemoths. His tendency to exaggerate in his stories, keeps his editor, Busby Chambers, who also owns the *Gazette*, ever vigilant when it comes to checking the facts in Murphy's work.

Unlike many of the Cedar Creek Lake residents, both full and part-time, Murphy hates to fish. He thinks it is the dumbest waste of time, and extremely boring. Instead of trolling for fish, Murphy prefers to build lightning-fast race boats, with big, blown engines that skim across the lake at a hundred miles an hour. He believes these water rockets will help get dates with attractive women. Unfortunately, his luck on that front is on a par with his luck getting a big city newspaper gig.

So, soon after the sheriff's crew snagged Young's body, Murphy was standing on shore talking up the local cops who gathered there looking for a little excitement to spice up their usually sedate shifts. It didn't look like much of a story to Murphy.

There were quite a few drowning deaths in Cedar Creek Lake every year. Drinking was usually involved, and this one didn't look to be much different.

While they passed the time on shore, the cops regaled Murphy with stories about what a drunkard and obnoxious guy Young had been, according to the people they had spoken with during their investigation. Murphy knew that editor Chambers would frown on any mention of that in his story about the drowning.

The sheriff's deputies' cursory examination of the body showed no obvious signs of foul play – no broken bones, no gun-shot wounds, and the dead man's lungs were filled with water. They'd take the body to the Henderson County Medical Examiner for further examination, but it looked like a routine drowning from all the obvious signs.

Murphy, grumbling to himself, headed back to the office to write still another boring story of a local man who had drowned in Cedar Creek Lake. He knew that he wouldn't be sending this story to the Dallas and Fort Worth newspapers as an example of his ster-ling work.

Murphy did place a call to Mindy Reese, the hotshot crime reporter for Dallas TV station, WDFW to tell her about the routine drowning. In his heart, Murphy knew that he would also be a great television reporter, so he was trying to get an audition by feeding news to Mindy. He also was angling for a date with the pretty blonde local television star. So far, he had made no progress on either of those fronts.

6

It was a gorgeous Sunday, late in the afternoon, 13 days after Claude Young's body had been recovered from Cedar Creek Lake. The Henderson County Medical Examiner had taken a look at the body and listed the cause of death as accidental drowning. There was a small story in the *Gazette*, and other area newspapers.

60-year-old Red Hammond, a bespeckled loan officer at a bank in the Dallas suburb of Garland, was firing up the gas grill on his lakeside deck. He looked like an accountant, slight of build, short in stature, a serious demeanor, with thinning hair on the top of his pointy head. His wife, Amanda, was preparing the chicken for grilling, along with a small salad for each of them.

They'd celebrate their 40th wedding anniversary this October. Amanda, who stood an inch or two over five feet, had aged well. She still weighed the same 100 pounds that she had on her wedding day. Routine trips to the beauty parlor assured that no gray hairs protruded from her brunette coiffure.

The Hammond's had a beautiful home on the lake. It was a big two-story with lots of glass windows facing the lake, and plenty of decking to enjoy the view. They'd been weekenders for about 20 years, and this was their third lake home. Each one had increased in size, ambience and value. Their three kids had grown up at the lake, but now had moved on with families of their own.

Amanda, unlike her quiet, some said boring, husband, had a real gift of gab and was a very successful real estate broker in Dallas. She'd worked hard for two decades to build up a big clientele and was always the top producer in her office. After having to miss many of those weekends with the kids due to the nature of her job, she was enjoying her reduced schedule at the age of 59.

It always allowed her to spend her weekends with Red at the lake. She was even learning to be more tolerant of her nosy neighbor, Patsy Aarons. Patsy, a widow, lived at the lake fulltime, and was the self-appointed security alarm for the neighborhood.

"Hello dear," Amanda heard as she walked onto her deck to give Red the chicken for grilling.

"Hi, Patsy," she said, "How are you today?" then bit her lip. Amanda knew better than to ask that question, because, as expected, it opened the floodgates for Patsy to expound in great detail about her various aches and pains. Amanda as she always did, patiently listened to the litany.

Then Patsy asked Amanda her usual question, "When are you heading back to Dallas, dear?" Amanda said it would be Monday morning, as usual. They'd be leaving early enough for both of them to get to work on time. Patsy promised to keep an eye on the place for them in their absence.

Meantime, Red gazed out at the beauty of Cedar Creek Lake, as wispy smoke and cooking aroma, seeped out the sides of the gas grill's cover. He loved it here, so serene, especially when the other weekenders headed home in the late afternoon every Sunday.

Red had expertly grilled the chicken breasts, and dinner was ready. The Hammonds contently noshed as they relaxed on their deck, gazing at the peaceful, shimmering water under a cloud-free Texas sky. This was the most wonderful time of the year, the spring shoulder season between the cooler winter weather, and the searing heat of summer. A heat that sometimes became so unbearable that you'd have to retreat to air-conditioned shelter in the middle of the afternoon just to cool off a bit.

This was also the time of the year when huge thunderstorms could roll across the lake seemingly at a moment's notice. Cedar Creek was not a large lake by some standards, but scary storms could kick up with very little notice, packing thunder, lightning and high waves that could capsize small boats, and especially a small wooden canoe.

The Hammonds were avid canoeists, possibly the only couple on Cedar Creek Lake who loved this slow, primitive means of travel. Those loud, obnoxious Jet-Ski people were always zooming past them, trying to splash them with their machine's rooster tails and waves, and just generally being a pain in the ass.

That is why they cherished these Sunday evenings, and put up with the hassle of rising very early Monday morning to make the 80-minute drive to Dallas, getting snarled in rush hour traffic on the edge of the city.

Sunday evening was their time. The weekenders were scurrying back to the big city, leaving a tranquil, deserted lake behind.

So, while Amanda took care of the dishes, Red carefully peeled the canvas tarp off their beloved canoe and prepared to put it in the water. This was no fiberglass canoe. "No character in them," Red muttered to anyone who was within earshot. No sir, this was a highly polished wooden canoe, lovingly kept in gleaming, pristine condition by Red. Every winter he carefully sanded it down to bare wood, and spent hours putting a fresh coat of water-repellant stain on it.

Red gazed out at the lake and smiled, as he thought to himself, "The water is calm, now that those bastards on the speedboats and personal watercraft had gone home." Those loud machines churned up the water more than even the most powerful storms could do.

There had been talk on the Dallas TV newscasts about the possibility of some thunderstorms late tonight – probably after midnight. But that was normal for this time of year. Red would always say, "Those weather people are always trying to cover all their bases on those forecasts. They never really know what's going to happen."

It was about an hour before sunset as Red and Amanda pushed off from the dock and started paddling. Patsy waved at them from her deck. They both waved back. They were kneeling on the ribbed floor of the canoe, and half-sitting on their life vests to cushion themselves against the hard-wooden bar that was the only place to perch in the ancient vessel.

Red and Amanda were accomplished and generally safe canoe enthusiasts. They normally paddled along the shore, contentedly watching the ducks and other sights along the way as they plodded along. But they had grown a bit bored after years of that, and every spring vowed to take one trip across the lake and back as kind of a rite of the season. The roundtrip was a little more than two miles.

To Red's practiced eye, the weather seemed fine. The water was very calm, so they had decided that tonight was the night for that annual trek. While they both believed in water safety, they had, in recent years, spent the last half hour or so of their weekly trips in the dark, just because they enjoyed the tranquility of it all. Plus, if the truth be known, they also thought it was being a "little naughty" and made them feel like the risk-takers they were not.

The canoe quietly cut through the water as the Hammonds headed toward the slowly dropping sun on the west shore of the lake. They were like a two-person symphony, in perfect sync as they paddled along, smiling and enjoying themselves. There was not another soul on the lake, except for a large pontoon boat far in the distance, trolling along the shore for sand bass.

Red had estimated that the trip would take about 20 minutes each way, since he figured the canoe traveled along at about three miles an hour. He was good at math, he'd always say, "It's what I do for a living."

Since they had a good hour or so before it really got dark, they decided to head down the shoreline for a while before going for the opposite shore. It would also keep their journey from the prying eyes of their nosy neighbor, who always warned them of the danger of paddling in the dark.

As the Hammonds peacefully paddled across the lake, the sky began to darken a bit, not just from the setting sun, but also from gathering thunderheads off to the west. They didn't look too fore-boding though, and the sunset was absolutely phenomenal as the clouds made for an array of blue, red and gold colors, with shards of light from the sinking sun peeking through.

The Hammonds easily made it to the opposite shore in less than a half hour. They turned around without dawdling, and headed back with a little more urgency, as it was beginning to darken more quickly than Red had anticipated. The dark gray and black clouds were beginning to boil up and thicken.

They were very practiced in their cadence, and made it back across the lake just as the darkness really settled in. Amanda breathed a slight sigh of relief, while Red launched into his usual, annoying "I told you we'd have no problems" rant.

The sky was beginning to flash in the distance, loud thunder echoed across the deserted lake, and big raindrops started to fall, but they just had a short trip home and felt safe along the shoreline. Red and Amanda needed to go just about a quarter mile, around a point, and then they'd be home and could put the canoe back under the tarp before the storm hit.

Even though the lakeside homes were vacant tonight, most had automatic electric lights on their docks or walkways that turned on at dusk, whose glow helped reassure the Hammonds as they paddled on.

Intent on their mission and with a wary eye on the approaching storm, Red and Amanda skimmed past a dock without noticing the tiny air bubbles popping the surface near the end of the pier. This dock, unlike most of the others, was dead dark, in fact the nearest lighted dock was about 100 yards in the distance, just before the point.

Suddenly, without warning, the canoe capsized, and an unbelievably strong man was pulling them both underwater. Just like he had with Claude Young, the silent intruder easily clamped both of them in his iron-like arms and legs, so there would be no bruises, no signs of a struggle.

He had fought two or three men at once during his Navy Seal days, many times before, much stronger men. Amanda was very petite, and Red was a pencil pusher, with less than average strength. The suddenness of the attack had completely caught them off guard. They were easy prey.

The Hammonds were trying to scream, but their efforts just sent soundless bubbles out of their mouths, bubbles that went nowhere under the murky water. They could not move. It was if someone had paralyzed both of them. Only their eyes moved, darting back and forth, and growing wider as their lungs seared, out of air. Soon, they both fell limp, as the powerful scuba-clad killer held them motionless under the water. Tonight, would be the Hammond's last canoe trek on Cedar Creek Lake.

Meanwhile ten feet above them, on the surface, the water was churning and rolling as huge waves crashed into the docks. The wind howled as the storm attacked the lake. It was pitch black, except when the brilliant flashes of lightning zapped across the night sky. White-hot fingers of energy were accompanied by deafening thunder loudly echoing from one end of the lake to the other.

As the canoe, still upside down, bobbed and bounced in the broiling water, the scuba diver released his victims, and then silently, unseen, swam away. Once again there was not a witness in sight. The lake houses were all empty. There were no other boaters on the now dangerous water.

It was the perfect crime. The scuba diver had watched this lake neighborhood, and the Hammonds, for weeks to be sure of that.

About 150 yards away, around the point that blinded her to the crime that had just occurred, Patsy Aarons was worried to death. She always sat in her rocking chair on the deck, admiring the beautiful sunset, and waiting for the safe return of her canoeing neighbors. But right now, it was dark and stormy with wind-blown sheets of rain pelting her windows as she peeked out from safely inside her house. "Where are they?" she thought to herself.

The storm had moved in pretty quickly, and it was a nasty one. The waves, topped by surging white caps, were two to three feet high. Patsy worried that if her neighbors were still trying to paddle in it, their vessel would most likely be capsized.

Many scenarios went through Patsy's mind. Had they seen it coming and decided not to come back across the lake? Had they made it back to this side, and then gotten out of the water before the storm hit? Were they safely waiting it out on shore, or at someone's house? She knew they would not call her. They thought she was just a nosy old bitty.

Patsy continued to peer into the blinding rain and gusty winds, as the white-topped waves crashed into the shoreline with a powerful whoosh cascading four feet high off her metal seawall. The sudsy, angry water was spilling over onto her lawn with every rolling wave.

Suddenly something caught Patsy's eye during a lightning flash. Was it their canoe? Was it upside down?

She dashed into the house and grabbed the light her son had given her last Christmas. It was a powerful searchlight-like device that could scan the water for a long distance.

7

Henderson County Sheriff Josh "Buddy" King cupped his hands around a steaming cup of coffee at the Shell gas station in his hometown of Eustace as the storm hit. This little whistle stop on Highway 175 between Cedar Creek Lake and the city of Athens, is another of those towns with one stoplight, a gas station, and a few old businesses on a rundown main street.

In an odd twist, the highway doesn't bypass this little town, but goes right through it. That's where the lone stoplight comes into play. Motorists grumble about the light that interrupts their speedy trip down the rural state highway. When the irritating light turns green, they quickly head out of town, giving little thought to the rundown restaurant on the side of the road that inexplicably always has stacks of tennis shoes for sale on an outside table in the summer.

Like a lot of small towns in Texas, Eustace was spawned by the railroad. Folks started moving there when the Texas and New Orleans Railroad extended its line east from Athens toward the town of Kemp. The post office was established in 1900, the same year the town's name changed from Jolo to Eustace. It was named for Captain W.T. Eustace, a popular Civil War Confederate soldier, or as people hereabouts referred to it, the "the war of Northern aggression."

Josh King was a "townie." He'd grown up in Eustace, in fact he'd been a local high school hero. Josh "Buddy" King was one of the most popular kids in his Eustace High School class, and an all-state catcher on the school's baseball team.

That was a dozen years ago, followed by an all too brief stint in pro baseball. His career lasted just two years, as King made it only to the Double-A level. The rap on him was one that's been heard for decades, "The kid just can't hit the pro curve ball."

So, Buddy, an avid bass fisherman, retreated back to his hometown and took police training courses at the local community college. Two years later he joined the Eustace police department, becoming one of its four officers. After nearly a decade in that job, King, at the age of 32, had been elected Henderson County Sheriff just four months ago.

King was the youngest ever to hold that position in East Texas. He'd done it on a lark after his buddies dared him to give it a shot. King won the election in a landslide over the crusty old sheriff who'd held the job for a decade. Buddy was handsome with short blonde hair, a muscular build and a quick smile that lit up his chiseled face. The sheriff stood 6 foot three and kept his tight athletic build by working out every day. King had used that quick smile and "aw shucks" demeanor as he shook hundreds of hands during his campaign. Buddy King was still very much the local baseball hero to the people who lived in this rural area.

That's why when the storm hit tonight; Buddy King was having a cup of coffee and telling fishing lies with Eustace police officer Darren Delaney. The young kid who was the cashier at the service station on this suddenly stormy Sunday night was eavesdropping, just trying to pass the time until he could escape at midnight when his shift ended.

Being single, Sheriff King always worked Sunday nights. It was one of the busiest nights of the week due to all the weekenders heading home, and it gave some of his men time at home with their young families on Sunday night. It was that thoughtful side that endeared him to the locals, and cemented friendships.

Officer Delaney, a weasel-looking man with pinched, beady eyes had a sweet scam going, and was regaling Buddy with the tale of his latest victim. He related how the speed limit is 55 for a short distance leaving Eustace, and then there is a sign about a hundred yards down the road that shows the speed limit increasing to 65.

Well, Officer Delaney said with glee, "I nail them poor bastards as they see the higher speed limit and begin to accelerate before they pass the sign."

Delaney, laughing, told King, "I sit in my cruiser between both signs and nail them suckers every time." It adds some serious coinage to the Eustace city coffers and provides great sport for Delaney.

Buddy was giving his friend a hard time, "You don't still use that old 'I'm a traffic specialist' line, do you?"

"Hell yes," Delaney retorted, "It leaves 'em speechless, and really pisses 'em off."

They had a good guffaw over that one, as the kid smiled from behind the counter and just shook his head.

8

About 15 miles away, Patsy Aarons shone the powerful light on the water. There it was! The Hammonds canoe was bouncing and rolling in the water about thirty yards offshore, just at the edge of the point.

It was upside down, and apparently empty. Patsy gasped and grabbed her telephone to dial 9-1-1 as the thunder and lightning boomed and flashed all around her.

The 9-1-1 dispatcher quickly put the word out, and Sheriff King roared toward Patsy Aarons' address, siren wailing and lights flashing, as Gun Barrel City police zoomed in from the other direction.

Cedar Creek Gazette reporter Dwayne Murphy had his ear glued to the police scanners as the storm hit, ever vigilant in the endless search for his story of the century. He grabbed his rain slicker and also headed for the Aaron's residence after hearing the address on his scanner.

While the law and the news hound were racing to Patsy Aarons' house, less than a half mile away, a dark figure was calmly, unhurriedly, stripping off his wet suit, and stashing his scuba tank, regulator, inflatable vest, rubber booties, rubber gloves, fins, and knife into the bright chrome steel compartment in the back of his dark blue Ford-150 pickup.

He had cleverly drilled a small hole in the bottom of the storage compartment, and the flatbed so the water from his wet gear could drain out, unnoticed. The chrome plated steel compartment was one you would see on most every pickup truck in Henderson County.

The unseen man took his time, methodically making sure everything was secured, and that there was no trail from the edge of the water where he emerged from the lake to his truck, parked about 30 yards away. Every lake house and mobile home in the vicinity was dark and empty, as he knew they would be.

After a few minutes he effortlessly hopped into the truck and drove away at a normal rate of speed. He was like a ghost. No one saw him enter the water. No one saw him emerge from the water. No one saw him drive away.

In fact, his first three victims had not seen him either – until they were in the last gasps of their lives. That was when they looked at him in wide-eyed fear, their terrified eyes asking "why?"

Patsy heard the sirens in the distance, and soon her yard and driveway were full of police cars and a rescue squad. Sheriff King, Patsy would later describe him to friends as a "muscular, handsome young man," quickly took charge. By now, the canoe had drifted past Patsy's dock and was banging into another dock about thirty yards down the way. The thunder and lightning was less frequent. The waves and wind were dying down a little too, but the rain was still pelting down in big, stinging drops.

A couple of firemen walked, and half swam into the rolling surf to pull the canoe to shore. The once spotlessly beautiful canoe had scratches and gashes everywhere, having crashed into docks and some rocks on its lifeless journey. There were no life jackets or paddles on board. There was also no sign of Red or Amanda.

Some of the police and fire officials raced along the shore around the point, shouting the Hammonds' names and shining their powerful flashlights looking for any sign of life. There was nothing but a whipping wind and rolling waves. They searched for several hours to no avail.

At first light, the search for the missing couple resumed. By then, the skies had turned to bright blue and a warm sun beamed down on a gently rippling lake. The tranquility had returned to Cedar Creek Lake.

Several boats dragged along the shore all day, while *Gazette* reporter Murphy looked on with Patsy, jotting down notes about the missing couple. A couple of Dallas TV stations sent crews, since the Hammond's were known by quite a few businesspeople in the Metroplex. Murphy was disappointed that Mindy Reese didn't deem it worthy of her presence, but he understood. She was, after all, the crime reporter and this looked like a drowning on an especially stormy night on the lake.

Finally, as the sun began to set, there was a shout from a Coast Guard Auxiliary boat. They had hooked a woman's body about fifty yards out from the last dock before the point. One of the Hammond's children identified the body as that of Amanda. The chief deputy told Sheriff King that the body was pretty battered from the storm, but there were no outward signs of foul play. King passed that information on to the Hammond's son in hushed tones.

It was late in the afternoon of the next day before they found Red Hammond's body a little farther down from where his wife had been located. It was the same story with him – no obvious signs of foul play, but some bruising and cuts, apparently caused by being banged around on rocks in the storm. His lungs were also full of water. The police stated it was an obvious sign of drowning.

The Hammond's untimely deaths received some pretty big play in the local media. It didn't look like a crime, so WDFW once again didn't send Mindy Reese, but another staffer did a live report from the scene by satellite during the evening news.

The story was perfect for the media. A couple goes out canoeing, a big spring storm brews up, and they drown as their anxious neighbor waits on shore. All the local TV stations from Dallas and nearby Tyler covered the story, as did Dwayne Murphy's favorite newspapers from Dallas and Fort Worth.

Dwayne himself got the front page of the *Cedar Creek Gazette*, with a big headline and color pictures. He was the only one who also mentioned that there had been another drowning just two weeks before this one. Dwayne wrote a sidebar story on the dangers of being on the lake when sudden spring storms crop up. He was proud of his work, feeling that his stories were clearly much better, and more detailed than those lazy reporters from the big cities to the west.

The Henderson County Medical Examiner did autopsies on the Hammond's bodies and ruled death by accidental drowning.

Less than a half hour away from the double drowning scene, the scuba diver sat in the cab of his dark blue pickup truck and read the story in the *Cedar Creek Gazette* with a satisfied smirk on his face. He thought to himself, "These yahoos have no idea who, or what, they're dealing with."

9

It was a Saturday morning, six days after the double drowning on Cedar Creek Lake. McDuff's Restaurant, just across the lake in Seven Points was packed as usual. They had the best biscuits in town, and the surliest waitresses. Locals and tourists alike found it to be a charming combination.

Sheriff Buddy King was sitting in a booth by himself. Melinda Sue, a gum chewing, sassy talking, fixture at the restaurant, had just served Henderson County's chief lawman his favorite order. Piled on his plate were a big greasy omelet, a side of grits, and some hot, fluffy biscuits. Buddy broke open a biscuit and smeared on some butter while the steam wafted out of the middle.

"Hey, Sheriff, what's up?" It was Dwayne Murphy. "Mind if I sit down?" he asked, already sliding into the vinyl-covered seat across from King.

King, smiled, "Looks like you already have, Murph."

Melinda Sue stopped by and dropped off a cup of black coffee for Murphy. She already had turned in his usual order, two eggs over easy, some bacon, and, of course, biscuits, with country gravy.

Buddy King didn't mind the interruption by Murphy. Although he could be a pain in the ass at times, like every one of those newshounds, King kind of liked the local newspaper pest. He also knew just how to use Murphy to get the right kind of stories in the *Gazette.* He believed Murphy's positive profiles helped King win the Sheriff's race, although he'd never confess that to the reporter.

Murphy, always nosing for the big scoop said, "So, any big doings last night? Had to be some with it bein' pay day, plus a full moon and all."

King shook his head, "Not really, surprisingly quiet for a Friday night."

Melinda Sue bounded toward the table her overly dyed platinum hair glinting in the restaurant lights, as she brought Murphy's heaping platter of food. The reporter and the sheriff sat in silence for a few minutes, enjoying the hot meal. Murphy was quickly devouring his food, piling one full fork after another into his mouth. Finally, he came up for air, and asked King if there was anything new on the three recent drowning deaths. When Murphy was around a conspiracy theory was never far behind.

"Nope, just looks like a couple of unfortunate, unrelated incidents to me," King replied. "But I'm sure you've got a theory Murph."

The *Gazette* reporter put down his fork and looked at King with a conspiratorial glint in his eye. He leaned toward the sheriff, lowered his voice, and took a quick glance around. The restaurant was packed with prying ears close by.

"Matter of fact, I do have some concerns," Murphy said in a professorial whisper. "First off, I've been askin' around about that loner feller, Claude Young. Folks tell me that even though he drank quite a bit most afternoons, he took his fishin' damn serious, and never had even one beer when they were out fishin' with him."

King glanced up from his food, his fork suspended in mid-air, "So?"

"Well," Murphy continued, "If he wasn't drinkin' how the hell did he fall out of that little boat?" He'd been fishin' like that for years."

Murphy went on without taking a breath. He was on a roll now.

"And those canoe folks who drowned, don't it seem a little strange that they both fell out of the canoe and couldn't make it to shore? They weren't that far away," Murphy asked the sheriff.

Buddy King put down his fork now and gave Murphy a look he reserved for the people who told him the craziest stories. His steel-blue eyes were shooting icicles at Murphy. He was well aware of the local reporter's penchant for whipping up big stories out of little stories. It was the last thing he needed on his watch, especially as the high tourist season was about to get into full swing.

"Murph," he said with heavy sarcasm dripping from his voice, "You telling me that what, some monster came along and grabbed all three of them? Maybe it was a 200-pound channel catfish that was hungry as hell?"

Murphy was undaunted. "Laugh. Go ahead," he snorted, "But I'm telling you two drowning incidents, with all three people fallin' out of their boats, in that short of a period of time, just don't make sense."

King just shook his head, left enough money for his meal and a generous tip for Melinda Sue on the table, rose to his feet, and hitched up his blue jeans.

He looked at the reporter and said with a smile on his face, and just loud enough for some of the prying ears nearby to hear, "Well Murphy, I guess an imagination like that is what makes you such a damn good reporter. See yah later." There were knowing smiles from those within earshot.

About eight miles away, on the west side of the lake, the rich folks in the Piney Woods Subdivision were getting ready for another beautiful Saturday of carefree lake living. This was an enclave of multi-million-dollar lake homes, and the snooty people who lived in them.

For many of them, these were their second or even third homes. They were huge structures with glistening glass windows everywhere, wide sweeping decks, fireplaces and big docks filled with expensive water toys of all sizes. Some estates had tennis courts, and even guest quarters that were larger than most of the common folk's homes along the lake.

The biggest manse of them all belonged to Fort Worth billionaire Franklin Bushman. It sprawled across three acres. Besides the main house, which was an exquisite 10,000 square foot, two-story beauty with custom stone exterior, a third floor observation deck and sliding glass doors giving a panoramic view of the lake, there was a detached movie theatre with plush leather recliners, a tennis court, a basketball court, and a guest residence that easily slept eight, and had its own kitchen.

In a Texas tradition, the dapper 47-year-old businessman had inherited his late daddy's oil money. With that came the requisite trophy wife, 30-year-old Misty, complete with big blonde hair from a bottle, and breasts from the skills of a plastic surgeon. She was perfect, a real Texas beauty, ogled by all the men whenever she wore that tiny black bikini, as she was this morning.

Franklin, a handsome man in his own right, with carefully coiffed salt and pepper hair, and a small mustache with flecks of gray, walked onto the huge deck carrying two cups of steaming coffee. He was wearing white tennis shorts, and a blue Izod polo shirt. Franklin worked out with his own personal trainer and watched every morsel of food he put in his mouth. That discipline showed in the nicely bulging biceps of his tanned arms, and his trim, very athletic figure.

Misty, who was languishing on a padded chaise lounge, stretched as he approached, threatening to pop right out of the small bikini top. Franklin admired the view. She was beautiful and had a terrific tan.

In the massive house, a maid service, and a caterer were busily cleaning up the remains of last night's party. It had been a fundraiser for the Cedar Creek Lake Cancer Society, graciously hosted by the Bushman's.

About a hundred people had swarmed over the estate with its impeccably manicured lawn and shrubbery. Like all of the Bushman's soirees it had been loud, with lots of free flowing booze, a live jazz trio on the outside deck and would be the talk of the lake's socialites for weeks to come.

Misty sipped on her coffee, made with the finest fresh ground, imported beans that money could buy. "Mmm," she purred, "This is really good honey, just what I needed to wake up this morning."

Franklin smiled down at his prized possession, "That's because Consuela put some Bailey's Irish Crème in it," he said, "A little hair of the dog never hurts."

Franklin sat on the chaise next to Misty, and she snuggled into his lap. They chatted about the party, laughing at some of their more obnoxious guests, and just enjoyed the warm, clear skies and their wide, unobstructed view of the sparkling lake.

Cedar Creek Lake was just beginning to fill up with snarling Jet Skis, some peaceful sailboats with their billowing red, yellow and blue sails puffing up in the morning's gentle breeze, and a few speedboats churning up the water as they pulled skiers and wake boarders. Sprinkled in amidst this busy scene were a few fishermen, trying to entice some big bass into their boats and silently cursing the noisy boats and Jet Skis that were scaring the fish away, and causing their fishing boats to bounce up and down.

The Bushman's planned to take it easy the rest of this morning, and afternoon, before heading out onto the lake this evening.

Their 65-foot yacht gleamed in the morning sun, moored to their massive wooden dock. Manuel, their gardener and handyman, was stocking the boat with fine food, and wine for tonight's excursion.

While Franklin and Misty were famous for their parties, they were equally well known for their lavish, million-dollar yacht. It was a craft that was far too big for this size lake, so it really stood out.

Franklin would have it no other way. He loved all the fancy cars and toys that money could buy, and he liked to flaunt his wealth.

Sometimes they used the fiberglass beauty, with detailed teakwood interior and fancy cabin, for all night parties, moored out in the middle of the lake. Most everyone had heard the rumors of just how wild those parties were, and many of the more adventurous wealthy folks around the lake were always angling for an invitation.

But there would be no wild party aboard "The Misty" tonight. Its namesake, and her rich husband were looking forward to a quieter, fun-filled night, just the two of them. It would be an evening that began with a fine meal, too much very expensive wine, and one of their favorite movies on the flatscreen TV, followed by passion as only Misty could bring it.

As the Bushman's lazed on their deck, they never noticed the sandy-haired man in a super fast bass boat slowly drift past their dock. The man had on a pair of denim shorts that were fraying on the bottom, a weathered Texas Rangers baseball cap and dark sunglasses. He was shirtless in the warmth of the morning sun. He had the rippled physique of a man who worked out endlessly with weights and probably ran many miles a week. The muscles did not bulge like a bulky weightlifter. They were sleek and defined, like those of a panther. This man looked fit and agile. He was nonchalantly casting a lure along the docks and shoreline. At the same time, the man's cold eyes, hidden by the sunglasses, were watching the Hispanic man load provisions onto the yacht. "So," the fisherman thought to himself, "It looks like I'm going to go on a covert mission tonight."

10

While the Bushmans napped, Sheriff King returned to the Henderson County Sheriff's Office to check in, and prepare to take the rest of the day off. He was going fishing with his buddy Billy Richardson. They were heading over to Lake Fork in search of some big largemouth bass. It was one of the best lakes in the country for those lunkers.

Richardson was a big man, still in good shape, with a goatee, keen eyes, and a face that was far too weather-beaten for someone only 53 years of age. It was a hazard of a life spent fishing and being a cop in the blazing Texas sun.

Billy Richardson was African American, a retired homicide detective from the Dallas County Sheriff's Department. He had seen it all during his 30 years with that big city crime unit. That's why he and his wife, Eunice, took his pension money at the first opportunity and moved into their peaceful, cozy cabin on Cedar Creek Lake.

They'd scrimped and saved to build the place, and lived frugally, but still needed extra money to make it on his police pension. That's why Eunice worked as a checker at the Wal-Mart Super Store in Gun Barrel City, and Billy was a part-time detective for Sheriff King.

He and King had teamed up on a couple of cases when Billy was working in Dallas, and the sheriff was still a police officer in Eustace. It was a common practice for the big city department to lend a hand to the smaller cities nearby during a big crime or difficult case. Billy and Buddy discovered their joint passion for fishing and had become tight pals. Before Billy retired, he had earned the reputation of being the guy who could always solve the toughest, most baffling crimes.

Buddy King, and Billy set off for Lake Fork, about 80 minutes to the north. As they passed the time on the drive, Sheriff King recounted Dwayne Murphy's crazy scenario for the recent drownings. They both had a good chuckle about that one.

"He's a newshound among newshounds," Billy said, "He never met a conspiracy theory he didn't like or embrace."

"Yah, he keeps waiting for the Big One, so he can get a job in Dallas."

"Never going to happen," snorted Billy, "They have real journalists at those big city newspapers. Murphy's an alright guy, but he ain't no Jimmy Breslin."

The rural scenery whizzed by and both men were silent for a while. Sheriff King was lost in thought.

"What you thinkin' about," asked the grizzled former big city cop, "Murphy doesn't really have you wonderin' about his theory does he?"

"Nah," King replied, "I'm just worried about him writing some crazy conspiracy story right as the tourist season takes off."

"First off," Billy said, "It is a crazy idea, secondly you know old man Chambers wouldn't print it in his rag anyway."

King nodded, "Yah, you're right. Let's go find us some big ole largemouth bass."

11

The sun had set in the west with little fanfare on this Saturday night. The cloudless Texas sky made for a run-of-the-mill sunset viewing, and now the full moon was beginning to rise, sending a silvery sparkling shimmer onto the quiet waters of Cedar Creek Lake.

There were a few fishermen working their lures near the lighted docks, as Franklin Bushman headed "The Misty" out toward the middle of the lake. It looked like a perfect night. The wind was calm. There was no rain in the forecast, and he knew Misty would make it a night to remember.

They were halfway through their second bottle of wine, a new blend Franklin had stumbled on during his weekly Internet searches, called Hang Time, a delightful Pinot Noir from Santa Maria Valley in California. It was almost two in the morning. There was a light warm breeze out of the south. The temperature was still in the 80's; the moon was brightly shining from a star-studded Texas sky, so Misty decided it was a perfect night to go skinny-dipping. Franklin smiled and said, "Let's go."

Misty jumped in first off the low boarding platform on the stern of the huge yacht, with Franklin quickly joining her. It was dark in the water, but the moon offered just enough light to see where they were, plus they had the comforting lights of the yacht's cabin glowing just a few yards away.

About fifty yards off the bow of the anchored yacht, the intruder silently treaded water, as he had been doing for the last hour. He was barely above the surface, and nearly invisible with his black equipment and wet suit.

While most swimmers would have been exhausted by now, the former Navy Seal had done this before, on many covert missions. He was able to effortlessly tread water with no hint of fatigue. He had spent hours watching the Bushman's frolic on their yacht over the past month or so. Tonight would be his night. The Frogman pulled his mask over his face, reached back to turn on his tank, and without so much as a ripple slipped below the surface.

Misty was teasing her husband, rubbing her naked body against his, and then quickly darting away like a nymph in the night. He loved this game, knowing that some passionate lovemaking would soon follow.

The scuba diver loved his game too. He could see the dim lights from the yacht penetrating the water just ahead of him, and the legs of the two rich people churning around just below the surface. He chuckled to himself, enjoying the fact that they had no idea they were taking their final breaths on this earth.

Misty was an excellent swimmer, in fact, had been a star on her high school swim team back in Georgia. She brushed her hair against his chest, and then quickly dove under water. It would be her final dive.

Misty liked to dive deep, so Franklin was unable to see her, and then she would suddenly break the surface in a different spot. It was part of their game. But the Frogman had a game of his own planned for her.

The killer and his steel grip were waiting for her about five feet below the dusky surface, and suddenly she could not move a muscle. She tried to scream but her effort went nowhere under the suffocating water.

Franklin, waiting on the surface, could see nothing in the smoky black water. He had no idea that his wife was fighting for her life just a few feet away.

Franklin, growing weary of the game, and wanting to save his strength for later, slipped out of the water, and sat on the swim deck at the stern of "The Misty" to wait for the boat's namesake to burst out of the water.

He watched, and waited, but saw nothing but the rippling water. "Where was she?" he thought.

There was no way she could hold her breath that long. Had she swum around to the bow, hiding from him, wanting him to go chase after her?

About ten yards away, and off to the side of the boat, out of Franklin's line of sight; Misty had lost her battle to escape the frogman's cement-like clutches. Her gasping lungs filled with water, and her killer took her to the bottom of the lake, forty feet below.

Back on the yacht, Franklin was growing more and more fearful that something had happened to Misty. He began to call her name. The only sound was the muted strains from the light jazz station coming from the yacht's expensive sound system.

He jumped into the water. That's when a dark figure suddenly appeared next to him and wrapped up his legs and arms. Franklin, a strong man in his own right, was no match for the killer. The billionaire could not move. Struggle was impossible. Death was inevitable.

12

The Texas sun rose over Cedar Creek Lake without a cloud to mar the deep blue sky. The only blight on the overhead canvas were white puffy contrails from jets hurrying to the sprawling DFW airport some 80 miles to the west.

It was a wonderful Sunday morning, and the weekenders, and their guests flocked to the water. They were anxious to squeeze every moment of fun out of the day before they had to head back to the reality of the big city.

At the far south end of the lake, quite a few serious fishermen had been on the water since dawn, looking for hungry Hybrid Stripers. Now, their once quiet lake was buzzing with Sea-Doos and speedboats, making the fishing a lot less enjoyable.

The Bushman's yacht was still moored out in the middle of the lake. Many a boater zoomed near it, wishing they had the money to own one, and at the same time wondering why someone would have such a large yacht on a lake. There was no sign of activity on "The Misty." It was now nearly noon.

Back at the Bushman mansion, about four miles away, Manuel was trying to decide what to do. Mr. Bushman had an appointment in an hour, so Manuel had expected him to be back by now. At the same time, he knew that Mr. Bushman had warned him never to call the yacht unless it was an extreme emergency, especially after a long Saturday night with Misty. He decided to wait it out.

The door chimes sounded, just as the grandfather clock's bell struck one at the Bushman residence. Manuel answered the door and ushered in two members of the Cedar Creek Lake Golf and Riding Club. They were on time for their appointment to discuss a donation for a new clubhouse to be named in Mr. Bushman's honor. But, Mr. Bushman still had not returned. It was very unusual for him to be late for anything, especially a business meeting.

Manuel apologized to the visitors for Mr. Bushman's absence, and made them comfortable on the sweeping wooden deck, with its panoramic view of the lake. As the visitors sipped iced teas, Manuel reluctantly dialed up the phone on the yacht, hoping the call would not anger his boss. There was no answer.

The Bushman's handyman was growing increasingly worried now. Had something happened to them? He had anxiously scanned the lake some time ago with powerful binoculars but could not see "The Misty."

Manuel called Tommy Smith's cell phone. He knew the Coast Guard Auxiliary volunteer would be chugging around the lake this Sunday, looking to help any stranded boaters.

Tommy Smith was just leaving the fuel dock at Wesley's Marina when the familiar strains of "*Anchors Aweigh*" sounded on his cell phone. His wife thought it was a cute touch. Tommy hated it, but knew better than to cross his wife over something like a cell phone ringer.

It was Manuel, the handyman for the Bushman's. He was worried because Franklin and Misty still had not returned from their overnight excursion on the lake. Tommy said he would go to check it out. He knew it would be easy to find the huge yacht; you could spot it a mile away.

It was less than twenty minutes later that Tommy eased his shiny old wooden Chris Craft up near the Bushman's yacht, the sun glinting off its smooth surface. He saw a couple of large, expensive beach towels lying on the swim deck at the rear of the yacht and noticed that all the lights were still on inside the beautiful vessel. But there was no sign of Misty or Franklin.

He shouted their names. There was no response. Tommy wondered to himself, "Are they still sleeping? It's nearly one-thirty in the afternoon?"

Growing more concerned, Tommy tied his boat up to the stern of the Bushman's yacht, so he could climb aboard.

Several boaters and people on SeaDoos had begun to gather. The Bushman's yacht was always a magnet, but when a boat with Coast Guard flags flying tied up to it, the magnetic field became more powerful.

Tommy walked along the swim deck, and then ducked his head into the cabin. He saw an empty bottle of wine on the table, with a half-filled bottle sitting next to it, along with two glasses. One glass was empty; the other still had a couple sips left in it. There was a banana on the table that had started to turn brown, and dirty dishes had been stacked in the small sink in the galley.

With increasing trepidation, Tommy walked through the entire yacht. It was undisturbed, but there was no sign of Misty or Franklin.

The beds had not been slept in. Had they had too much to drink and fallen overboard last night?

The thought of robbers crossed Tommy's mind, but another quick search of the cabin found Misty's jewelry undisturbed on the nightstand, as well as Franklin's Rolex and wallet, stuffed with hundred-dollar bills and credit cards.

That snapped his thoughts back to the falling overboard theory. Had they both drowned? It seemed impossible, not only because the Bushman's were the richest couple on the lake, but how could five people drown in a just a few weeks?

13

Meanwhile, over at Lake Fork, Sheriff King and his buddy Billy Richardson were working the shoreline hoping for one last large-mouth bass strike before they had to head back home. They had boated nine of the beautiful fish on Saturday, spent the night in a little motel down the road, and headed back out at dawn.

Most anglers believed in the "catch and release" approach on Lake Fork, assuring that the bass will continue to grow fat and feisty. The fishing buddies had released all the fish they'd caught, including just three so far today. The bite had been a bit slow on this Sunday.

As King retrieved his lure, his cell phone suddenly rang. King put down his pole and answered. It was the Coast Guard volunteer Tommy Smith.

"Sorry to bother you sheriff," Smith said, "but I think we may have a real problem here on the lake. I thought it would be best to keep it quiet right now."

"What's up Tommy?"

Smith then filled in the sheriff on the missing Bushmans and their yacht moored out in the middle of the lake.

Sheriff King's stomach knotted up. Could there possibly be another pair of drowning deaths? And this time involving the richest couple on the lake? He knew his fishing day was abruptly over.

King told Smith that he'd done the right thing, and to just stay on the yacht until he called him back. Smith said he would, and then told the sheriff that quite a few boaters had gathered to see what was happening. King told him to tell them nothing was wrong, to just move on their way.

Sheriff King called the Gun Barrel City police chief, filled him in, and told him to maintain radio silence on this one.

"Let's do everything by cell phone," King said, "We need to keep a lid on this situation until we figure out what the hell is going on. If it is what it appears to be, the media will be swarming all over us in no time."

Sheriff King and Richardson quickly put their bass boat on the trailer, and left it at a nearby marina. They'd come back for it later. Right now they had to speed back to Cedar Creek Lake as rapidly as possible.

Back at the Bushman's mansion, Manuel told his visitors that the meeting would have to be cancelled. He was sorry but something had come up. The two men grumbled a bit, and then left. This was most unusual. Franklin Bushman had never stood them up before, and Manuel was acting very strange.

Manuel called Tommy Smith back. He was clearly upset, "Tommy, did you find the yacht? Are the Bushmans alright?"

Tommy, remembering the sheriff's caution said, "I think everything's fine Manuel. We'll know more in a little bit."

Smith's comments struck Manuel as being vague, and very strange.

"What does that mean?" he asked.

Tommy was evasive, "Nothing, everything's fine, they should be along shortly." He hastily hung up the cell phone.

Meanwhile, there was a buzz starting to go around the lake. A lake community is a friendly community, and everyone likes to nose around in everybody's business. It is a natural extension of a small town, plus an atmosphere where everyone sits around on their deck, or on their boats, waving and saying howdy to each other, just "bein' neighborly."

Mike, the grouchy old proprietor of the Full Moon Marina, on the north side of the lake, started to hear the buzz as he pumped fresh gasoline into a couple of boats that had ventured out to the middle of the lake where the Bushman's extravagant yacht was anchored. Something was going on out there, nobody exactly knew what, but it seemed like the Bushman's yacht was empty. Where were its rich owners?

With a loud chug-chug-chug signaling his approach, Dwayne Murphy pulled his latest water-borne rocket ship up to Mike's fuel dock.

"Hey, Mike," the nosy reporter shouted, "What's up?"

Mike quickly served up the latest gossip on the Bushman's. That changed Murphy's agenda. He quickly re-fired up the blown hemi on his ultra-speedboat.

"Gotta go," Dwayne said excitedly, "I'll be back later for gas."

He slowly chugged his way out of the "no wake" zone of the marina. When he was clear, Dwayne's sleek boat leaped forward shooting a huge rooster tail stream of water six feet high behind it, as he headed for the middle of the lake at full tilt.

There were now about a dozen boats gathered in the vicinity of "The Misty," including the sheriff's department boat, and one from the Gun Barrel City police. Dwayne joined the group and got tight-lipped "no comments" from his usually talkative police sources.

Dwayne's heart was racing, this could be THE BIG ONE, that story he had been searching for, to get out of this small pond and play with the big boys in Dallas. He called the weekend editor at the *Dallas Morning News*. He quickly filled him in and offered to team up on this big story. The editor was reluctant to do that, but he also knew that Dwayne knew everything and everybody around Cedar Creek Lake.

"Ok," the editor said, "I'll send someone right away."

The screaming siren and pulsating lights signaled Sheriff King's return to Cedar Creek. He had made the usual 90-minute trip from Lake Fork in about 50 minutes. King asked Richardson, the former Dallas County detective, to work closely with him on this one. He knew it would be a media circus.

Dwayne Murphy pushed the number four button on his cell phone's speed dialer, and heard the sultry, professional voice of WDFW reporter Mindy Reese. Murphy excitedly rushed through his story of the missing rich couple, and their abandoned yacht.

Reese, who did not trust Murphy's reportorial instincts, knowing of his tendency to exaggerate, asked him some very pointed questions.

"Now Murph, are you sure they've disappeared?"

"I'm tellin' yah Mindy, I am sitting in my boat, just a few yards away and there is no sign of them on that yacht."

Satisfied with his answers, Mindy too believed this could be a big story – especially on a usually slow Sunday night in the news business. She'd take this one herself. It might even attract the attention of the networks, she thought.

Mindy made one more call, just to be sure of Murphy's information. The TV reporter called the Henderson County Sheriff's office and got stonewalled. That only raised her sense that this was a big story.

She phoned the Gun Barrel City police department and received the same closed-mouthed response initially. But then Mindy turned on her southern charm, and finally got confirmation of the missing couple from the dispatcher, a young part-timer who had been smitten by seeing her on television.

The TV news business is obsessed with being first on the air with a big story, so Mindy quickly called her news director at home, filling her in on the mystery unfolding at Cedar Creek Lake. The news boss dispatched a satellite truck to pick up Mindy at her downtown Dallas loft apartment. She also called the newsroom, and quickly got a bulletin on the air.

The world was about to hear about the missing rich couple, and their empty expensive yacht bobbing around in the middle of Cedar Creek Lake, about an hour out of Dallas, Texas.

WDFW was showing Tiger Woods about to try to sink a birdie putt, when the announcer voice said, "This is a Breaking News from the WDFW News Now newsroom." Within minutes the story was being broadcast on every radio and TV outlet in the Dallas-Fort Worth area. Soon the totally connected electronic planet that is the news business had beamed the report to every corner of the country.

14

Sheriff King pulled out all stops on this possible drowning, and police-trained and volunteer scuba divers were soon everywhere in the area of the yacht. The word had spread, and there were so many boats trying to get close for a look, that the sheriff's department and Coast Guard Auxiliary had to keep shooing them away. Many of the boats had been rented by the media horde, shoving hundred-dollar bills into recreational boaters' eager hands to get a lift out to the yacht.

A grim-faced Sheriff King watched the search from the deck of the Henderson County patrol boat. His buddy, Billy Richardson had an equally stern look on his seasoned face, as they spoke in hushed tones, out of earshot of everyone else.

"What are you thinkin' Billy?" King asked the veteran Dallas police detective.

"This is a strange one. Two people just don't disappear from a yacht in the middle of a quiet lake. The odds against them both drowning are also astronomical."

King asked, "What if they were drunk, and just fell in, and couldn't swim?"

Richardson shook his head from side to side for emphasis, "Not likely. From everything I've heard over the years they were both excellent swimmers and did these overnight lake journeys many a time."

Sheriff King nodded, "Your right, in fact I remember readin' somewhere that Misty was on some swim team in high school or college."

The conversation stopped, as the two lawmen silently surveyed the scene before them. There were a dozen scuba divers in the water, spread out in a methodical grid pattern under the surface. There was also a small armada of boats dragging outside of the circle of scuba divers, trying to snag what they presumed to be the Bushman's bodies lying somewhere under the forty feet of cloudy brown water.

Sheriff King looked at his buddy, "You don't suppose that Murphy's crazy theory could be true? Could these five drowning deaths be connected?"

With a sideways glance, Richardson replied, "I'm not buying it. First off, we don't know whether the Bushman's drowned or decided to head off by themselves and left the yacht here. Secondly, those first three drownings were totally unrelated. There is no connection between a lonely old drunk fisherman, two people who like to canoe, and a rich couple on their yacht."

King nodded, "Your right, we need to see how this plays out before we go jumping to any conclusions. Lord knows the news media will do enough of that."

One of the unobtrusive observers, lost among the many boats circling or floating near the search scene, was a well-muscled, well-tanned man in denim shorts, wearing a Texas Rangers ball cap, dark sunglasses, and no shirt.

This was a new experience for him. Usually his missions ended when a helicopter or ship picked him up and whisked him away from the scene. It was kind of exciting to watch all these cops, and all that news media, trying to find the victims he'd left behind just a few hours ago.

The killer chuckled to himself, as he thought, about the twist he'd engineered at the last moment. He was anxious to see how all these law enforcement rocket scientists handled his little diversionary tactic.

The Frog Man's training had warned him how police agencies liked to take pictures and video of bystanders at these crime scenes, so he nonchalantly started the motor on his bass boat and unhurriedly left the scene and went fishing a mile or so away, just in case, anyone was keeping an eye on him.

It was about five o'clock when a diver found the body of Misty Bushman, in about 33 feet of water, only about 40 yards from the yacht. With news helicopters hovering overhead, and snoopy reporters craning their necks from nearby boats, the lifeless body of the 30-year-old former beauty queen was brought to the surface. Sheriff's deputies quickly covered her with a sheet to keep the naked corpse from the prying eyes of the news hounds and other equally snoopy lake residents.

As in the other three recent drowning deaths, there was no sign of foul play, no bruises, and no outward sign that this had been a murder. Billy Richardson, calling upon his well-honed detective skills, took a close look at the nude body. There was no skin under her fingernails, which would have indicated a struggle. There was no sign of trauma anywhere. Her lungs were filled with water, bloating the lifeless body.

Richardson's police mind was working overtime as it processed this latest apparent drowning. Even though he had shrugged it off a few hours ago in talking with Sheriff King, he had that familiar nagging feeling in the back of his brain. Could they be connected? Is it possible that someone is murdering people by drowning them? If that's true, why is there no sign of a struggle? Richardson was stumped, but he was not one to believe in coincidences, and this sudden spate of drownings would be a bizarre co-incidence.

The divers searched relentlessly until the lake water became too dark. They had only been able to see about three feet in front of them with the bright sun's shafts of light penetrating the cloudy water during the afternoon. Once the sun started to set, it was an impossible task.

Sheriff King called off the search for Franklin Bushman until dawn on Monday. He posted a guard on the yacht and left it moored at its present location to help them pinpoint Bushman's body the next day, and to preserve the crime scene, if that was indeed what it turned out to be.

Mindy Reese and the other reporters were scurrying everywhere trying to get reaction from neighbors of the Bushman's, and other movers and shakers in the Cedar Creek Lake area. They did a profile of the couple, recounting their charitable work that had resulted in millions of dollars in donations. A police car was stationed at the entrance to the Piney Woods Subdivision to keep the nosy reporters away from the Bushman's home and rich neighbors.

By the 10 o'clock newscast the media was putting a new spin on the story. Mindy Reese led the way with a live report, standing next to the lake, with the Yacht's lights in the distance. Like her colleagues, she raised the specter of doubt about foul play.

"With still no sign of Franklin Bushman," she reported, a serious, concerned look on her perfect TV face, "some police have told me privately that they also have to look at this as a homicide. It would be unthinkable for Mr. Bushman to have killed his young wife, but until they can talk to him, police cannot rule out anything in this baffling case."

15

Thirty-five miles to the east, Cody Martin watched the flickering television set while sitting in the dark in his secluded cabin on the shore of Lake Athens. He smiled at the Reese report. Part of Martin's Navy Seal training dealt with diversion and subterfuge. He was taught ways to throw the enemy off the scent.

That's why Martin, swimming below the surface, had dragged Bushman's body about a mile away from the yacht before dropping him in about 15 feet of water, about 200 yards off the shoreline. It would take them a few more days to locate Bushman, probably not until his bloated body had floated back to the surface.

Meanwhile the police and media would be raising all kinds of speculation, as they tried to guess just what the hell was going on in their normally sedate and peaceful part of East Texas.

The news media sunk its collective teeth into the Bushman double drowning story like a hungry pit bull and refused to let go. Soon the national cable news channels joined the local media.

CNN, MSNBC and the Fox News Channel set up shop, brought in legal experts, and speculated endlessly about what really happened at Cedar Creek Lake. Because a semi-celebrity billionaire couple was involved, and Franklin Bushman remained missing, the TV magazine programs like *Inside Edition* also took up the story. Suddenly the lake was not the sleepy place it had been just a few days before.

Meanwhile, Sheriff King led the search party trying to locate Franklin Bushman. The search had to be on two levels. While boats dragged the lake, and scuba divers logged many hours searching underwater for his body, the FBI and other law enforcement agencies were on the lookout for Bushman to turn up on the lam somewhere.

They pored over Bushman's business dealings, wondering if he was in trouble financially. He was not. They interviewed hundreds of colleagues and acquaintances of the couple looking for signs of trouble. They found nothing. Everyone described them as a couple that was very much in love. Bushman, they said, would do anything to keep his beloved wife happy. His cellphone and credit cards were still on the yacht, leaving police no chance to trace his whereabouts through those paths.

Cody Martin kept a low profile at his cabin on Lake Athens. He was excited about the hullabaloo he had caused and amused by the way the police and the media were acting like fools.

So far, no newshound or police agency had linked the four, and possibly five drowning deaths. And why should they, each seemed to be an unrelated event.

Billy Richardson, the ace detective baffled by this case, had a long conversation with Sheriff King about the five drowning deaths. But, though his antennae were up, and Richardson felt that it was rare to have five people drown in such a short time frame, he could find nothing to link the victims.

"There is just no common thread," Richardson told the sheriff. "The first victim is a drunk and a loner, the next two victims are a quiet couple whose canoe capsized in a storm, and then there is the rich trophy wife, with a missing husband – who may have killed her, or may have drowned himself after they consumed lots of wine."

Richardson was clearly at a loss for answers, just as Cody Martin had planned it by making these murders appear to be a series of random, disconnected events.

Now the lack of a common thread did not stop Richardson from a full-scale attack on the backgrounds and any other information he could gather about the victims. But each piece of information led nowhere.

16

Cody Martin was 28 years old, stood six feet tall, and was strong as an ox with a rippled body that would make a weightlifter turn green with envy. He had cold blue eyes that could penetrate steel, and a tough, no nonsense demeanor. Martin had graduated from Mabank High School, just down the road from the lake.

But, even though it was a small school, he doubted that anyone remembered him. He never joined in any of their stupid sports, or dances or partying at the beer busts in the woods of Henderson County. He was a quiet loner back then, studious, and a bit of a wimp.

The other school kids picked on him mercilessly. He literally ran home from school every day, hiding in his room. He had no friends and no relationship with his parents. Every day, his anger grew, but he kept it suppressed. He was boiling on the inside, but never let on, just kept to himself as the demons grew within his soul.

Martin joined the Navy right after high school. He did it to get as far away from all those irritating hicks in his hometown as possible. He had grown taller, but still was anemic-looking with a very non-athletic body. Even in the Navy, he kept to himself, never made any friends, and just spent his time alone. Everyone seemed to avoid him and his brooding personality.

Then Martin read about the elite Navy fighting specialists called Seals. He became obsessed with the idea. He wanted to become a Seal.

Martin had always enjoyed swimming in Cedar Creek Lake and was a pretty strong swimmer despite his otherwise frail body, just because he swam every day. He always swam alone. He never had a girlfriend. He never wanted one. Never wanted any friends either - too much work. He just liked to be left alone.

Despite his other shortcomings, Martin had always been single-minded. When he decided to become an elite Navy Seal it truly became an obsession. He lifted weights every free moment, spending hours a day in the base gym. His body changed dramatically. The loner became a certified scuba diver and swam for even more and more hours to build his stamina. Every day, he practiced his ability to hold his breath underwater for longer and longer periods of time.

It took two years of hard, relentless work in the weight room, the pool and running mile after mile every day, while he maintained his Navy day job – a low-level, unknown and unappreciated filing clerk.

Though his commanding officer noticed an impressive change in Martin's physique, he still smiled broadly and chortled out loud when the sailor told him he wanted to be a Seal. That lame reaction raised the temperature a few more degrees deep in the seething furnace inside Martin's soul, driving him even stronger toward his goal.

It took three months of cajoling before Martin's superior reluctantly let him fill out the paperwork for Seal training. The commanding officer was afraid he might be embarrassed by Martin's attempt, but he also didn't want to lose one darn fine filing clerk.

To the commanding officer's great surprise, Martin was eventually accepted for Seal training and quickly became one of the best of the best in his class. For the first time in his life Martin the loner had found a skill that earned him admiration from others. He pretended not to care, but he was bursting with pride inside, even as he kept his distance from the rest of the Seals.

Navy Seals are modern day warriors who volunteer to fight as commandos, doing the dirtiest, toughest and most miserable jobs imaginable. These are jobs that no other soldier wants to have anything to do with. Navy Seal missions require unimagined stamina and an enormous tolerance for pain.

Seal training is the most intense in the military. Only five percent of the men who enroll in the training course hang on through graduation. Hell Week, alone, consists of five days and five nights of non-stop training drills with a total of only two hours sleep.

His commanding officer was shocked when Martin survived the intense training, and then began to volunteer for the most dangerous missions. For the next few years he rescued hostages, killed people when necessary, and did all the inhuman tasks that make the Navy Seals the elite fighting unit that it is.

But then, he became a little too intense. Suddenly he went from inhuman to an animal. Martin's concerned superiors continually passed him over for the missions that used to be a part of his almost daily routine. They felt, rightly so, that he had gone over the edge to the dark side. Martin was killing people unnecessarily during his missions. The Frog Man retreated further into his shell. When a fellow Seal made him angry during a drill Martin killed him. He was cleared in a military trial as the judge chalked it up to "just a Seal being a Seal." Like many Seal discretions, the whole episode was hushed up and never made public. But for Martin's commanding officers it was the final episode. He was quietly and unceremoniously drummed out of the Seals. Once again he was as useless to them as a lowly filing clerk.

Martin was furious. How could they treat him like a worthless piece of crap after his superior work on their behalf? It was as if the Frog Man were back in high school – a useless, unappreciated lump of nothingness. The fire in his belly that had stoked him to make the transformation to a Seal in the first place was now roaring at full flame, this time in unimaginable anger. His first reaction was, "to hell with them!"

But as the days and weeks passed, Martin decided that his commanding officers had simply made a huge mistake. His warped mind determined it was his obligation to the country and to the Seals to continue to hone his skills so when new leadership came to the front, he'd be ready when they wisely called him back to serve his country.

Six months after his severance from the Seals, Martin wrote a long, rambling letter, pleading to be allowed to return to the service of his country. He was quickly shunned in a form letter. So, once again the former anemic boy who turned into a killing machine had been rejected, this time by the only life he ever truly enjoyed.

Martin knew too much about the Seals and their secret activities, so they paid him a hefty pension so he could go away, keep quiet, and fade into the woodwork. And, so he did, even as he secretly vowed to himself to be ready when they corrected their mistake and begged him to come back.

Martin's mother and father had split up years before. His Mom had re-married and moved to Houston. His Dad died at the age of 47 in a car accident in Louisiana. Martin had never talked to either of them again after he joined the Seals. He had no brothers or sisters.

The former Navy Seal decided that the best place to disappear would be the Piney woods of East Texas. So, when he became a civilian, Martin moved to Athens. It is a city of 13,000 about a half hour from Cedar Creek Lake, and about 15 minutes from Eustace. He could be invisible there.

Athens was the biggest city in the region, outside of Tyler. It had several traffic lights. It was a pretty little town, the county seat, with a large courthouse in the center that formed part of an old-fashioned town square.

Established in 1865, it was named after Athens, Greece. Athens became famous in the early 1900's when its black-eyed pea business took off. The town is credited with starting the Texas tradition of eating the black-eyed peas on New Year's Day for good luck.

Today tourists flock to Athens twice a year, for the annual Memorial Day Weekend Fiddler's Contest, and its hamburger festival. The city claims that resident Fletcher Davis invented the hamburger and shipped it to the 1904 World's Fair in St. Louis.

Cody Martin rented a small, non-descript cabin on Lake Athens, a few miles out of town. It was on a secluded part of the small lake, and his neighbors were not close enough to snoop, or to try to get to know him.

He swam for hours every day, lifted weights at home doing one angry rep after another, after another, and stayed in great shape. He was self-sufficient. Martin even purchased his own equipment for re-filling his scuba tanks. Tanks he had purchased in Plano, a suburb in far north Dallas, far from the quiet life in East Texas, making his activities more difficult to trace.

Martin also started to stalk his victims – 35 miles away at Cedar Creek Lake. He did not know any of his victims, didn't care about them really. After all, they were just targets. The Navy had taught him well, once a Seal heartless killing machine, always a Seal heartless killing machine.

No, Martin had no revenge motive on all the stupid people he had to put up with while he grew up. No rhyme, nor reason in choosing his victims. In Martin's twisted world he was simply staying in top form until the Seals realized his value and called him back into service. He chuckled to himself, "won't that drive the cops, those know-it-all profilers, and the media crazy."

Meanwhile over at Cedar Creek Lake, WDFW crime reporter Misty Reese, and *Gazette* reporter Dwayne Murphy worked long and hard to uncover a possible link between the drownings, and to scoop the world on the whereabouts, and fate or Franklin Bushman.

Reese was an accomplished reporter who had won numerous EMMY awards for her investigative work. She was tall, lithe, almost gaunt in the way of many TV performers, and had fine facial features that were perfect for the television camera. Reese also had the big hair, favored in the great state of Texas. Reese was a graduate of Texas A&M. After working less than a year at a small TV station in Waco, Texas she made the leap to Big D and WDFW-TV. Just a year ago, the station had rewarded her tenure, and hard work, by naming her co-anchor of the weekend newscasts.

But, despite her strong reporting skills, Reese and Murphy were getting nowhere, and neither Reese's news director, nor Murphy's editor would let them run in print or on air, with simply speculation that the deaths were actually murders, and were somehow linked.

After a week of intense media pressure, but no progress by the baffled police officers or the army of reporters, The Frogman decided that it was time to turn up the heat.

17

Forty-seven-year-old Anthony Runyon was an ambitious media consultant based in Dallas. A former state politician, he had launched a thriving political consultation business after losing his race for governor of Texas about five years ago.

Runyon, who had never married, flew from coast to coast to assist in political campaigns, working with the candidates and their handlers on how to deal with, and manipulate the news media.

He was also an unabashedly avid fisherman. He never traveled without his custom-made pole and travel case, and always found time to sneak away for a day of fishing, no matter what part of the country he was in.

That passion led Runyon to buy a small lake house on Cedar Creek Lake. He put in an office, and left his downtown Dallas loft behind whenever possible, to work in the tranquility of his lake house.

Runyon worked long, hard hours even at the lake, often late into the evening, but he always found time at the end of the day to grab his pole and fish off his dock.

Even though the lake was a hotbed of media types chasing the Bushman story, Runyon had the lake to himself after eleven o'clock at night as he stood in the dark shadows, and made cast after cast across the bright swath of water illuminated by the spotlights shining down off the end of his dock.

It was approaching midnight, on a very dark, moonless night, as Runyon battled about a six or seven-pound hybrid striper that had lunged at his shiny Spinnerbait lure as it flitted across the lighted stretch of water. The fish leapt out of the water a couple of times, and still had some fight left in him. Runyon was having a blast, when his quiet night was suddenly shattered. He was so busy battling the fish, he didn't notice that death was lurking nearby.

The Frogman surfaced just off the end of the dock, in about six feet of water, grabbed Runyon's ankles and in one powerful motion jerked him quickly into the night air. As he fell helplessly into the water, with a big splash, Runyon's pole slipped out of his hands, and the powerful fish swam away with it, as both the fish and the fisherman disappeared into the dark water.

Just as suddenly the still night returned to this dark corner of Cedar Creek Lake. The Frogman's surveillance showed that every resident along this section of shoreline was a weekender, and none of them, except for Runyon, were at the lake on this night.

Sheriff Buddy King rolled out of bed early on Wednesday morning. He showered quickly and headed out the door to meet Billy Richardson for breakfast. King needed a sympathetic ear and some advice. The search for Franklin Bushman was still coming up empty, and the media was accelerating the drumbeat.

King was also getting an earful from local merchants in Henderson County. They were not pleased with all the negative media attention just as their prime tourist season was heating up. They had helped Sheriff King win the election and they were letting him know about their displeasure in no uncertain terms.

As he hopped into his squad car, Sheriff King had no inkling that his world was about to get really turned upside down in unimaginable ways today.

18

On the west shore of Cedar Creek Lake, Shirley Hermann, was out for her daily morning stroll, her trusty pooch Versace at her side. Shirley, at age 76, took a brisk walk every morning to keep herself in the spry shape her friends all admired her for.

She walked along the road near her lake house, and then cut into the small park area a half block away that bordered the water. It was a small patch of grass with one lone picnic table. The table was chained to a tree near the boat launch, so no one would be tempted to throw it in the back of their pickup truck. Shirley always picked up any trash left behind by careless boaters and park users, trying to keep her neighborhood clean.

She stooped down and tossed a discarded beer can into the garbage bag she always carried along on her morning walks. She also had her trusty "pooper-scooper" to assure that Versace did not pollute the landscape either.

It was a beautiful morning, with the sun beginning its journey from the far eastern shoreline to its eventual perch high in the sky by noontime. There was just a smattering of puffy gray-white clouds to spoil the otherwise clear Texas sky. The weatherman had said there was a slight chance of a thundershower by late this afternoon.

As Shirley gazed out at the lake, something caught her eye. It looked like a big garbage bag, or something, floating about 50 yards offshore in the calm water. She walked to the very edge of the rocky shoreline and tried to focus on just what it might be, but the rising sun in her eyes turned the object into a silhouette.

Her curiosity aroused, and her anger rising with the thought that someone had dropped some big trash into her beloved lake, Shirley guided Versace back to her lake house. She grabbed her binoculars, left Versace behind, and hurried back to the small park for a closer look, grumbling to herself all the way about those damn weekenders who pollute the lake and then head back to Dallas.

As she brought the binoculars into focus, Shirley was startled to see that it was not some big trash bag, as she had suspected. There was what looked like a person, floating face down in the water, and he was naked!

With a gasp, Shirley walked briskly back to her home, and dialed 9-1-1.

"Good morning, this is the Henderson County 9-1-1 dispatcher," answered the voice on the phone, "what is your emergency?"

"I think there's a dead body floating in the lake," Shirley blurted into the phone. She added, "and it's naked as a jaybird."

"What is your name, and your location, madam?"

As she wrote down the information, the dispatcher's mind was racing. Could this be the body of Franklin Bushman?

At about that same time, Sheriff King and Billy Richardson were digging into greasy eggs, sausage, grits, and of course, steaming hot homemade biscuits at McDuff's restaurant. They were going over details of the missing billionaire for the hundredth time. Richardson, who had solved many tough cases in his Dallas detective career, was stumped and getting more and more frustrated.

"I've tapped into every source I have," he said, "and it keeps coming back the same. No money problems, a rock-solid marriage to a wife he clearly adored, and not even a traffic ticket to his name."

Just then, Sheriff King's cell phone rang. It was the 9-1-1 dispatcher. The frustration level was about to go off the charts.

"Sheriff, this is Molly. You told us to call you directly and not to use the police radios in case something important came up in this case of that missing Bushman fellow."

"That's right Molly. What's up?"

"Just got a call from a woman on the west shore who says she thinks there's a body floating in the water about 50 yards off of Canton Park, right near the boat launch. She says it's naked too."

Sheriff King quickly scanned the area she was talking about in his brain. It did not make sense.

"Molly that park is at least a mile from where we found the abandoned yacht isn't it?"

The dispatcher assured him that was true. King must have raised his voice a bit, because Richardson gave him the "pipe down" look, as a lot of ears perked up all around him in the restaurant.

King got the message and lowered his voice as he told the dispatcher that she had done the right thing by calling him first, and warning her not to tell anyone else.

"No one, Molly, not even in our own office, until I can personally check it out," he admonished her, "I'm on the way right now."

King and Richardson both rose from the battered booth of the restaurant and tossed money for their half-finished meal and a tip on the table. They briskly walked out of the place and got into their police car. King decided against the siren, wanting to maintain a low profile, away from the prying eyes of the media.

As soon as the lawmen left, waitress Melinda Sue dropped a couple of coins into the restaurant's pay phone. *Gazette* reporter Dwayne Murphy answered on the other end of the call.

She was almost speaking in a whisper, "Murphy, this is Melinda Sue. I got a hot tip for yah." Murphy had a network of snoops all over the lake area. He was always recruiting new spies to join his team. Most of the tips turned out to be worthless, so Murphy was expecting nothing, but he was in for a big surprise.

"I think somebody might've found the body of that Bushman guy whose wife drowned the other day."

Murphy, who had been half asleep at this early morning hour, jolted to life.

"What makes you think that Melinda Sue?"

She glanced around, then said, "Well, the sheriff got a call on his cell phone, and he got real serious, told whoever was calling not to tell anybody else, and said 'how could that be, it's a mile from where we found the yacht.'"

Murphy got excited. It must be Bushman's body. But where was it?

"Melinda Sue, did he say where this happened?"

"No, but he sure did rush outa here in a hurry."

Murphy thanked the waitress and ran the scenarios through his head. A mile away from the yacht? Which way? It could be either side of the lake. How would the body get a mile away?

King's cruiser was heading rapidly, but without lights and siren down the side streets that would take him to Canton Park. Richardson was frowning, "There are no big currents in this lake. How the hell would a body drift a mile away, and stay under water?"

King glanced over at the detective, "Don't know, but I don't like it. There's something fishy going on here."

"I tell yah Buddy, I've been penciling out all kind of possibilities for these strange episodes, and this development definitely wasn't on the list."

The sheriff's patrol car pulled into the park. He assumed the lady sitting at the picnic table, with the dog on the leash, was the woman who called in the sighting.

King and Richardson hopped out of the car, and slammed the doors shut, moving briskly toward the woman. King spoke first, "Howdy ma'am, I'm Sheriff King, and this is detective Richardson. Are you the one who called 9-1-1?"

"Yes sir. There's a body floatin' right out there," she replied pointing a gnarled, bony finger at a spot about fifty yards offshore, "Here take a look see."

Sheriff King took her binoculars and focused on the spot she was pointing out. "Yup, that sure looks like a body all right. Did you tell anybody else about this, ma'am?"

"No sir, the dispatcher lady told me it was important to keep it quiet, so as not to disturb the crime scene," she said with a touch of pride in her voice.

"You did just great, ma'am. Thank you very much," Sheriff King praised her while he looked around for a boat to use to reach the body.

Meanwhile, nearly straight across the lake, about two miles as the crow flies, Patricia Schmidt was pulling into Anthony Runyon's driveway. He paid her $40 a week to come in and tidy up the place for him every Wednesday.

Patricia got out of her battered 15-year-old station wagon and lugged her various cleaning ingredients and a big pail to the door of Runyon's lake house. She plopped the load down on the porch and knocked on the door. There was no answer.

She thought to herself, "That's odd, Anthony knew I was coming over at nine this morning. He said he'd be working in his office."

Back on the opposite side of the lake, Sheriff King called the Gun Barrel City police chief on his cell phone, and filled him in, cautioning him to keep this between only them at this point. He asked the chief to bring a boat to the park, but to do it without arousing any suspicion.

The police chief quickly left the office, backed his squad car into the department's garage, and hooked up a trailer with a small fiberglass runabout on it.

19

Dwayne Murphy was stumped. He'd looked at a map and found no less than five parks that could be within a mile or so of where the yacht had been moored, and they were on both sides of the lake.

Murphy stopped at the Sonic drive-in across the street from the Gun Barrel City police station to grab a cup of coffee. It turned out to be a lucky decision.

He was trying to pinpoint which park to head to first, when Murphy spotted the police chief's car leaving the station, towing a runabout behind it. A big grin crossed his face, as he thought to himself, "Rather be lucky than good."

Murphy pulled out of the drive-in, keeping a discreet distance behind the police cruiser. He was sure it would lead him to the crime scene.

While Murphy was following the police chief, Patricia Schmidt, tired of knocking, decided to try the door at Anthony Runyon's home. It was unlocked, as usual. She'd warned him many times about keeping the door locked, but he said it was safe around the lake, not like in Dallas, where he always kept his doors locked and bolted.

She stepped inside and found the lights on in the living room and kitchen, with the TV blaring in the den.

She called out Anthony's name. No answer. Patricia peeked into his office. Empty.

The police chief pulled into the park, and quickly backed the boat down the ramp, and into the water. Detective Richardson grabbed the rope and held it at the dock, while the chief parked his squad car and the boat trailer.

Murphy had stopped about two blocks away from the park, not wanting to be spotted by the police chief. He parked his car, walked through the yard of a neighboring home and peered around a tree toward the park.

Patricia Schmidt couldn't figure out where Anthony was. His car was in the driveway, and it wasn't like him not to be slaving away at his computer this time of day. He always seemed to be a workaholic to her, although he did always set aside some time for fishing. But she knew that was usually late at night.

Patricia decided to walk out to the dock, just to see if Anthony was taking a break for some reason. She headed down the path but couldn't see anyone on the dock that stretched about 40 yards into the water.

At Canton Park, the three lawmen had piled into the small runabout and fired up its motor. They chugged quickly to the spot where the body was lying face down in the water.

Reporter Murphy had grabbed his trusty binoculars as he left his car, and was intently following the action from shore, hidden behind a tree.

Patricia Schmidt walked to the end of the wooden dock. There was no sign of Anthony Runyon. She walked past the small fish shed that sat next to the boatlift and turned right to walk to the end of that portion of the dock. No sign of Runyon.

Patricia was about to turn to head back to the house, when something caught her eye in the water. It looked like a large piece of blue cloth, there seemed to be a little air bubble in it, as it floated near the surface, barely visible in the murky water. The water was only about three feet deep right off the shore side of the dock.

The runabout reached the body and Richardson, using rubber gloves, carefully rolled it over. There staring back at him with wide-open, but very dead eyes was the man he knew from pictures as Franklin Bushman.

Patricia Schmidt was frightened. She had seen Anthony wear a jacket of that same color on many occasions. Just then, the wind picked up a bit, sending a ripple through the water. The piece of cloth rolled over. It was a body.

Patricia screamed and ran around to the ladder a few feet away. She took off her shoes, and waded into the chest-deep water, rushing as fast as she could, fighting to move quickly through the water.

She grabbed the body, and nearly fainted. It was Anthony Runyon, and he was very dead. She screamed again, dropped the body and rushed her way back through the water.

Patricia scrambled up the ladder and sprinted to the house. She quickly dialed 9-1-1, and breathlessly told the dispatcher what she'd just seen.

Across the lake, the lawmen carefully held the body, and decided to gently drag it to shore behind the small boat since the small watercraft was already filled with the three of them. They slowly creeped back toward the dock.

Murphy strained through his binoculars to see the face of the lifeless form but could not make it out. He ran back to his car. He thought to himself, it's time to drive to the dock and greet the lawmen, with his camera in hand to get the award-winning pictures of their catch.

At that same moment, Sheriff King's cell phone began to ring.

"Damn it," he said, "Now what?"

The boat was about ten yards from the dock, and King had just spotted Murphy, camera in hand, snapping away as they neared the shore. What could go wrong next?

With much irritation in his voice, Sheriff King punched the call button on his phone and fairly shouted into it, "Yah, what is it?"

"Sheriff King this is the 9-1-1 dispatcher. I have a hysterical woman on the phone who says she has just found a body floating in the lake."

King's stomach almost fell through his feet. His face must have twisted into a horrendous form, as detective Richardson quickly said, "What it is Buddy, you look like you're about to pass out?"

Murphy was now less than fifteen yards away, still snapping pictures with a vengeance. King lowered his voice into a hoarse whisper, "We just got a report of another drowning."

Richardson shot a look at his pal, and then at the *Gazette* reporter now just a few feet away. "What the hell?" was all he could manage to get out. The man who had seen it all during decades solving the most hideous and difficult crimes in a metro area of five million people was shocked. He thought to himself, "What the hell is going on?"

The emergency dispatcher was still on the cell phone. "Ah, sheriff," she finally said, "you want the rest of the information? I need to know what to do."

That snapped King out of his trance. "Uh, just hang on a minute and I'll call you back. I have a situation here that has to be taken care of first."

The small motorboat was now at the dock, and the police chief was holding the edge of the structure, while Richardson maintained his grip on the corpse of Franklin Bushman. King hopped onto the dock.

He directed his anger at the newspaper reporter.

"Murphy, what in the hell are you doing here?" he screamed, "Hand that camera over to me right now!"

The reporter had never seen Sheriff King so angry, his sculpted jaw was thrust forward, and he was moving quickly toward Murphy with his hand out.

Murphy started to back away from the advancing sheriff.

"Sheriff King, I know my rights. This is public property, and I have every right to be here," he shouted, trying to sound as forceful as possible but his voice squeaked and cracked. He was clearly afraid of the menacing look on King's face.

"And I have every right to slap you in handcuffs and toss you in jail for interfering with a police investigation," King shouted back at him, still striding forward while Murphy scrambled backward as fast as he could.

Now Murphy was both scared and excited. Scared, because he felt that King might snap him in half, he was so crazed. Excited, because his mind was racing with the national exposure, he would get for being thrown into the slammer for taking pictures of a story that would soon be capturing more national attention. This could be his big break, whether he had the pictures or not.

Patricia Schmidt was pacing back and forth on the deck of Runyon's lake house, staring at the portable phone in her hand. She was trying to will it to ring. The emergency dispatcher said she would call right back. It had been almost five minutes. It seemed like five hours.

She dialed 9-1-1 again. The same dispatcher answered the call. Patricia was talking in quick bursts, "It's been a long time, why haven't you called back, what should I do, I'm scared, I don't know what to do, poor Mr. Runyon is out in the awful water, he's not moving…"

When Schmidt paused briefly for a quick, sobbing breath, the dispatcher jumped in, with the most soothing voice she could muster under the circumstances.

"Ma'am, I know how difficult this is. The sheriff has promised to get back to me right away. He is dealing with another matter right now that demands his full attention. You hang tight, it'll just be a minute."

Meanwhile at Canton Park, Sheriff King was now within a foot of the *Gazette* reporter. It was about to get ugly. Behind him, Richardson and the police chief were struggling to drag Franklin Bushman's waterlogged body onto shore, so they could cover it with a blanket.

King's cell phone started to ring. He stopped to answer it, as Murphy continued to back away, trying desperately to put some more space between himself and the seething sheriff.

It was the 9-1-1 dispatcher, "Sheriff I'm sorry to call you again, but the woman is really losing it. Can I send a car to the location?"

King quickly ran through the options in his head, as the dispatcher filled him in on the full story. "No," he said to the dispatcher, "Tell her I will be there as soon as possible, probably about 20 minutes. And tell her not to tell anyone else about this, just have her sit tight. Got it?"

He jammed his phone back into his pocket, and turned his attention back to Murphy, who was looking at him with a very curious look. The reporter was thinking to himself, "What the hell is going on here? What was that call all about?"

The sheriff said firmly, "Murphy you get in the backseat of my squad car. Right now. You sit there until I get there. And hand over your cell phone to me now!"

Murphy, who was thinking the sheriff was going to maybe kill him just a few moments ago, let out a sigh of relief. This reprieve was a good alternative, and he still had his camera with the pictures. He handed his cell phone to the sheriff and walked over to the squad car, clutching his camera with both hands, cradling it like a small brick of gold.

King strode back over to Richardson and the Gun Barrel City police chief. They looked at him with puzzled and very concerned stares. The sheriff took a big breath, checked to be sure that Murphy was out of earshot, and turned back to the lawmen.

"That was Molly, a woman by the name of Patricia Schmidt says she found the body of a guy named Anthony Runyon floating in about three or four feet of water, just off his dock. What the hell is going on here?"

Richardson furrowed his brow; his well-lined face was a mask. He knew he had to calm down his friend, who had never faced a crisis close to this in his entire life.

"Buddy, first off take a deep breath. We need to decide some next steps here. Who is this woman who called 9-1-1?"

"Don't know her, Billy," the sheriff replied, trying to speak with a calm voice, "She's apparently a cleaning lady who showed up at Runyon's home, didn't see him anywhere, and then found him floating in the water. That's all I know."

20

Murphy sat in the sheriff's squad car about a hundred feet from the trio. He had left the door open, as he strained to hear what they were talking about. Sheriff King hollered at him to shut the door, which he did. Murphy couldn't roll down the window, it was electric, and the sheriff had the ignition keys. He sat back in the seat, arms crossed and fumed to himself.

"OK," Richardson offered, "Let's leave the chief here with Bushman's body. He can get his most trusted deputy out here to help him until we can get back. That way we can keep a lid on finding Bushman. We'll call Doc in to examine the body before we move it anywhere. Be sure to warn him to not talk to anyone, he loves to talk."

King nodded, "Good plan, so far, what else?"

Richardson looked over at the newspaper reporter, and said, "Have him get out of your squad and into the back seat of the police chief's car. That will keep him on ice until we figure out how to handle this with the news hounds. Let him keep his camera for now, I think we're going to have a hell of a lot more to worry about than his pictures."

The other two lawmen nodded in unison, Richardson continued, "The sheriff and I will head over to this new location and try to make sense of all this crap. We only communicate by cell phone, no police radios. Got it?"

The veteran detective and sheriff hopped into the county squad car, and raced out of the park, spewing stones from the rear tires as they fought for traction. Richardson called the 9-1-1 dispatcher to get Runyon's address.

As soon as the county squad car was out of the immediate neighborhood of the park, King flipped on the emergency lights and siren. He wanted to get to Runyon's house as soon as possible but didn't want to raise the suspicion of neighbors near the park.

Cars moved over one by one, as the sheriff's car, siren wailing raced down the highway and across the bridges between Seven Points and Gun Barrel City. As he neared the neighborhood that contained Runyon's residence, he cut the siren and lights, and slowed down, again not wanting to draw undue attention to where he was headed.

Patricia Schmidt saw the sheriff's police cruiser pull to a stop on the road near Runyon's garage, and let out a huge breath. "Thank God," she thought to herself. It had been less than an hour since she spotted the body, but it had seemed like a week.

The sheriff and detective introduced themselves to Schmidt, and she quickly walked to the dock to show them where Runyon's body was floating motionless in the calm water. The wind had now diminished, and not a breeze stirred on the lake.

Richardson emptied his pockets, took off his shoes and clambered down the ladder to retrieve the body from the shallow water. The sheriff helped him lift the lifeless form onto the dock. They took a cursory look, before covering him with the blanket they had brought from the squad car.

"No outward signs of violence or injuries," Richardson sighed and said, "Looks like he could have drowned."

That did not sit well with his housekeeper. "He was in great health, and fished off this dock most every night," she said sharply looking the sheriff in the eye, "How could he drown in four feet of water? All he had to do was stand up!"

Both King and Richardson shook their heads; the sheriff spoke first, "I have no idea ma'am. He could have had a heart attack, or passed out for some reason and fell into the water."

Richardson looked at her, "How well did you know Mr. Runyon?"

"It's not like we were friends or anything," she quietly replied, "I just cleaned his place once a week, but he was a nice man, always very friendly, and a hard worker too."

Sheriff King walked away from them, to the end of the dock near shore. He called the police chief on his cell phone.

"Bad news," he said, "We've got another one here. Looks like he may have drowned, just like all the others. Doc get there yet?"

The chief informed the sheriff that the medical examiner had indeed reached the park and had looked at the body of Franklin Bushman. The chief said, "There were no signs of a struggle, no bruises, no wounds, looks like he had water in his lungs."

The sheriff gave the chief Runyon's address and asked him to send the medical examiner there. They'd wait for him.

The sheriff was uncertain of what to do next. They clearly had a puzzling situation, a horrible situation, with six deaths in a short time span. They needed help. This was bigger than King's small department could handle. Maybe it was time to call in the big boys from Dallas, maybe even the FBI.

King strode back to the end of the dock, and gently suggested to the cleaning woman that she wait in Runyon's house for a few minutes. She silently nodded her head, and gladly moved away from the covered body of Runyon.

Sheriff King turned to his friend, the veteran of many horrible cases in Dallas, and said, "I need some ideas, what the hell do we do now? We have to keep these bodies from the news media, but we need to start crime scene investigations at both locations. Maybe we need some help from Dallas or the feds?"

Richardson had also been thinking of the next steps. None of them would be easy.

21

It was nearly three in the afternoon, and the killer was getting anxious. He had been watching the local TV channels all day and had the Dallas news/talk radio station on too. But there was no word of either body being found. There was nothing on the Internet, or social media either. He was looking forward to the confusion these discoveries would cause, to the rush to speculate by the local and national media, but there was nothing on TV but game shows and soap operas.

King and Richardson decided it was time to call for limited help. The former Dallas detective called one of his buddies in the forensic unit and asked him to come to Cedar Creek Lake to help in the investigation and detailed examination of the two latest bodies. Danny Cates quickly got approval from his boss, grabbed his crime kit, and left Dallas using his siren to get to the lake as quickly as possible.

Murphy was much less afraid of the Gun Barrel City police chief than he was of Sheriff King, who was much stronger and had clearly gone ballistic an hour or so ago. He opened the door of the squad car and started walking toward the chief.

The chief told him to get back in the car. Murphy stood his ground, "No way in hell. You can't hold me here indefinitely. I'm leaving." He started to walk away.

The chief reacted quickly, and in a frightening manner. He pulled his gun out of its holster and with a stern voice hollered after Murphy to halt in his tracks or he would shoot.

Murphy, startled, spun around and saw the gun leveled at him. The chief was serious. He quickly crawled into the back seat of the city squad car, and rapidly closed the door. The police chief locked the doors this time.

Sheriff King decided he had to call in some of his most trusted officers to begin to secure this potential crime scene, and also the scene at Canton Park. Although the city police chief had helped him out by bringing the boat, the park was technically located in the county, outside the city limits.

Suddenly the harsh ringing of a cell phone interrupted his thoughts. But it wasn't the sheriff's phone. It was Murphy's. He'd stuck it in his pocket after taking it from the reporter.

Lost in his thoughts, the sheriff grabbed the phone from his pocket and answered it with a brisk, "Yeah."

The voice on the other end was southern and silky, but firm, "Hey, Murphy what the hell's going on? I haven't heard from you all day."

Sheriff King listened intently. He knew that voice but couldn't place it.

"Hello! Talk to me, Murph. Are you there?"

A flicker of recognition crossed the sheriff's face. Damn, he thought, it's that TV reporter, Mindy Reese. Now what should he do? He disconnected the call.

Sheriff King's world was spinning out of control. This was not like making an error in a minor league baseball game that caused his team to lose the game. This was suddenly a chain of events that he was not prepared to handle. He'd only been sheriff for a few months.

He had to lean on his friend, Richardson to help him get a grip on the situation. He didn't have to look far; Billy Richardson was right at his elbow, with a worried look on his craggy face.

A couple of Sheriff King's senior officers arrived at the home of the dead consultant. They were told to secure the area, keep it low profile, and to thoroughly search the water, the dock, and the property for any clues. King and Richardson drove back into Gun Barrel City, grabbed a couple of coffees at a gas station, and headed back to Canton Park where the billionaire's body had been found.

Canton Park was a busy place, and the lawmen knew the lid would blow off this situation pretty soon. There were a few nosy neighbors standing around the outskirts of the park. The lawmen did manage a smile when they saw a thoroughly angry Dwayne Murphy, the reporter, still held captive in the back of the city police chief's squad car.

Bushman's body had been loaded into the ambulance. Detectives were everywhere searching the park for evidence, with a few members of the scuba team looking for clues under the lake's water.

Sheriff King and detective Richardson sat the at the lone picnic table. Richardson had a yellow legal pad. The Gun Barrel Police Chief sat down to listen in. The reporter was pounding on the window of the squad car, saying something they could not hear.

"Alright," Richardson said, setting down his coffee. "First off we have a mess here. Two crime scenes spread out on opposite sides of the lake, six unexplained deaths, and the national media ready to pounce on this story like white on rice."

"Plus," Sheriff King added, "We have no idea how the hell Bushman's body got over here, a mile or so away from where his wife's body was found, and," he nodded over to the angry reporter, "We can't keep him on ice much longer or we'll have a civil rights suit on our hands."

"OK, let's make a list of priorities," Richardson said, pen poised over the legal pad. "First off, we need to schedule a news conference so we can put our own spin on this situation before the media starts speculating like crazy."

"I agree," King offered, "But I'd like you to handle the news media. I'm not good in front of all those news hounds. You've been there many times before. Can you be the spokesman for the investigation?"

"No problem," Richardson replied.

"Good, the next question is what the hell do we tell them?"

Richardson put down his pen, gazed out over the lake, took a peek at the gathering crowd at the park, and let out a big sigh, "Well, I guess we can only tell them the facts as we know them. Which ain't a hell of a lot at this point."

King nodded grimly, "We gotta be careful not to scare the hell out of people who live around here, and the tourists too. These business owners do eighty percent of their business from now until Labor Day."

The Gun Barrel Police Chief chimed in, "And you know the news media will be speculating like crazy about a serial killer being on the loose around here."

Richardson looked at his watch. "Let's have a news conference at seven o'clock tonight. That's about four hours from now. That gives us enough time to put a plausible report together, and it gets us past the early evening local newscasts, and the network newscasts."

King nodded his agreement.

"Now," Richardson said, "We need to call in the FBI, and Danny Cates should be here any minute from Dallas County to help us start putting the pieces together."

King looked at his friend, "I hate getting the FBI involved, they'll trample all over us."

Richardson shot King a reassuring look, "No they won't. Leave those blue suits to me. I know them pretty well, and we have some mutual respect. I'll handle them."

"Great."

"Now here's the plan," Richardson said as he scribbled on the note pad, "We announce that there have been a number of apparent drowning deaths. We explain that there has been no sign of foul play in any of them. That there is nothing we have uncovered so far to link any of the deaths to any one event, or any one person, or to each other. At the same time, we are not naïve enough to believe that six drownings in such a short period does not raise concern that something unusual might be causing them."

Sheriff King flashed a tight smile, "That sounds reasonable."

Richardson snorted, "Yeah but there is no reasonable when it comes to the news media horde on a story like this. I think at this point we take no questions. I will use a map to lay out where the drowning deaths occurred, and I'll say we will have more information in another day. We also announce that we have formed a joint task force with the Henderson County Sheriff's office, the Gun Barrel City Police, the FBI, and a special assistant from the Dallas County Sheriff's office."

As this discussion went on, Murphy, the trapped reporter started banging on the window of the squad car. He'd had enough of this imprisonment.

At that moment, a solid white car, obviously an unmarked police cruiser pulled into the park. It was Danny Cates from Dallas County.

Richardson gave his former partner in crime solving a hearty handshake and introduced him all around. Cates heard the pounding coming from the squad car and gave Richardson a questioning look.

"No, that is not a suspect," Richardson said to his friend, "Just the local newspaper reporter we've been keeping out of circulation for a spell."

Cates laughed, "He is not a happy camper."

The Gun Barrel City police chief strolled over to his squad car, unlocked and opened the door. The reporter got out. He was fuming. Murphy stormed over to the picnic table, still clutching his digital camera, but not daring to take a picture at this moment.

The lawmen had thought of a way to appease the newspaper reporter. They'd give him word of the sixth death, if he agreed to keep a lid on it until after the news conference. That way he would have a head start on that aspect of the story in return for his discomfort the past few hours.

Sheriff King motioned for Murphy to sit down, "Listen Murph, sorry about that little detention, but we've had a busy couple of hours, and really needed some time to do some police work without being trampled on by the other news media."

Murphy was having none of it. "I'm going to sue you personally," he fumed, "And the county and the city of Gun Barrel for false imprisonment, and for civil rights violations. This is a public park, and," he pointed a finger at the police chief, his voice rising, "He threatened me with a gun."

King and Richardson looked at the chief, who shrugged, "He said he was leaving, and you told me to keep him here, so I did."

The two lawmen stifled an urge to let out a tension-easing chuckle. They were afraid Murphy was going to come over the top of the picnic table. He was hot.

King said in a calm, conciliatory tone, "Look Murph, I know you're pissed, but we're willing to throw you a bone to make your wait worthwhile. But you have to agree to sit on it until after seven o'clock tonight."

Murphy crossed his arms, trying to maintain his anger, but the sheriff had obviously piqued his interest. "I'm listening," he said, jutting out his jaw a bit.

Sheriff King explained to Murphy about the sixth drowning. He offered the dead man's name and address, on one condition. He admonished Murphy, "In exchange for this information you agree to drop any talk of a silly lawsuit, you do not tell anyone about this latest death, especially that TV reporter Reese, and you don't publish anything on the newspaper's web site until after the news conference."

Murphy uncrossed his arms, leaned forward and said, "OK, but I get to dig into who this guy is, interview whoever found him, and I can send the story out to the wire service and over the newspaper's website right at seven o'clock sharp. Deal?"

The sheriff nodded, "Deal."

Richardson said, "We'll alert the media about 5:45 about the news conference. That'll be too late to dig into it in time for the six o'clock news, and they'll have to scramble to get here by seven."

Murphy, now feeling like a police insider, chuckled, "You guys play a tough game when it comes to the news media."

22

While Richardson filled in Murphy on the sixth victim, a solitary figure sat in front of his TV set on the shore of Lake Athens, waiting for the five o'clock news to begin.

Cody Martin had hoped that his latest victim would send the police into a dazed state and incite the hungry news media. He had no idea that the police had also discovered the body of the billionaire today.

The killer was disappointed. There was no mention of the drowning deaths at all during the newscast.

He thought about calling that hot crime reporter, Mindy Reese, but caught himself before he made what could have been a fatal, traceable, mistake.

Dwayne Murphy was beside himself, as he furiously wrote the story of the dead media consultant. The ambitious *Cedar Creek Gazette* reporter had a "world exclusive!" He also had the only pictures of the dead billionaire's body being removed from the lake, as the sheriff seemed to forget about his digital camera as they made their deal on the timing of the news reports.

His crusty editor had even been impressed. They were poised to release the information on their website just as the news conference began, complete with the exclusive pictures. They would also be splattered across the front page of the *Gazette* tomorrow morning. What a break that all this happened on the same day the weekly paper went to press. The editor/owner had even bent the tight budget of the little newspaper to allow Murphy to have eight color pictures on the front page, including his exclusive pictures of the dead consultant's lake home, and the cleaning lady who found the body. He would have the only interview with her too. Murphy was salivating. Was this the break he had been striving for all this time?

Murphy was jarred out of his daydreaming by the sharp ringing of his office phone. He answered it and found the angry voice of Mindy Reese on the other end of the line. Murphy glanced at his watch. 5:50 p.m. The police had just alerted the media to their news conference set for seven o'clock that night.

"Murphy," Reese was nearly shouting into the phone, "What the hell is going on? What is this big news conference all about? The cops aren't saying anything."

A thousand thoughts rushed through Murphy's head at once. He was sitting on the biggest scoop of his life, but he'd made a deal with the sheriff, and he feared what the muscled lawman would do to him if he broke that vow.

But he could also share his scoop with Mindy which might lead to a job at the TV station, would certainly gain him national publicity as other media outlets hungrily picked up the story, and maybe, just maybe, get him a date with the beautiful crime reporter.

"Murphy, you still there?"

"Ah, yeah." He paused, shook his head, and said, "Don't know Mindy they just called and said there was a news conference at seven."

Reese was hot, "You're holding out on me Murphy. I can hear it in your voice."

"Not true, Mindy. Hey I gotta go. See you at the news conference." He gently hung up the phone, his heart pounding. He knew there was going to be hell to pay with Reese when he broke the story in about an hour.

He went back to work, finishing his big scoop so he could head to the library for the news conference.

Thirty-five minutes away, Cody Martin was reading *Soldier of Fortune* magazine, and half-watching the Dallas television news in his cozy cabin. He perked up when the anchorman reported that the Henderson County Sheriff had called a news conference for seven o'clock tonight. The anchorman said that crime reporter Mindy Reese was on her way to the news conference right now. He continued, "Mindy reports that police are tight-lipped on the exact information to be relayed at the news conference, but we believe it has to do with the drowning death of Misty Bushman, and the disappearance of her husband, billionaire Franklin Bushman." He reminded viewers to stay on this channel because the station would broadcast the news conference live in about an hour.

As the Dallas satellite trucks and news vehicles raced toward the Cedar Creek Library, Sheriff Buddy King paced back and forth like a panther in a cage. Richardson had never seen his longtime pal so nervous. King had a death grip on a piece of paper, mumbling to himself as he worked to memorize what he was going to say to lead off the news conference.

"Relax Buddy," Richardson said in a soothing voice.

"Easy for you to say. You've been through these kinds of ordeals a lot. I'm just not good at trying to stay out of the traps these reporters try to set for me."

Richardson smiled, for the first time all day. "It's easy," he told the rookie sheriff, "You just smile at 'em, duck every question they ask, and make sure you get out what you want to say. Then turn it over to me."

In the main meeting room of the library cables were snaking everywhere as the media set up their equipment. Outside the building satellite trucks covered the parking lot with their colorful logos from Dallas TV stations, the Tyler TV stations, and even one from CNN. The national cable network would beam the news conference live around the country, with Fox News Channel and MSNBC also picking up the satellite feeds from their affiliated stations from Dallas.

Murphy finished his worldwide web exclusive on the body of the billionaire being found, along with the drowning death of the political consultant. As he drove the mile or so from his office to the library, Murphy placed phone calls to Mindy Reese's cell phone, as well as CNN, and the big newspapers in Dallas and Fort Worth.

He excitedly told them to go to the Gazette's web site at 6:58 p.m. to get a heads up on the main points of the news conference. This would give the electronic channels a chance to break the story on their own right before the news conference began, with proper credit to Murphy, of course.

The excited newshound was bending the rules a bit, and he knew the sheriff would be angry. But this was the break Murphy needed. His name would be mentioned from coast to coast as news outlets used his exclusive information.

Cody Martin looked at his watch as he sat in the den of his secluded home, the dark black curtains pulled tightly closed to shutout the sunlight – and the world. It was almost time for the live news conference. He turned up the volume on the TV, leaned forward a bit in his overstuffed leather recliner, and waited.

Sheriff Buddy King strode to the podium in the library meeting room and gazed across the crowded scene. It was a sea of TV and still cameras with the whirring of their automatic advance mechanisms echoing throughout the library. He cleared his throat and asked everyone if they were ready. Suddenly the noisy din was overtaken by silent anticipation. A chair scraped on the concrete floor with the sound reverberating through the sudden silence.

The sheriff had never stood before such a large gathering. He took a deep breath and plunged on. "I'm Henderson County Sheriff Josh King," he began. "I've called this news conference to bring y'all up to date on a number of drowning deaths that have occurred in Cedar Creek Lake over the past few weeks. At this point, we believe that all of the unfortunate deaths have been accidental." The sheriff paused as a low murmur came from the skeptical news media, then he forged on. "But due to the unusual number of these occurrences in a relatively short period of time, I have formed a task force consisting of my department, plus representatives from the Gun Barrel City, and Seven Points police departments, the FBI, and detective Danny Cates, on loan from the Dallas County Sheriff's department."

Sheriff King, paused, and turned to look at his friend. "I have appointed Henderson County detective Billy Richardson to head this task force. He is a retired veteran of the Dallas County Sheriff's department and is my lead investigator here in Henderson County. Billy."

Billy Richardson moved to the podium, as the sheriff stepped off to the side. He peered into the bright lights and glanced down at his prepared remarks.

"Ladies and Gentlemen, I have some information to relay, and then I'll take a couple of questions. Today we recovered the body of Franklin Bushman from the lake about fifty yards off Canton Park. There were no outward signs of foul play, and the death has tentatively been ruled due to accidental drowning.

On the other side of Cedar Creek Lake, we also recovered the body this afternoon of Anthony Runyon. He apparently was fishing off his dock last night, fell into the water, and drowned. Again, there is no sign of foul play."

The low murmur reached a crescendo and shouted questions started erupting from the media. Richardson, a cool veteran of these media circuses, calmly put up his hand for quiet. He glared at the media, as if daring them to interrupt him once again. Richardson looked like an angry father taking his unruly children to task, as his piercing eyes bored holes in one news person after another.

"Now," he continued in a modulated, almost soothing, voice, "I know y'all have questions, and I'll take some of them in a moment. Before that, I just want to emphasize that although we have had a number of drowning deaths in a relatively short period of time, that at this time, we have no reason to believe that any of them are anything more than unfortunate incidents. None of them are related in any way, and each circumstance is totally different."

The killer's ears perked up at that statement. A satisfied look spread across Cody Martin's face as he watched the televised news conference. They don't have a clue, he smugly thought to himself, sitting alone in the semi-darkness in his small cabin on Lake Athens.

Back at the news conference, the din increased as hands, some bearing notepads, shot into the air like bottle rockets on the Fourth Of July. They all wanted their questions answered now. Billy Richardson pointed at Mindy Reese to go first. Beauty had its privileges.

"Detective," the TV reporter fairly shouted with disdain in her voice, as the room began to quiet, "How do you explain the fact that Franklin Bushman's body was found over a mile from where he disappeared from his yacht, from where his wife's body was found?"

Billy waited for the noise to abate a bit, "Miss Reese we just found the body of Mr. Bushman several hours ago. We have just begun the investigation."

Standing to the side, Sheriff King marveled at how his self-assured pal had sidestepped that potentially explosive question. More hands shot in the air, as reporters clamored for Richardson's attention, shouting down the attempted follow-up question from Mindy Reese.

The detective pointed at the man he recognized as a CNN national correspondent. The reporter asked if the lake was a safe place for residents.

Richardson gave a reassuring smile, and in a very calm voice said, "We want everyone in this area to know that while these are unfortunate incidents, that Cedar Creek Lake is a safe place to live and to have fun on the water. We have no evidence to suggest otherwise."

As the volume peaked again from the reporter's shouted questions, Sheriff King stepped in, as they had rehearsed, and said, "Thank you ladies and gentlemen." With that the lawmen turned and left the podium as the shouted questions rained down on their backs.

Thirty miles away, the serial killer pulled back the heavy curtains and gazed out the window as the reporters began their speculation speaking into the multitude of TV cameras. He was pondering whether to let the reporters stir the boiling pot on their own for a while, or to add to the confusion by having them find another victim.

23

In the crowded library meeting room, *Gazette* reporter Murphy was having his fifteen minutes of fame, and he was lapping it up. The local TV stations and the national cable channels were taking turns interviewing the only reporter to have been at both crime scenes, and to have interviewed the woman who found Runyon's body. The TV-types had taken the photographs off the newspaper's website and were showing them as background graphics as the reporters interviewed Murphy live. Surprisingly, for a newspaper guy, Murphy proved to be a glib and enlightening live interview subject. For his part, Murphy was anxious to get home and watch the recording of his moment in the sun.

Sheriff King, detective Richardson, Dallas County detective Cates, and a number of other lawmen were back in the sheriff's office, talking about the case. King congratulated Richardson on his handling of the news conference. "Didn't lay a glove on yah," King said as he slapped his friend on the back.

Richardson was not smiling. He said in a low, concerned voice, "It went okay, but we need to get a handle on this situation, and quick. With six deaths in a few weeks, the media will sink their teeth into this one and not let go. That includes the national media too."

Detective Cates nodded in agreement, "We all know that these have to be connected in some way, and the news media is always big on conspiracy theories. It is going to get real nasty, real fast. The circus has come to town in a big way."

They spent the next couple hours going through each death, each incident, searching for some small thread, anything to connect them. The baffling part was that there were no signs of foul play, no signs of a struggle, on any of the bodies. They simply could not find any links between the deaths.

Meanwhile, Cody Martin hopped into his truck, and headed for Wesley's Marina for a beer and a grilled chicken sandwich. He sat alone on the outdoor patio of the second-floor restaurant that offered a wonderful view of the docks below, and the moon shining on the lake as it stretched toward the distant east shore.

It wasn't too busy tonight, but the few occupied tables kept waitress Crystal scurrying around. Without trying to be too obvious, Martin enjoyed the view of the diminutive brunette with the short cutoff jean shorts, and a t-shirt tied up to give a glimpse of her flat, tanned stomach.

The serial killer wondered to himself what the media and the lawmen would do if she were his next victim. Everyone in the area knew the waitress and animal lover was the sheriff's girlfriend. She'd been with him everywhere on the campaign trail. He motioned to Crystal for another beer.

In the Henderson County Sheriff's office, Buddy King, Billy Richardson, and Danny Cates were working on a big bulletin board. It was rapidly being covered with pictures of all six of the drowning victims, a thumbnail sketch of their lives, a description of the location of where their body was found, and any autopsy information.

Richardson was putting pushpins in various locations on a large blown up map of Cedar Creek Lake. Each pin represented a victim, and where the drowning occurred.

Cates, a tall, thin man with a pointed beak for a nose, close cropped curly, sandy brown hair, very pale skin, and classic thick coke-bottle glasses, was poring over the autopsy findings and the reports on each of the victims put together by the county investigators. He was the ultimate computer geek and one of the best in the entire country at mining data bases. If there was a link between the cases, Cates would eventually find it. He was tireless and would work the keyboard for hours and hours without even taking a bathroom break.

As the lawmen scoured the paperwork for some clue about the apparent drowning deaths, some 15 miles away, Cody Martin sipped his beer, trying to fade, totally unnoticed into a corner on the outdoor patio at the marina.

Like all the other patrons, he leaned a bit over the rail to watch as the huge catfish broke the surface of the dark water churning it up as they grabbed the table scraps being dumped from the restaurant into the lake. It was always fun watching the plump two to three-foot-long catfish fighting over the uneaten food. Martin smiled to himself; the scrambling catfish reminded him a bit of the news media trying to get a handle on what was going on.

Billy Richardson yawned and stretched as he glanced at the clock on the cracked gray wall with the peeling paint in the sheriff's office. It showed that it was 9:25 p.m.

He looked at his old friend who was on loan from the Dallas County Sheriff's department, "Got anything Danny?"

"Nah, it just doesn't add up,' Cates replied, 'It is far too big of a coincidence for six people, including two couples, to drown in such a short time. The odds say it is simply not possible"

Cates motioned to his laptop computer, and shook his head, "Statistics for the past 25 years show that an average of two to three people have drowned in Cedar Creek Lake a year. The most ever was seven in 1983, and four of those victims were in a boat that capsized, and they were all drunk as hell. It was a bachelor party for a guy who never made it to the altar."

Sheriff King had a big frown on his face as he looked at the two veteran crime solvers shook his head and said, "You guys are the experts, and you're telling me we have six unrelated accidental drowning deaths, but they can't really be accidental drowning deaths?"

Richardson, yawned again, "Buddy it beats the hell out of me, but I guess that's what we're sayin'."

Sheriff King glanced at his watch, "Oh hell, I gotta go, I'm supposed to pick up Crystal in ten minutes, and she's twenty minutes away. I tell yah what, I'll just call her and cancel it." The detectives convinced King to get away for a few hours.

Over at Wesley's Marina, Cody Martin's quiet night was shattered by a group of five couples who pulled up in a 25-foot party barge, and noisily clambered up the steps from the dock to the second-floor restaurant. They sat just ten feet away from him and Martin knew it was time to quietly fade into the night.

He motioned to Crystal to bring him his tab. She smiled and brought it over to his table. Martin pulled out a few bills, left a fair, but not overly generous tip. His Seal training taught him never to do anything that would draw attention to himself. The goal was to be a phantom, an unmemorable person in everything he did.

As Martin pushed back his chair to leave, he spotted Sheriff Buddy King ascending the scuffed, dusty wooden stairs of the Marina restaurant. Martin glanced at him but tried to be as inconspicuous as possible as he watched the county's chief lawman arrive.

King nodded a greeting at a couple sitting at one of the outdoor tables, and then headed straight for Crystal.

"Hey darlin'," the sheriff said, "Sorry I'm late."

"No worries Buddy," Crystal replied, "I'm going to need just a few minutes to finish up anyway. Want a beer or something?" She gave him a quick hug.

As the serial killer drove his pickup truck home, his mind was racing in overdrive. "This is as good as it gets," he thought to himself. He could really throw things into a frenzy if the sheriff's girlfriend drowned. On the other hand, it could really bring more heat than he wanted. This was supposed to be a stealth mission. He wrestled with these divergent thoughts as he headed for his Lake Athens hideaway.

Crystal Disborn was born in Dallas 24 years ago. Her family moved to the Cedar Creek Lake community of Mabank when she was twelve. She was voted Miss Cedar Creek Festival four years ago. Crystal was a water rat which explained her great tan, and why she worked as a waitress/bartender at the marina, instead of using her brains and beauty to get ahead in the world.

A world-class water skier, Crystal was also learning a lot of new tricks on a wake board. There were plenty of good-looking, well-muscled guys who were willing to take her out on their super-fast boats. Not only was Crystal an excellent athlete, but she filled out a bikini in a manner that attracted stares from men wherever she went on the lake.

But there was much more to Crystal than good looks. While it was true she never had the urge to attend college, she had been a straight A student in high school, and also was in the top 2% academically of her graduating class.   Crystal had a very kind heart and worked tirelessly on behalf of the local SCPA.

She helped them rescue abused and abandoned dogs and cats, volunteered at the SCPA kennels as much as possible, and helped at every fund-raiser she could attend.

Crystal had a dog and a cat co-existing in her apartment. The dog, a beautiful collie she named K.C., after the 60's rock group K.C. and the Sunshine Band, was the smartest and friendliest animal she had ever seen. Crystal had rescued him when he showed up outside the apartment complex one day. All efforts to find his owner had failed, so she took him in. She was enamored by his gentle demeanor, and the tip of his tail, a little puff of white fur that looked like he'd accidentally dipped it in a can of paint. K.C. also had what Crystal called, "Moony eyes" when he wanted her to feel bad about leaving him in the apartment as she left.

Crystal also had a ball of white fur called Fluffy. The cat got into a lot of mischief, but amazingly was best friends with the dog, K.C.

Crystal, unbeknownst to the Sheriff, was also taking a few night courses at the community college on law enforcement. She felt it might help her down the road to create a security business for her and Buddy when he tired of being Sheriff. Crystal was enjoying the classes, especially the one on self-defense, a requirement for the course. She had easily mastered the moves that would allow her to hold her own in most situations.

Some called Crystal and King, Ken and Barbie behind their backs. They made quite a striking couple, the handsome, former athlete with the well chiseled body, and the former beauty queen. It was too much for many jealous gossips on the lake, although many others thought they were an ideal couple.

They had met three years earlier at a Baptist church picnic, of all places. Crystal was working at the SPCA booth, as usual, and Buddy King was there with some buddies checking out the classic car show that was part of the event.

The fetching beauty caught King's roving eye as he walked past the booth. Crystal was well aware of the hero from Eustace. They began to chat and had been inseparable ever since.

24

As the serial killer parked his truck and headed into his lake cabin still mulling the pros and cons of making Crystal his next victim, she was enjoying a beer with Sheriff King at Joe's Pub in Gun Barrel City. It was Tuesday night, and the weekly dart tournament was in full swing at the windowless tavern. Interestingly, none of the drinking establishments in the little city had windows. There were two schools of thought on why that was. The first was that it got too expensive to keep replacing the windows after the usual weekend mini brawl. The other was with no windows, neither your boss nor your wife could see that you were inside having a cold one.

The debonair, handsome young lawman, and his beautiful, brunette girlfriend made quite a few heads turn in the crowded bar. As usual, they also were winning the dart tournament, but Crystal noticed that Buddy was being awfully quiet tonight. He threw his darts with little of the flair and banter that usually accompanied his expert tosses.

"What's wrong Buddy?" Crystal asked her companion, but she already knew the answer. "It's these drowning deaths isn't it?"

Buddy looked into her clear blue eyes, let out a big sigh, and nodded his head. "Yah, when I ran for sheriff, I never thought anything like this would happen. We have no damn idea what's going on, but there could be some maniac running around drowning people." He looked up at the ceiling, then back into those terrific eyes that were intently focused on him, "It's driving me crazy."

She gently took both of his hands into hers, and said softly, "Do you really think somebody is killing these people?"

"I know it sounds crazy, but it can't be a coincidence that six people have drowned in such a short period of time," he said almost whispering.

Crystal lowered her voice even further in the crowded bar, "How many people have this theory? It could cause panic all over the lake, right during the height of the tourist season."

"I know, that's the other side of this damn mess. I'm trying to keep the newshounds from making some sort of a connection and creating a big ass deal out of this thing."

Crystal spotted *Gazette* reporter Dwayne Murphy on the other side of the crowded, smoke-filled room. She nodded at the local pot-stirrer, "What about Murphy? I'm surprised he hasn't written that story already."

King glanced at the local reporter, "Well, he actually tried to link them in a conversation with me a couple weeks ago, before we found the last one."

"How'd you keep him from writing it?"

King allowed a small smile, "Well I had a long talk with Busby Chambers about the need to keep that kind of talk out of the media. As owner of the paper, he has an interest in keeping people from panicking too. It could cost him a lot of advertising revenue from the local merchants."

Just a few miles away, the lights were still burning in the meeting room at the sheriff's office, as detectives Richardson and Cates worked late into the night. They were at the big board that contained all the information on the six deaths.

Billy Richardson said, "This is a damn puzzle with a very big piece missing. What the hell connects these victims? There is nothing here."

Danny Cates, pointed at the timeline of each death, "The only links are they all drowned, and, while we don't know for sure, it seems that they all happened at night, with no witnesses."

Richardson stroked his chin, stared at the big board some more, and shook his head, "You don't think it's possible that someone is intentionally drowning these people, do you?"

Cates shook his head, "It seems far-fetched. None of the bodies showed any bruises or anything else that would indicate a struggle, and they all had water in their lungs. Besides that, how could someone drown two people, like happened in two of the cases, without any bruises?"

"Yah, got me, Danny. That's the disconnect for me on these deaths. Who could do something like that? It seems almost physically impossible."

While the top detectives pondered the clues, Cody Martin was sweating profusely in his cabin, twenty miles to the east. He was intensely lifting weights as he followed his nightly routine to keep his physique in top shape.

As his muscles rippled and glistened with perspiration, Cody's face twisted into a straining mask, as he worked to lift the weights. His thoughts were on Crystal. He decided he needed more surveillance in case he decided to make her his seventh Cedar Creek victim.

Back in Gun Barrel City, the sheriff and the serial killer's next possible target left the bar and headed to King's place for a late night workout of their own. One that would be much more tender than Cody Martin's.

The two detectives snapped out the lights in the situation room at the sheriff's office and called it a night. Billy Richardson knew he would be tossing and turning for a couple hours before falling asleep, as his brain wrestled with the dilemma of the Cedar Creek deaths.

Above them all, the moon shone brightly in the clear Texas night sky. Stars twinkled. A gentle breeze sent a small ripple across the peaceful lake creating a dazzling silvery sheen. But many lake residents were worried as their heads hit the pillow. A trip around Cedar Creek Lake tonight would have shown that few boats were out looking for largemouth bass, working their lures around docks strewn all around the lake in the darkness, and most decks and backyards were more empty than usual. Residents were quietly dealing with the deaths in their own cautious manner.

25

It was ten in the morning, a Wednesday, with the big Memorial Day weekend just over a week away. Ace TV crime reporter Mindy Reese, and *Cedar Creek Gazette* reporter Dwayne Murphy were huddling in Reese's crowded little office at WDFW-TV in downtown Dallas.

They were trying to connect the dots that would link the six drowning victims. The national media's interest in the story had waned, as two weeks had passed with no additional dead bodies turning up. But Mindy and Dwayne remained hot on the trail. They just knew this was a big story, and they wanted to be the duo to break it wide open.

Murphy leaned closer to the blonde TV star as they compared notes. Her scent was wonderful. He was excited just having this private time with the love of his life. Reese was oblivious to all his thoughts as she frowned and concentrated on the information.

Memorial Day Weekend was the first big holiday of the boating season, and the two reporters were working on a joint project. They would co-author a front-page article in the *Gazette*, and a lead story report on the television newscast next Thursday, the day before thousands would flock to Cedar Creek Lake for four days of fun and relaxation. Murphy's editor had reluctantly agreed to the project, with the proviso that he would do heavy editing if need be.

Mindy Reese said, "Here's the deal Murphy, we need to come up with a plausible theory of how these deaths are connected. Let's spend the rest of the day tapping our police sources and running some scenarios past them."

Cody Martin was up before dawn. This was going to be a day of heavy reconnaissance. He needed to pin down daily movements of the waitress. This was also going to be a difficult hit because she was not one to ever go on the water alone at night. Crystal's activities usually involved skiing and wake boarding during the daytime. The cold-blooded killer smiled to himself. He loved a challenge.

The morning sun shone rudely into Crystal's eyes. She lazily rolled over and snuggled into the strong arms of Buddy King and kissed his ear.

King, smiled, and kissed her back, a long lingering kiss on her warm, full lips. "Good morning," he half-whispered, as he tried to shake the deep sleep from his contented body.

"Morning," Crystal purred back. Last night had been the most fulfilling of their short relationship. They were both naked under the thin sheet and enjoying the intimacy of this morning moment.

A few miles away, retired Dallas County detective Billy Richardson watched a male and female duck waddle past as he sipped his morning cup of decaf coffee on the deck of his lake house. It was a gorgeous morning, blue sky as far as the eye could see, with just a hint of a breeze.

Suddenly Richardson slammed his coffee cup down hard on the table and grabbed his cell phone. His mind had been racing all night, and now he had a thought about the case that needed to be discussed. Right now.

"Cates," came the sleepy reply on the other end of Richardson's phone. Cates had been hammering away on his computer until almost four in the morning.

"Danny, I think I may have something that we can work with. It is a question that we never have answered, and it could be the clue to help us get on track with this damn thing."

Cates tried to focus on the conversation. It was barely seven o'clock, and he'd had only a few hours of sleep. "What's that?"

Richardson was excited, and the words came tumbling out, "Okay. With all the confusion of the consultant's body being found the same time we found the billionaire's body, we never really poked into how the hell the rich guy's body could have traveled a mile or so from the yacht. Every other body has been found pretty much where it went under the water. How the hell does a dead body float that far away? It's not like this is a river with a big current or something."

Richardson paused to catch his breath, and then plunged on, "Doesn't that mean that somebody had to drag that body to the spot just off the park, or dropped it in the water right before we found it? How the hell do you drag a dead body that far without anyone seeing you? How do you place it in the water without being seen?"

Cates was trying to digest the torrent of words from Richardson. "Yah know Billy, you might be onto something. We definitely need to spend some time on that one today."

Cody Martin decided to stake out Wesley's Marina, so he could begin to work up a profile of Crystal's usual routine. He wanted to be very careful, but he'd also glanced at his calendar before leaving home this morning. It showed him that the big Memorial Day holiday was just over a week off. That would be the perfect time, he thought to himself, to add Crystal's name to the list of victims. The publicity would be huge.

Meanwhile the object of the killer's thoughts had just finished a leisurely shower and was getting dressed. It was Wednesday, her day off, so Crystal wasn't in a hurry. But King was suddenly in a rush after getting a call from detective Richardson.

Sheriff King brought three steaming cups of Starbuck's coffee into the situation room. It was still a novel treat for lake denizens, as the chain coffee purveyor had only opened shop in Gun Barrel City a month ago.

Billy Richardson and Danny Cates were in an animated conversation. They seemed quite excited, not even glancing up as King shut the door.

"What's up guys?" the sheriff asked. Billy had been vague on the telephone, saying only that they finally might have something to go on.

Richardson looked up, and with a small smile, said, "Buddy we may have a clue to get us rolling on this case, and to prove that these drowning deaths may not be accidental."

Cates excitedly chimed in, "It was right there in front of us from the get-go, but we all missed it in the craziness of the two bodies being found the same day."

"What is it?" King said through clenched teeth, his voice rising, the sheriff was getting impatient for details.

Detective Richardson pointed at the map of Cedar Creek Lake, using his big beefy index finger to guide the sheriff's eyes. "This is where Bushman's yacht and wife were found."

King nodded. Richardson moved his finger to the right and down a few inches on the map. "This is where we found Bushman's body. That's about a mile away."

Sheriff King was not grasping the significance of the finding, so Richardson was impatient now, his voice rising, "Don't you see Buddy, there is no way that in this lake a body floats under water, or on top of the water for that matter, for a mile from where a person drowned. Somebody had to take the body to that spot."

Buddy King had been a little foggy due to his lack of sleep after a wonderful night of making love to Crystal, but he was suddenly very clear-headed at this instant. He looked sharply at Richardson, and then Cates, "Are you guys saying that somebody drowned Bushman, and then dragged his body a mile away in the water?"

Cates jumped in, "Or somebody drowned Bushman and dumped his body in the water off the park. The bottomline, we believe, that there is no way that Bushman's body ends up in that area without somebody taking it or placing it there."

The sheriff's analytical mind was whirring with possibilities now. He responded to Cates, "What if Bushman drowned his wife, and then tried to swim to shore, but never made it?"

Richardson answered that one, "We cannot rule that out as a possibility right now, but it seems far-fetched. Bushman was not known as an athlete, even though he had a personal trainer. He was a businessman. His wife was the ace swimmer"

Cates jumped in again, "Besides if he just wanted to swim to shore, it was less than a half mile away from the yacht as the crow flies. Why would he try to swim so far away?"

The sheriff was deep in thought, digesting what the experienced detectives were telling him. "So, what you're saying is that, at least in the Bushman case, the evidence would suggest, that someone was involved in their deaths?" He was carefully choosing his words.

Richardson picked up on his good friend's concern, "Look Buddy, I know that you don't want to cause a panic or hurt business as we get into the summer season, but we think, realistically, there is something to this. It gives us a direction to go in. We need to go back through the evidence of all of the deaths and see what we can piece together."

King, grim-faced, nodded, "It is a big concern. The media is hovering like vultures, looking for some link in these deaths to trumpet 'serial killer' and really make things miserable around here. Dig into it, but no one outside of the three of us, is to know anything about this theory." He stared into their eyes for emphasis. Both men nodded in understanding.

Eighty miles to the west, Mindy Reese and Dwayne Murphy reconvened to continue work on their joint report on the six drowning deaths that was scheduled for release the next week. Much like the lawmen in Henderson County, they had assembled a map with colored push pins marking the locations of the six drowning deaths. The special report would air on the TV station next Thursday night, and then be the subject of a big front-page splash in the *Cedar Creek Gazette* for its usual Friday morning edition.

The print journalist, Murphy, was very excited about the opportunity to appear in the television report. He just knew this was the big break that would catapult his career.

The TV reporter broke into Murphy's dreams, "Listen Murph, we can't just make this a long re-hash of the information that has already been reported by the both of us, and the other media. We need a fresh hook, something to make people sit up and take notice."

Murphy eagerly nodded his head, "I know. I have had the theory from the third death that there is someone out there killing these people, but no one will listen to me."

The TV star bore her bright blue eyes into Murphy's and shook her head sideways, "There is nothing I have seen to support that. Now, I have my suspicions too, but we need something to hang that theory on, and I can't find a damn thing."

Murphy was lost in those baby blues for a few seconds until Reese said, "Hello, Murphy. Where are you?"

He snapped out of it, "Sorry, just thinking. Well, let's look at the list again. It has to be there somewhere."

It was close to eleven o'clock the next morning, a Thursday, when Crystal Disborn parked her green, 10-year-old Mustang convertible outside the Marina, unlocked the door of the restaurant, and walked in. If she had taken a look around, she might have noticed the blue pickup truck parked toward the end of the parking lot, just past a couple of SUVs with empty boat trailers attached.

Cody Martin smiled as he watched the lovely waitress disappear into the Marina. He, as always, was impressed by her beauty, and the way those tight, very short blue jean shorts, and midriff-baring t-shirt showed off her tight body, and wonderful tan.

Martin had her routine down on days that she worked. He knew she was also off on Wednesdays. But he was still wrestling with how to kill her. The others had been easy. They were all alone, under the cover of darkness, on the lake. There were never any witnesses.

The only time that Crystal was on the lake was when she was skiing or wake boarding with a small group of people. It was always in broad daylight too. Still pondering this difficult dilemma, he started the truck and drove away.

Crystal had a busy Thursday. Memorial Day would be here next week, and business was picking up at the Marina and the grill. She kept glancing at the clock as the day dragged on. Buddy had called, and said he was going to pick her up tonight. Crystal couldn't wait to be alone with the handsome sheriff.

The sun was just sliding away into the horizon, as Cody Martin's pickup truck slowly, unobtrusively, drove back into the parking lot at the marina. He knew that Crystal's shift would soon be over, and she'd be jumping into her car. It was time to continue his surveillance, his methodical preparation for his next stealth mission. Martin did not like to deal with any surprises. They could compromise his mission.

Martin parked the truck at the far end of the lot. It was a crowded place tonight. He lowered the driver's side window, turned off the engine and waited.

A little after eight o'clock, Crystal walked out of the marina door. Just like clockwork, Martin thought. It was the same routine every time.

But instead of getting into her Mustang, Crystal fussed with her hair, glanced at her watch, and stood there waiting just outside the marina door.

A few minutes later, the sheriff's car pulled into the parking lot and stopped next to her. She gave Buddy King a multi-megawatt smile, slid into the passenger seat, and then gave him a big hug and lingering kiss.

Martin sat upright in his truck, the veins in his bull-like neck popping big time. "Damn her," he seethed to himself, "How can I plan this hit if she's heading off with the damn sheriff, instead of doing her usual routine?"

Cody Martin was extremely agitated as he drove out of the marina parking lot, and back toward Seven Points. His heavily muscled arms and shoulders were popping out of his tight tank top as he kept a death grip on the steering wheel, his jaw set in a tight line, and his eyes fixed straight ahead. He did not like it when plans took a sudden unexpected turn. It drove him absolutely crazy. It was that quick-to-boil temper that had cost him his Navy Seal career.

The killer turned on his truck's radio. The announcer was in the middle of the hourly news update, "and it has now been over two weeks since the last of six unexplained drowning deaths on Cedar Creek Lake. Police officials say they are continuing their investigation but point out that they have uncovered nothing to link any of the deaths. They call it a series of unfortunate accidental incidents that happened to come in a short time span. In other news…"

Martin roughly snapped off the radio. Now his anger was boiling over. The sheriff was underestimating his skill, mocking him. He needed to shake things up. Now.

As Martin's truck turned onto the bridge that crossed the lake from Seven Points to Gun Barrel City, he spotted a solitary fisherman, barely able to be seen from the road as darkness, with no moon in sight, enveloped the lake. There was even a little fog rolling in for good measure.

He drove past the man, who was all alone with his truck parked in the grass just off the road, only a few feet from the end of the embankment where the bridge began. Martin finished the trip into Gun Barrel City, and then on an impulse wheeled his truck into the Big Brave Marina parking lot, turned around, and headed back across the bridge in the opposite direction.

The fisherman had moved under the bridge and was casting out into the lake using a long pole, the kind you'd usually see if someone were fishing in the surf in the Gulf of Mexico. He was hoping to hook a big catfish. He'd used this rig in the past to haul in some channel cats that weighed twenty pounds or more.

Suddenly the fisherman heard a rustling behind him in the darkness. It startled him. He'd read all about the mysterious drowning deaths.

The fisherman spun around to see what he guessed to be a relatively young man walking toward him in the darkness. He could make out that the man was carrying a tackle box and a pole. The fisherman relaxed a bit.

The man was about ten feet away when he said, "Howdy. Doin' any good tonight?"

The fisherman replied, "Not yet, only been here 'bout an hour." He was beginning to relax a bit more, but remained wary, this was a scary time to be on the lake alone in the dark.

The road was only about ten feet above them. But the light traffic whizzing by could not see the men on the embankment below.

As the fisherman made another cast, Cody Martin put down his tackle box and sneaked a peek, sizing up the man. He figured him to be about five-ten, and about a hundred sixty pounds. He looked to be in his early 60's.

Martin opened his tackle box. He was still about ten feet away from the fisherman. "What yah usin' tonight?" the killer asked.

"I'm trying some crawdads. The guys at Big Brave said the big cats were hitting them right now." The fisherman watched his line, hoping for a strike.

Suddenly the killer dropped his own pole and sprinted toward the fisherman. He was on top of the startled fisherman in a matter of seconds. The killer tackled him from behind, snapping his head back, and pinned his arms to his side his momentum thrusting the two of them toward the water. The terrified fisherman let out a yelp, and the two men hit the water with a loud splash.

In his haste and anger, the killer did not have his scuba gear with him, but he had long ago taught himself to hold his breath for a very long time. He used to win contests against other Navy Seals by going over five minutes without taking a breath.

That skill came into play now as he held the fisherman in his vice-like grip under the inky lake water, the two men sheltered

116

from any curious eyes by the bridge, even as cars and trucks continued to speed by overhead.

The killer eventually felt the fisherman's body go limp, as he lost the fight for his life. By trying to get a breath, he had gulped his lungs full of water. Martin took the body to the bottom of that stretch of lake. It was about ten feet deep.

The killer splashed out of the water, grabbed his pole and tackle box, and walked quickly, and quietly to his truck that was parked about 200 yards away. He left the fisherman's pole and gear right where it had fallen during the attack.

The parking lot was empty. Martin glanced at his watch. It was almost ten o'clock. He hopped into his truck, quickly toweled himself off, and drove away at a casual, unobtrusive speed.

The antique clock on the mantel struck midnight with a dozen loud chimes. 67-year-old Betty Alcott awoke with a start. She had fallen asleep during the ten o'clock news and had missed the weather forecast.

Betty wondered where Herb was. He would have awakened her when he returned from his nightly trip to the bridge looking for big catfish. Where was he?

Betty worried about Herb, especially with those people who had drowned lately at Cedar Creek Lake. He always came home by ten o'clock, even if the fish were biting. Herb had to get that weather report every night. Betty was very anxious as she looked at the clock. It was now a little after midnight.

She decided to call the Gun Barrel City police, to have them check on Herb, and to tell him to come home.

26

Cody Martin sat in the dark in his Lake Athens hideaway. He was very angry with himself for allowing his temper to force him to take such a big risk. He shook his head, as he thought to himself, "Hell, I don't even know who the hell I killed. I never even watched his patterns. Somebody could have come along. Damn, this is the kind of stuff that got me in trouble with the Seals."

Gun Barrel City Police sergeant Kelly Brooks got the call on his cruiser's radio. It was a small department, and formalities weren't needed. "Kelly," the dispatcher said, "Can you swing by the park just across the bridge, and check on a Herb Alcott who should be fishing right next to the bridge, on the shore? His wife just called, says he's always home in time to see the weather on the late news, but he's still not there."

"10-4 Russ," the officer replied as he swung his squad car into a driveway, turned around, and headed across the bridge. He saw a pickup truck parked in the weeds next to the road as he drove by and turned left into the parking lot.

He radioed in, "Russ I see a truck parked here. I'm going to get out and see if the guy is still here." Sergeant Brooks parked his cruiser and grabbed his big spotlight.

His heavy work boots crunched the gravel along the pathway toward the truck. It was the only sound. He waved the flashlight all around. No sign of any fisherman.

A half-hour away Cody Martin had begun to lift weights. He was angrily jerking the heavy bar. Sweat was glistening off his naked chest. He was working to calm himself by pushing hard with the weights, trying to drive the anger away.

Sergeant Brooks flashlight found a large tackle box, an old plastic five-gallon paint pail filled with crawdads, and a few feet away a fishing pole, lying on the edge of the water. He also noticed some heavy footprints in the slightly muddy path near the shore. Had the fisherman slipped and fallen into the water? Had there been a struggle with someone else?

Brooks keyed his portable radio, "Russ, check out this Texas license plate for me. It's RCT899 on a white Dodge pick up. Not sure of the year."

"10-4."

A few miles away, Betty Alcott paced the floor. She called the Gun Barrel City police again. After about eight rings, the dispatcher answered. He asked her if her husband drove a white pickup truck. Betty caught her breath, "Yes. Did you find him? Is he okay?"

The dispatcher replied, "Ma'am, I have an officer on the scene, and as soon as we assess the situation, I'll call you back. Just sit tight." He hung up the phone.

Then the dispatcher keyed the police radio, "Kelly, that plate comes back to a Herb Alcott. Just talked to his wife again, that would be her husband's truck. Any sign of him?"

"No," the sergeant replied, "I've checked out the truck. It's unlocked, his wallet is in it, and it is undisturbed. But he is definitely not here. It looks like he could have slipped into the water, or he may have had some company, there's some heavy foot marks in the path which is kinda muddy."

It was now almost 12:30 in the morning. Gazette reporter Murphy was startled awake by the incessant ringing of his telephone. He fumbled for the handset in the dark and knocked it onto the floor. Murphy leaned out of bed, picked it up and sleepily mumbled, "Hello."

It was one of Murphy's scanner freaks, a disabled guy who sat up most of the night listening to the crackle of the police radios.

"Murph," the man said on the other end of the phone, "Sorry to wake you up but I figured you'd want to hear about the missing guy just across the bridge from Big Brave."

At the same time, the Gun Barrel City police dispatcher was dialing up his boss, to alert him to the situation. "Yeah," he was telling the police chief, "it looks like we might have another mystery drowning on our hands, or the guy could have just walked away or something, but his wallet is still in his truck, undisturbed."

The police chief rubbed the sleep out of his eyes, "Better call Sheriff King too."

While the police chief and the newspaper reporter struggled to wake up, get dressed, and head to the crime scene, the killer finished his fast-paced weightlifting, and sat in the dark of the still night, gulping a sports energy drink. His mind was racing as fast as his heartbeat had been a few minutes ago during the strenuous workout. The white-hot flame burning in his gut had begun to diminish.

He thought to himself, "How could I have let my temper jump out of control like that? It got me in trouble with the Seals, and now it could put me in prison for murder. What was I thinking? Didn't even do any reconnaissance on that mission, it was just a spur of the moment attack, all because that damn waitress took off with the sheriff."

120

Martin's brain was processing the crime scene, trying desperately to recall if he had left anything behind, carelessly dropped anything, or done anything that could trace the crime back to him.

It was nearly one in the morning when the phone rang at Sheriff King's home. He and Crystal had just fallen asleep. It was the Gun Barrel City Police dispatcher.

"Hey Buddy, sorry to wake you, but we have a missing fisherman down by the bridge just before Big Brave."

That snapped the sheriff's brain to attention in a hurry, "What do you mean missing?" The dispatcher filled him in.

The police chief and reporter arrived at the scene almost simultaneously, in fact Murphy almost ran into the police cruiser as it turned sharply into the parking lot at the park. This did not make the chief happy.

He jumped out of his car and shined his flashlight into the eyes of the startled newspaperman. "Murphy, what the hell? I oughta toss you in jail for that move."

"Sorry chief, I didn't know it was you," was all Murphy could manage. He was still groggy and trying to get his mind to focus on where he was and what was going on. Murphy was not one to easily jump out of bed and be wide awake.

The chief was not appeased, "What the hell are you doing here anyway?"

Murphy's brain was beginning to defog, and his sharp tongue was waking up to, "I guess I could ask you the same thing at one o'clock in the morning? I heard there was a call about a missing man."

The chief shook his head in disgust, "This is a potential crime scene, so I don't want you to traipse around here and destroy any evidence in case it is. You sit right here until I get back." He gave the nosy news hound a menacing stare, "Got it?"

Murphy nodded. The chief continued, "I'll be back over here as soon as I know something."

Buddy King gently removed his arm from around Crystal. She was a sound sleeper, and the phone call had not interrupted her rhythmic, deep breathing. He got dressed in the dark, left her a note, and headed out the door.

King crawled into his truck and called the chief on his cell phone. They decided that since the crime scene was secured, and there was little they could do until daylight that the sheriff would head to the Alcott residence and try to console Mrs. Alcott until they had a better grasp on just what they were dealing with.

Betty Alcott was pacing the floor, and wringing her hands, her face a mask of worry and fear as she glanced for the hundredth time at the mantel clock which now showed it to be 1:25 in the morning. Where was her husband? What happened to him?

She jumped when the doorbell clanged, but then went quickly to the front door. Sheriff King was standing on the porch, his badge in clear view. As Betty Alcott opened the door she started to cry and panic, "Oh, no is he dead? What happened to him?

Sheriff King tried to calm her down, as he slowly guided her to the overstuffed and well-worn sofa in the family room of the small residence. In a soft, soothing voice he said, "Now, Mrs. Alcott we just don't know anything right now, and that's the truth. We did find your husband's truck, but so far, we don't know where he might be, but we're looking for him as best we can right now."

She was sobbing with fear and the words came gushing out, "He would never just go off somewhere without calling me from a pay phone or something. He never drinks or anything. Just loves to fish. I told him to be careful with those drowned people and all, but he wouldn't listen. Had to go fishing tonight."

Sheriff King took her shaking hands, and gently broke into her non-stop delivery as she stopped to sob briefly. "Now, Mrs. Alcott we have no reason to believe that anything happened to your husband. We just need some time to look into this situation. I'm guessing it will be daylight before we can really get a handle on things."

She turned her terror-stricken eyes to the sheriff, "I can't wait. You have to find him right now." Her voice was rising, her hands trembling.

At first light a small army of police vehicles, officers, and the news media gathered at the edge of the lake. Murphy had alerted the two big city newspapers, and his favorite TV reporter.

The media was kept at a distance, in the parking lot, about a hundred feet from the missing man's pickup truck. Detective Richardson, as head of the task force, was directing the operation with an iron fist. Sheriff King had convinced the missing man's wife to wait at home until he had more information.

The sun shone its face as an orange orb on this clear morning as it rose in the distance. Scuba divers waded into the water from the shore, and a couple of police boats worked the area where the fisherman disappeared.

The water was murky, but only about ten feet deep under the two-lane bridge that spanned this portion of the lake. It was a favorite fishing spot for crappie at this hour of the morning, but police kept all boats away from the possible crime scene.

In his cabin on Lake Athens, Cody Martin sipped a special herbal breakfast drink as he flipped around watching the local TV news programs. They all reported that a fisherman was missing from under the bridge near Gun Barrel City on Cedar Creek Lake. Police did not know if he was somewhere in the water or had left the area. They were concerned because his fishing gear and pickup were still at the scene, untouched.

Martin went over the events at that scene in his mind for the thousandth time since last night. He had not slept as he tried to picture what happened and wondered if he had made a mistake on his hasty, unplanned mission.

The police detectives tried to get usable casts of footprints at the scene, but it was a heavily trampled area. This was a favorite part of the lake shore for fishermen.

It was about 8:15 when a sheriff's department scuba diver broke the surface about 20 yards offshore, and shouted, "I think we have him here." That created a scramble by the media and the police. The media were kept away by a couple of officers, as the sheriff's department diver brought the body to shore where other officers held up a big tarp to keep the prying media eyes and cameras from getting a glimpse of it.

Detective Richardson held Herb Alcott's driver's license in his right hand. They had found it in Alcott's wallet, on the dashboard of his unlocked truck. Richardson looked down at the body lying near his feet, the eyes were wide open, as was the mouth. It was the same face that smiled back at him from the driver's license, only the face on the ground was frozen in death.

Detective Richardson noticed something else, so he knelt next to the body for a closer look. It seemed to him that the dead man's neck was tilted at an odd angle. He caught the eye of Sheriff King, trying not to draw anyone else's attention.

King stooped down next to Richardson, and quietly, almost in a whisper asked, "Whatcha got, Billy?"

124

Richardson pulled on a pair of rubber gloves and gently lifted the head of the dead man. He half-whispered, "Buddy I think his neck is broken."

King immediately grasped the significance of this finding, rose to his feet, and instructed his men to cover the body and load it onto a gurney to transport to the county morgue.

Sheriff King told detective Richardson to give a brief statement to the media as head of the task force. As they gathered around Richardson, King hopped into his truck and drove to Betty Alcott's house.

Betty Alcott was sitting on the swing on the porch of her neat, but small home when the sheriff drove up. She was quietly talking to the police officer who had been posted to keep any nosy news media away. Two of her neighbors were also there trying to lend comfort as they waited for word on Herb.

As King got out of his truck, Betty Alcott hurried toward him, leaving the others behind. "Do you have good news," she asked, more of a hopeful plea than a stated question, her red eyes were drilling into those of the sheriff.

King stepped forward and put his arm around her. She immediately knew that her fears had come true, "Is he gone?" was all she managed as she started to sob.

"I'm afraid so Mrs. Alcott. We found his body in about ten feet of water a few minutes ago."

"How did he get in the water? He was fishing on shore like always, wasn't he?"

"It looks like he was. We found his fishing gear on the shore."

A flood of emotions hit Betty Alcott at once, as she cried out, and then collapsed into the sheriff's arms, crying uncontrollably. King tried to calm her down as best he could, but it was no use.

Back at the crime scene, detective Richardson finished his briefing of the news media. He had provided little information. Richardson told them they had recovered the body of a fisherman who was reported missing last night around midnight. They had no cause of death, and the name was being withheld pending notification of next of kin.

He ignored their shouted questions and said they would know more when he knew more.

Cody Martin was in the middle of his 200 daily sit-ups when the voice on the TV set made him abruptly stop, "We have just received word that the body of a missing fisherman has been found by scuba divers off the shore of Cedar Creek Lake just outside Gun Barrel City. The man's name and any other information are not being released by police at this time. They refuse to say if this latest death is in any way connected to the recent drowning deaths of six other people on the lake about an hour east of Dallas."

Martin stared at the TV set. Once again, he played the episode through his mind, second by second, trying to remember any mistakes he may have made during the attack brought on by his outrage caused by the sheriff's girlfriend changing her routine. Something was nagging him in the back of his mind, but he could not clear up the fuzzy recollection that kept the information from coming into focus.

Detective Richardson followed the hearse to the county morgue, where he was met by the county medical examiner. Sheriff King and detective Dan Cates joined them.

Doctor Perry Millinberry was in his mid-60s. He had retired from his family practice in Athens just this year but remained the county medical examiner. He'd held the post for over two decades. It was his way of giving back to the community, and usually it was a pretty peaceful job with little call for his services. He certainly had never seen anything like this spate of drowning deaths.

Doctor Millinberry limped as he walked toward the body of Herb Alcott. He was a part-time rodeo cowboy in his youth until a bull had wrecked his knee, leaving him with a permanent limp. His hair remained jet black, making him appear ten years younger. He had huge bushy eyebrows even bigger than that guy on *60 Minutes*, and his eyes were brown and clear, he did not need glasses at his advanced age. His hands were a bit gnarled, but he could still wield a scalpel with the best of them. He was also very thorough, some called it plodding, when examining a corpse.

"Doc, I think this guy has a broken neck," Richardson said as Millinberry stood over the body and removed the covering.

The doctor said nothing, but gave Richardson a sideways glance with his eyes and eyebrows that said, "Now you're a doctor too?" He'd dealt with all kinds of lawmen during his long tenure, and he refused to let anybody rush him through an examination, "Well, I'll just have to check that out Billy." He also didn't cotton to all these high-tech crime scene investigator shows on television. The good doctor felt they were all fiction, totally out of touch with the real world.

He methodically removed the clothes from the corpse, carefully taking notes as he worked. The medical examiner gave the impatient lawmen a bit of play by play as he went through his practiced routine.

"OK, no outward signs of gunshots or any other wounds. The skull is intact," he said in a monotone, as his steady, practiced hands started to explore the head and neck area of the victim.

"It does appear that there is an injury to the spinal column at C4 through C7." He jotted down some notes, and then gently eased the body from its back onto its front with the help of Sheriff King, who had hustled to the morgue after speaking with the victim's widow.

There was a dark bruise on the back of Alcott's neck, just below his hairline and above his shoulders. The doctor probed the area with his fingers, and slowly intoned, "I believe your field assessment was correct detective Richardson. His neck appears to be broken. I would assume that it was snapped backwards, cracking the vertebrae."

The room was suddenly enveloped in stony silence. Everyone gathered around the body of Herb Alcott was thinking the same terrible thought.

The group remained mum as Doctor Millinberry resumed his examination, "I don't think the broken neck caused his death. There is water in his lungs." He looked into the grim faces gathered around the examination table, and took a slow, deep breath.

"Gentlemen," the doctor said, "My preliminary finding is that this man drowned. But he also has a broken neck. The only thing I can assume is that he was standing on shore fishing and someone rammed into him from behind and violently pushed him into the water."

Detective Richardson spoke first, "So, doc what you're saying is that someone hit him hard enough from behind to snap his neck, and then took him underwater and held him there until he drowned?"

There was a long pause as the doctor looked at Richardson. Finally, Doctor Millinberry shook his head, "I didn't say that. I'm not sure how he drowned. He could have been semi-conscious and took in water as he struggled to breathe. He could have been knocked out and ingested the water. Someone could have held him under until he drowned. I really don't know. Just like the other drowning victims there aren't any visible bruises on his arms or body, outside the hemorrhage on the back of his neck. I can't say from what I've seen so far that anyone grabbed him and held him under. I can say with pretty good certainty that someone plowed into him from behind with sufficient force to break his neck and propel him into the water where your diver found him this morning."

27

Back in Dallas, Dwayne Murphy had rejoined WDFW crime reporter Mindy Reese as they continued to work on their big special report which was now due in just one week. The latest unfortunate death might have provided the hook they needed for their special.

Detective Richardson called a special meeting of his task force. Armed with the information that he had been expecting, and fearing at the same time, it was time to pore back over every piece of evidence in these drowning deaths.

"Gentlemen," Richardson began, eyeing each person in the room one by one, "There is a very good chance that all of the drowning deaths were not accidental, as I think deep down, we have all suspected."

There was a murmur of assent and the nodding of heads in the room. The attention of the men also cranked up a notch or two, many sat up in their hard-plastic chairs as Richardson continued in somber, measured tones, "The ramifications of this information are far-reaching. It means we need to carefully go over every little detail in each of the incidents. It means we need to keep a lid on this information or there could be panic across the area. It means we have to move with urgency before the killer strikes again."

As the task force dug in for a long day and night, Cody Martin finished gassing up his pickup truck at the Shell station in Gun

Barrel City and headed for his favorite marina for lunch. It was time for more reconnaissance.

The killer parked in the mostly empty lot at Wesley's Marina and climbed the weather-beaten steps to the second-floor restaurant. He was greeted at the top of the steps by Crystal, looking beautiful in her usual work attire, a pair of white, very short and tight shorts, and a short blue halter-top.

She had a flicker of recognition on her face as Martin had become a semi-regular at the busy, open-air eatery, "Grab any table you'd like. Can I get you something to drink?"

Martin smiled, "Just a glass of water would be fine."

The killer walked over to an umbrella table, on the front edge of the outdoor patio of the restaurant. It was a beautiful day. The skies were cloudless and blue, the breeze was gently coming out of the south, and the lake was sparkling below the patio.

As Crystal brought his water, Martin noticed that they had the place to themselves. There was not another customer, or employee in sight.

"Pretty quiet here today," Martin said, "Thanks for the drink."

"No problem, ready to order?" Crystal thought to herself that even though he'd been here quite a few times, she did not know his name. She was impressed with his muscular build and clear, deep blue eyes.

"I'll just have a Cobb salad," Martin said. Crystal nodded, "You know I've seen you here before, but I don't know your name. I'm Crystal."

Martin gave her a small, friendly smile, "I knew that from being here a few times. I'm Joseph."

"Well," Crystal smiled back reaching out to shake his hand, "It's good to officially meet you Joseph. Do you work around here?" She was impressed by the steel-like grip, even though he clearly wasn't trying to make it that way.

The Seal training bells clanged loudly in Martin's head. He must remain as invisible as possible. It was time to cut off this conversation. "No not really," he said, "But I am kinda in a hurry."

Crystal caught his "end of conversation" signal, nodded, and headed off to prepare his order.

Once again the serial killer took a careful look around the restaurant. There was not a soul in sight, and no one at the gas pumps on the dock either. He knew there was one woman working the counter downstairs, inside the marina's general store. There was no one else around.

At WDFW-TV, Mindy Reese and Dwayne Murphy continued to work on their special report. As Reese reviewed video, Murphy was burning up the phone lines back to Henderson County. He knew that the autopsy must be finished on the latest drowning victim and wanted to know what they had found.

Murphy called Sheriff King's cell phone. King answered on the second ring.

"Sheriff, this is Murphy."

"How the hell did you get this number?" an obviously very irritated sheriff shot back.

"Ah, I don't know. You must have given it to me once," Murphy lied. He actually had paid a deputy sheriff one hundred dollars for the number about two months ago.

Sheriff King was abrupt, "Well, what the hell do you want, I'm very busy."

"I was just wonderin' what you found out in the Alcott autopsy?"

King paused only briefly, "Nothing there, Murphy. Looks like a drowning."

Murphy decided to plunge on, "Do you really believe this is still another accidental drowning, sheriff?"

"I believe I have better things to do than to talk to you, and don't ever call me on this number again." The cell phone connection went dead.

Murphy might not be the world's best reporter, except in his own mind, but he was dogged. He tried other Henderson County detectives, and some other county contacts. He learned nothing. There was a tight lid on this one.

Back at Wesley's Marina, Cody Martin slowly worked his way through the Cobb salad. Crystal spent her time cleaning up behind the bar and doing other busy work. She felt that her lone customer had been a bit rude, so she decided to leave him alone. Martin was still the only person there. His mind was racing.

Should he kill her right now? How could he do it and still make it look like an accident? He took another forkful of salad, calmly gazing out on the lake, as he mulled his next move.

Dwayne Murphy was clearly frustrated. He walked over to Mindy's video editing station and plopped down heavily in a chair. She stopped the machine, "What's up Murph?"

"I just have a feeling that there is something going on. All my usually very talkative sources are clammed up." Murphy pounded his fist on the work desk in frustration, "Damn it Mindy, I just know there is some new evidence based on that Alcott death, and nobody's talkin'."

"What do you think we should do, Murph?"

The newspaper reporter looked up at his fellow journalist, "I think we need to spend the day at Cedar Creek Lake. We've got to find out just what the hell they're hidin' from us. Maybe you can take a shot at the widow Alcott, see if she knows anything?"

Mindy nodded, "OK, let's go. I'll get Zeke to come along with his camera just in case we turn up something."

In the Henderson County task force office, Sheriff King poured another cup of coffee, and sat down next to detective Richardson. His friend looked tired, with dark lines under his eyes, and his weathered face looked a bit drawn.

"Billy, you're not getting enough sleep, are you?"

Richardson, looked up at the sheriff, stretched his arms and neck, and said, "This is driving me crazy. We all were worried that these weren't accidents, and now we know they aren't. There's some wacko out there, and we have not one piece of evidence except for a broken neck on one of the victims."

King just nodded. His face was grim, and detective Richardson thought his friend had aged a bit in the past few weeks.

King asked, "Do you think we should go visit Mrs. Alcott? We really need to dig into whether her husband had any enemies and see what else she can tell us in light of this new evidence."

"Yeah, good idea. It'll get us out of this stinking room and out in the sunlight for a few minutes too. Just be sure not to tell her about the broken neck. We need to keep a very tight lid on that information."

"Got it," King agreed, "let's go."

Crystal walked over to Martin's table and picked up the remnants of the salad. She gave him a small, more guarded smile and asked, "Anything else for you?"

"No thanks, just the check."

She walked back toward the bar, and Martin got up to follow her. There was still not another person in sight.

Crystal walked around the corner of the bar, picked up the order form, and turned around. She was startled to see that the customer had silently followed her.

"Oh," she said, and backed up a little, her eyes growing wider.

Martin said in a soothing, non-threatening voice, "Sorry, I just thought I'd save you the trip."

The waitress relaxed a bit, and handed him the bill, "That's seven-dollars and sixty-one cents."

Martin slowly took his wallet out of the back pocket of his blue jeans, as his mind wrestled with his next move. He could swiftly grab her and throw her off the deck into the water, race down the stairs and hold her under the water until she was dead. No, bad idea, there was a woman in the general store on the first floor of the marina, and lake houses across the narrow channel with a clear view.

Sheriff King and detective Richardson pulled up at the Alcott residence. Mrs. Alcott was outside on her knees, tending to her rose bushes, hoping to take her mind off the death of her husband for a few minutes. She quickly jumped to her feet and began brushing off the soil from her hands when she saw the sheriff's car pull into her driveway.

The men got out of the car and walked toward her.

"Do you have news for me?" the widow asked, her eyes darting nervously from one man to the other.

Sheriff King took her arm and gently led her toward the porch. "Not really," he said, "But we would like to ask you a few questions to help in our investigation."

Mrs. Alcott let out a big sigh, and took a seat on one of the battered, padded porch chairs.

She first looked the sheriff in the eye, and then the detective, "You mean you still don't have any idea who killed my husband?"

Detective Richardson answered in a hushed voice, "I'm afraid not Mrs. Alcott, but maybe you can help us find him."

Martin pulled a ten-dollar bill out of his wallet and set it on the bar. Just as Crystal reached for it, the door opened downstairs at the marina store, and there was the sound of feet scuffling up the wooden stairs.

Martin heard the intruders, and said, "Just give me one dollar back."

Crystal said, "Thanks," and gave him his change, just as two men reached the top of the stairs.

One of them said, "Can we still get lunch?"

28

Sheriff King and detective Richardson settled into a couple of chairs on the porch of the widow Alcott's aging, but comfortable home. She had flowers everywhere in pots on the floor and hanging from the ceiling. There was a myriad of bright colors. Colors that were in sharp contrast to the grim discussion the three of them were having.

"Mrs. Alcott," King began in a quiet, gentle tone, "Are you sure that your husband had no enemies? He hadn't gotten into a spat with anyone recently?"

Mrs. Alcott shook her head emphatically, "No," she almost shouted in frustration, "I've told you that before. He kept to himself, puttered around the house and in his woodworking shop, and went fishin' by himself at night. Why do you keep asking the same questions?" Then she put her clasped hands in her lap and sat still, staring straight ahead, looking at neither of the detectives.

Detective Richardson felt her frustration, and unwisely, on the spur of the moment, decided to level with the woman, "Mrs. Alcott your husband was apparently shoved into the water by someone with such force that it snapped his neck backward hard enough to crack some vertebrae."

Shock passed across the widow's face as she looked in horror at the detective, and then the sheriff, "Oh, my god, who would do that to my poor Herbie?" She began to weep softly.

As the WDFW news vehicle left Dallas in its rearview mirror and headed toward Cedar Creek Lake, Dwayne Murphy was on his cell phone, placing a call to the Henderson County Medical Examiner. He had known Doctor Millinberry for years and had found him to very talkative when the mood struck him. Murphy knew how to push his buttons and hoped he could do that now to get more information on the death of Herb Alcott, and the other drowning victims. Maybe he'd consent to an interview on camera to talk about the baffling deaths.

The irascible doctor picked up his phone on the third ring, "Yeah, Doc Millinberry here."

"Hey Doc, this is Dwayne Murphy, how yah doin?"

"Murphy, yah old sonofagun, haven't talked to you for a minute."

Murphy started right in on a subject he knew would get the medical examiner riled up, "Hey, I was watching *CSI* the other night, and they showed how the medical examiners used this new technique to track who killed a factory worker…"

Doctor Millinberry stopped Murphy in mid-sentence, "Don't get me started on that damn *CSI* crap Murphy. We both know that's a bunch of TV B.S. that has nothin' to do with the real world."

Murphy was pleased that the medical examiner had jumped at the bait so easily, now to set the hook, "Well, I was just thinkin' that this might help you guys figure out what happened to that Alcott fellow and those other drowning victims at Cedar Creek Lake."

Doctor Millinberry fairly shouted into the phone, "Murphy I don't need any fancy TV mumbo-jumbo to figure out what happened. They all drowned with no signs of foul play or other injuries." The medical examiner paused, and before Murphy could jump back in, he volunteered, "Except for that Alcott fellow, of course."

Murphy sat straight up in his rear car seat, startling Mindy Reese who was riding in the front seat ahead of him. Murphy always slouched in the car. She looked at Murphy with quizzical eyes.

The newspaper reporter quickly decided to try and bluff the doctor into giving him more information before he realized what he had just said, "Well, I just thought it might help you in determining how Alcott got his injuries, that's all."

Doctor Millinberry was wound up now, and not being careful with his words, he indignantly shouted into the phone, "Well, damn it Murphy, I've been doctoring for forty years, I know a broken neck when I see one." The doctor then fell silent; he had just realized he'd said much more than he was supposed to. Sheriff King would be furious.

Murphy was quickly processing the information. He knew his time was just about up, "So, that means someone shoved or tackled Alcott from behind, broke his neck, and then carried him into the water so he would drown?"

Doctor Millinberry was angry with himself for letting Murphy trick him into saying more than he should have so he tried to backtrack, "Murphy I am not saying anything like that. I have to go, and I expect you will not quote me on any part of this conversation. It was all off the record." The phone line went dead.

In the news car, Mindy Reese was turned all the way around in her seat, facing Murphy. They were both beyond excited.

Reese spoke first, "Did I just hear you say that someone hit Alcott from behind so hard that it broke his neck?"

Murphy was grinning even wider than the proverbial Cheshire cat, "Yes, little lady, we have a big scoop for our special. The old doctor fell for my trap and gave us information that will blow the lid off this investigation."

"So, that means that at least in Alcott's case, this was no accidental drowning, and it sure makes you wonder about the other deaths too. Is there a serial killer out there who is making it look like these people drowned?" Reese asked.

"Yeah, absolutely. We've known all along that these couldn't be from natural causes, the odds are too strong against that happening," intoned Murphy, he clearly was very proud of his work with the talkative medical examiner.

"OK, Murphy," Reese was planning their next move, "Let's visit the widow Alcott. Hopefully she'll do an interview and confirm what's going on."

Back in Athens, Doctor Millinberry was staring at his office phone as if it were a gun that had just accidentally discharged. "Damn," he thought to himself, "How could I have let that damn newspaper guy lead me into saying what I said." He decided to hide this conversation from the sheriff. He had warned Murphy not to quote him. Maybe it would just blow over.

After the lawmen left her home, Betty Alcott returned to her rose bushes, but she was just going through the motions. Her mind kept playing their conversation over and over. Someone had killed her husband.

About 20 minutes later, Mrs. Alcott looked up to see the news van from WDFW pulling into her driveway. It stopped, and Mindy Reese jumped to the ground and began to walk toward her.

Betty Alcott had always admired the TV reporter's work and found her charming. She was struck by how much prettier she was in person and such a tiny thing too.

"Hi, Mrs. Alcott," Reese said as she extended her right hand, "I'm Mindy Reese from WDFW."

Mrs. Alcott smiled; it was good to have some company after just hearing the awful news about her husband. "I know who you are, Miss Reese, I watch your reports all the time."

"Well, I am so sorry about your husband's death," Reese said, as she cradled the widow's hands in her own following their handshake. "I was wondering if we could do a short interview with you, on camera, so people could learn more about what a fine man he was?" Reese said with sincerity, looking Mrs. Alcott in the eye with a well-practiced look of complete empathy and understanding on her face.

Mrs. Alcott paused for a few seconds. The sheriff had said not to talk to the media, but this Reese woman was a favorite of hers, and it would be great to say some good things about Herb. "OK, but can I wash up first, I've been tending to my roses?"

"Sure, take your time; we'll just get set up on the porch so you're good and comfortable."

Mrs. Alcott headed into the house.

About fifteen minutes later, the cameraman had set up a couple of fill lights and placed his camera on a tripod on the Alcott porch. Mindy Reese was sitting next to Betty Alcott, who had combed through her graying, naturally curly hair, and put on a pale blue sundress.

The camera started to roll, and Mindy Reese expertly and gently prodded the widow Alcott through a series of softball questions about her husband. Then, she decided to ask the bombshell.

"Mrs. Alcott, have you been told by the police that your husband apparently suffered a broken neck, before he drowned?"

Betty Alcott stared at the TV reporter for a few seconds, and then decided to talk about what the sheriff had warned her not to because everyone must know how her dear husband lost his life,

"Yes, the sheriff just told me that terrible news a few minutes ago actually."

She began to tear up, and the cameraman zoomed in closer on her face, "I can't believe that someone would want to do anything bad to my Herbie. He did not have an enemy in the world. He and I never had a cross word in 40 years. He was just a wonderful man. We all loved him so much."

Mindy Reese's voice was very sympathetic as she said, "Mrs. Alcott we're all sorry for your terrible tragedy. Did the sheriff mention what they think happened to your husband?" The cameraman pulled back from a solo shot of the reporter, to include both of them in the picture.

The widow looked down at the ground for an instant and drew in a sharp breath. Eventually she raised her head to look at Mindy, as a few more tears trickled down her cheeks in long rivulets, "He said that someone apparently pushed him from behind," she stopped and sobbed softly as the cameraman zoomed tight on her pained expression, "Pushed him from behind so hard that his neck snapped back and he broke some vertebrae's."

Mrs. Alcott looked right at Mindy, asking in hushed tones, "Why would someone want to do that to my Herbie? Why? Why?" She started sobbing softly again, holding a pink handkerchief to her face.

Mindy Reese and Dwayne Murphy where heading back to Dallas after their interview with the widow Alcott. They were excitedly talking about their worldwide exclusive. They now had two sources, the Henderson County medical examiner, and the widow of a victim, who corroborated that at least one of the deaths had been murder.

Their joint TV special was tomorrow night, with the newspaper portion coming out the next day, heading into the busy Memorial Day weekend. Both reporters were confident that no one else had the information, so they could hold off on breaking this story until the special the next evening.

They also debated how the murderer had killed his other victims. Had he used a boat to get close? He couldn't have swum to the middle of the lake to kill the Bushman's. The discussion raged all the way back to Dallas as both reporters beamed and basked in the warm glow of such a coup.

While the two reporters wrestled with the question of how the murders had been committed, detective Billy Richardson was holding a meeting with his key investigators on the same subject. They too were stumped. How had the murderer approached his victims, apparently without being seen?

Cody Martin spent this day driving around Cedar Creek Lake. He was on a reconnaissance mission. The campgrounds were beginning to rapidly fill in anticipation of the holiday. Martin smiled to himself, "This is a target-rich environment."

The killer had stopped fixating on his mistake in murdering the fisherman. Days had passed with little news about the death, so apparently, he had not made a major mistake, as he had feared. Martin felt it was time for another covert mission, but at a different lake. It was time to change his pattern, and further befuddle the sheriff and his men.

Purtis Creek State Park was a pretty little campground on its own small lake about fifteen miles from Cedar Creek Lake. Families flocked to the camp sites for the Memorial Day weekend. It was a beautiful setting, very woodsy, with special programs for the kids, and a couple of large wooden piers that were perfect for young fisherman.

Each pier had special catfish feeders that spewed food into the lake a couple times of day, attracting hundreds of the hungry whiskered fish. It made it easy for young and old fishermen to snare a catfish with a hook and some stink bait.

Cody Martin's cold killer eyes took in this idyllic scene as he drove through the park, ostensibly searching for a campsite. The lake was small enough that only electric-powered outboard motors were allowed. About one-third of the lake was filled with tall spikes of wood sticking four and five feet out of the water. These were small trees, the branches shorn off that were used as habitats for the numerous bass that lived in the lake.

At this hour, several boats were on the lake, a rope tied to the trees to keep the fisherman locked in one spot. One that caught Martin's eye was a boat with a rather rotund man who seemed to be in his late twenties, with a full red beard, and a floppy hat to protect his head from the hot Texas sun. A young boy, maybe five or six years old, was fishing too, proudly using his own little pole.

"Dad, there ain't any fish in here," said the young boy, pouting as he reeled in the line on his little plastic pole, and peered at the worm still wriggling around on the hook.

Dan Welman smiled at his seven-year-old son and said in his usual laidback manner, "Kevin you have to be patient when you go fishin'. We've only been out here a few minutes. The fish probably don't even know we're here yet."

"Come on Dad, I'm hungry, can't we go eat lunch and come back later?"

Dan Welman's protruding stomach was growling too, "OK, let's get some grub, finish putting up the tent, and then we'll come back out in a little while."

The young father started the trolling motor on the small two-man inflatable boat and headed to shore. Welman was a computer programmer in Dallas, separated from his wife; he had his son for a rare long weekend visit. They'd been planning this camping trip to Purtis Creek State Park for weeks.

Cody Martin continued to slowly drive around the park, trying to be inconspicuous as he kept an eye on the father and son. He wanted a campsite near theirs.

29

Sheriff's department investigators continued to re-study evidence sheets, and debate scenarios using the big board with pictures and maps showing all the victims. The door opened, and Jarred Peters strolled into the room, coffee cup in hand. "We're all out of java in the squad room, hope y'all don't mind if I steal some of yours," Peters said as he moved toward the big coffee urn in one corner of the room. Peters had a shaved head, muscular build, and confidence of someone always in control of every situation.

Sheriff King smiled at the lead diver on his scuba team, "Nah, help yourself. Just leave a buck or two per cup." Peters filled his oversized coffee cup and took a sip as he scanned the big board.

Detective Richardson, not pleased with the interruption, picked up the discussion once again. "OK, we need to come up with some possibilities here. How the hell does the killer get close to his victims when they're out on the lake?"

The men were clearly stumped, and the room was silent. Peters moved closer to the evidence board. He stroked his scruffy 5-inch long blonde goatee and stared at the different sites with the multi-colored pins.

"Could be a scuba diver," he mused aloud.

Fifteen pairs of eyes immediately focused on the visitor. Sheriff King spoke first, "What are you sayin' Jarred? Some scuba diver is swimming out to the middle of the lake and drowning these people?"

Peters, continued to scan the board, "I'm sayin' it's a possibility. I'm sayin' that an expert scuba diver could swim a great distance, pop out of the water, and grab somebody."

Detective Richardson jumped in, "Peters may be onto something. But, Jarred, how could he drown these people with no sign of bruises or a struggle, except for the last guy with the broken neck?"

Peters, as was his habit, stroked his goatee again, paused for a moment and then said, "Well, about the only man capable of doing that would be a Navy Seal. They're specially trained to swim long distances and kill without leaving any evidence."

The room fell silent. It seemed plausible. But if it was true, what kind of animal were they dealing with?

In Dallas, the two reporters were struggling with the same conundrum? If there were a serial killer, how was he getting close enough to his victims without being detected?

They were feeling the pressure now. The special aired tomorrow night. Time was running out.

Cody Martin continued his slow drive on the small roads that snaked through the park, keeping an eye on the small boat as it neared shore. He wasn't alone; there was a small parade behind him. There were a lot of people looking for the perfect campsite for the long Memorial Day weekend.

Martin kept tabs on the man and boy as they pulled their inflatable boat onto shore and walked to their nearby campsite. He turned left, took a right at the next intersection, and found himself driving right by their campsite. The killer drove past four campsites that were already taken and pulled into a vacant spot. He would be far enough away from his next victims, so he would not arouse suspicion, but still close enough for reconnaissance. Martin dropped his tent and other gear to claim the campsite, and then drove to the ranger's office to pay.

Mindy Reese's frown suddenly turned into a eureka moment. "There's only one way that a serial killer could be knocking off these people Dwayne. It has to be someone who is a really good swimmer. They can't just pull up in a boat. They have to swim. But how could they swim to the middle of the lake, and once they get there, how the hell could they grab these people and kill them without any marks, unless the cops are lying about that?"

"How about a scuba diver?" Dwayne asked, "Could that be it?"

Mindy picked up the phone and quickly dialed a number.

The hot Texas sun was beginning to head for the horizon under a clear blue sky. The only break in the endless blue were puffy white contrails from jets that had passed over. It would be dark in about an hour.

Cody Martin grabbed his metal tongs and flipped over a couple of chicken breasts sizzling on the heavy rusted grill that was sitting on a steel pole cemented to the campground. He was also keeping a surreptitious eye on the father and son a few campsites away.

Dan and Kevin Welman tossed their paper plates in the trash and headed back onto the lake. Dad pushed the boat off the shore, while Kevin strapped on his lifejacket. They'd fish until it was dark, oblivious to the muscled stranger with the cold narrowed eyes following their every movement.

Cody Martin smiled. This was going to be an easy mission.

At WDFW television, the two reporters were furiously writing the lead segment of tomorrow night's special. They were now sure a serial killer was on the loose at Cedar Creek Lake. Mindy Reese's discussion with a friend who was a scuba master had convinced them that the killer was probably using an underwater breathing apparatus to silently approach his victims.

The scuba expert told her how a skilled diver could move effortlessly, and silently through the lake water with nary a ripple and no sign of their presence, other than tiny bubbles popping the surface.

The station's news director walked into the room. The reporters stopped their typing and looked up. They'd informed her of their exclusive interview, the confirmation from the medical examiner, and their theory about the scuba diver. The news manager gave them permission to sit on this startling information until the newscast that aired two hours before their special tomorrow night.

The news director said, "Two things. First off, we need a title for this special program, and I need it now. Secondly, I think we should get Sheriff King to appear live during the program, so we can spring our information on him for a comment. That way he can't dodge our questions."

Mindy and Dwayne smiled at that one. "Great idea," Mindy said, "It'll be fun to watch him squirm a bit. He is so sure of himself all the time."

"Alright," the impatient news director continued, "We need a name for the special right now."

Dwayne piped up, "How about 'The Scuba Serial Killer'?"

"No, that doesn't work for me. What's another name for a scuba diver?"

Mindy spoke up, "Well, they call them divers, or frogmen?"

The news director smiled and nodded her head, "That's it, 'The Frogman of Cedar Creek.'"

Purtis Creek Lake was like a sheet of glass as the sun settled into the horizon sending beautiful shafts of red, blue and gold into the darkening Texas sky. There was no breeze, and not a ripple on the water. Dan Welman loved the serenity as he waited patiently for a fish to take his bait.

The setting sun had turned the lake into a giant mirror with sparkling bursts of color everywhere like Fourth of July sparklers, as the still water reflected the trees that dotted the shoreline. There were several boats within fifty yards of Welman and his son.

Back at his campsite, Cody Martin grabbed his fishing pole and walked a short distance through the woods to the edge of the lake. He furtively surveyed the situation while casually casting his lure across the peaceful water.

The killer's trained eyes homed in on his quarry, sitting in their small boat about 100 yards away. He smiled to himself at how peaceful they seemed to be, unaware the world was about to come crashing down around them.

Young Kevin Welman kept asking his dad where the fish where. The father shook his head, "Don't know son, they sure don't seem to be very hungry tonight, do they?"

"Sure don't dad. Let's go back to the camp and try again tomorrow. Maybe we can make some s'mores?"

"No," the father shook his head while smiling at his offspring, "not yet son, let's wait until the sun sets. I'll bet they start hitting our bait then."

As the orange glow of the sun was swallowed up by the horizon, darkness began to descend on the small lake. Cody Martin walked back to his tent, tossed his fishing pole inside, and opened the shiny steel compartment in the bed of his pickup truck.

He glanced around. There was no camper close enough to see what he was doing, as the campsite was now quite dark, and the people on either side of him were apparently away at dinner or doing other things outside the park.

Martin took out the bag with his mask and fins and walked back into the woods. He'd decided that no air tank was needed for this mission. The lake was small, and he could use a snorkel without being detected.

Dan Welman turned on the running lights on the small boat, as required by law. He was smiling as his son reeled in a small mouth bass. Kevin was excited now about their fishing excursion.

The killer sat on the shore, pulled on the wet suit and fins, and adjusted his mask and snorkel. He was protected from prying eyes by a thicket of trees, even as he watched his next targets floating in their boat with the small lights glowing in the darkness. It was time to head out on his mission.

Sheriff King answered his office phone on the third ring. WDFW-TV reporter Mindy Reese was on the other end.

"Hey Sheriff, how's it going?"

"Okay, Mindy. What's up?" King warily asked the pushy reporter. He knew this was not a social call. It was about the series of killings. He desperately wanted to keep the latest revelations quiet through the Memorial Day Weekend.

Reese plunged into her request, "Dwayne Murphy and I are putting together a special report that will air tomorrow night about the," she paused, searching for the right word so she didn't tip off the sheriff, "Ah, drownings on Cedar Creek Lake, and we're hoping to do an interview with you as part of the program. You know, get the latest on the investigation."

King inhaled sharply. A special television program? He didn't need this right now. The sheriff also wondered just how much they knew about the situation. He did know that she and Murphy were real bulldogs when it came to sniffing out what was really going on in big cases.

"Well, I don't know, Mindy. I'm pretty busy with all the folks heading to the lake for the holiday weekend and all."

Reese had a ready answer, "Oh, I'm sure you are, sheriff. That's why we thought it would be easiest to just do a live interview for a minute or so during the program."

King quickly weighed that idea. The good part of that is viewers would hear what he had to say without the reporter editing out some of his comments. The downside was she could pin him to the wall with her questions. Damn, he thought, what does she really know?

"Sheriff?"

"Uh, yah Mindy. I guess that's alright, as long as it's a short interview. There really is nothing new on the drowning deaths to report anyway. Why are you doing a special?"

Cody Martin was waist deep in the water, moving without a sound. He fit the mask snugly over his face, and silently disappeared under the water. Only the small tip of his black snorkel protruded a couple inches out of the water. It was nearly invisible as he swam toward the unsuspecting father and son.

Dan Welman's son was really having fun now. The bass were hitting pretty well, and he'd boated four of them in the past few minutes. None of the fish were large enough to be "keepers" but he was having a great time just the same. Dan smiled contentedly as he watched his young son. He had often dreamed of moments like this during the four years Welman and his wife had tried to have a baby.

The killer swam slowly and stealthily just using his powerful legs to propel himself noiselessly through the water just below the surface. He was in total darkness except for the green glow of his underwater compass. Martin had set a course that would take him right to the unsuspecting father and son for his quick, surprise attack.

He figured that he was about halfway to the boat now, and it was time to barely break the surface for one final look around before completing the mission. The scuba divers mask peeked above the surface. It too was black, and invisible to all but the most perceptive onlooker.

Little Kevin Welman, like most young fisherman, became bored quickly, even though the fish were biting. He looked at his father, "Hey, Pop, let's go make s'mores around the campfire."

Cody Martin, without a ripple, slipped back under the water. His reconnaissance showed no obstacles to completing his mission. It would be over in less than three minutes.

Less than twenty miles away, Sheriff King placed a call to Doctor Millinberry. He had agreed to the live interview during the TV station's primetime special tomorrow night. Now he wanted to be sure there would be no surprises.

"Hello, Doc Millinberry here."

"Hey Doc, this is sheriff King. Sorry to bother you after hours."

Millinberry chuckled, "There are no 'after hours' in this job sheriff." Then he paused, wondering if someone had told the sheriff that he'd spilled the beans on the investigation. There had been nothing on the local news about it tonight, and he had felt better, even relaxing a little, hoping for the best.

King replied, "Ain't that the truth. Hey, Reese and Murphy are doing a special report tomorrow night on WDFW about the drownings, and I'm doing a live interview. Just wanted to make sure you haven't talked to them and given them any information we don't want to get out."

The elderly doctor paused for just a few seconds. Apparently, he thought, they were going to keep their word since they'd talked to the sheriff and did not mention anything to him about the doctor's huge mistake. "No," he lied, "haven't heard from either one of them for quite awhile."

"Okay Doc, thanks." The sheriff hung up.

The killer figured he was within twenty yards of the boat. His body began to tense for the quick fury that was about to come.

Suddenly he heard the sound of a small outboard starting, and then the noise began to move away. Martin stopped and began to tread water, still staying below the surface, and out of sight.

After waiting a few more seconds, he warily stuck his mask above the waterline. The small boat with the father and son was heading toward shore.

Martin was furious. His mission had to be aborted. He took a few deep breaths to gain control, and then turned and swam back to shore. He'd have to wait until tomorrow night. Martin fought to control his anger. He did not want to repeat the mistake he'd made of rushing that fisherman near the bridge without doing his reconnaissance, although apparently it had turned out alright. There'd been nothing on the news to suggest he'd left any evidence behind.

30

The Thursday before Memorial Day Weekend dawned to another clear blue sky. It was a picture-perfect day for the lucky ones who could sneak away early to their lake retreats and the campgrounds to get a head start on the long holiday weekend.

The early morning sunlight shined through Cody Martin's thin tent right into his sleeping eyes. The bright beam of yellow woke him up. It was a few minutes before six.

He stretched and turned on the small high-tech portable radio he always had with him. It brought in all the local radio stations, but he also had programmed in the important police frequencies. It seemed to be a quiet morning.

Martin partially opened the door of the tent and saw one his next targets was also up at this early hour. The father was cooking breakfast on the small camp stove. There was no sign of the little boy. The killer wanted to keep a sharp eye on their movements today. It was imperative he complete his mission tonight.

Two hours later in Seven Points, sheriff King was having breakfast with detective Richardson. They were eating mostly in silence, not wanting to discuss the case with so many prying ears around.

"So, you're going to do that interview tonight, huh?" the police veteran asked the young sheriff.

"Yeah, I figure it'll be short, and they can't spin anything I say or take it out of context," the sheriff replied. "I guess they're just doing a special program on the eve of the first holiday week-end of the season."

The wily former Dallas detective looked at his friend, "Buddy just be careful. That Mindy Reese can be a barracuda especially when she's grandstanding live in prime time."

"I know. I'll watch what I say."

The peaceful sun-filled day in East Texas quietly disappeared into darkness. Cody Martin was crouched down near a big cottonwood tree, watching the father and son as they fished aboard the small boat on the tranquil lake. The quarter moon was beginning to rise, and the huge Texas sky twinkled with thousands of bright stars on the cloudless night.

The killer had his scuba bag right next to him. The mission would be carried out tonight.

The production assistant was helping sheriff King put a small plastic earpiece into place, as he sat at his desk in the Henderson County Sheriff's Office. This would allow him to hear the questions from Mindy Reese who would be sitting on the news set in WDFW's Dallas studio. His pal, detective Richardson was sitting in a nearby chair, just out of camera range.

Cody Martin decided to let it get just a little darker. He was confident his prey would not be leaving so soon tonight. They had only been on the water about twenty minutes.

"Son, be sure to put the light brown end of the night crawler on the end of your hook," Dan Welman instructed, shining his small flashlight at his son's hook, "The fish like to bite that end, not the dark end."

"Okay Dad," Welman's seven-year-old son replied, "I'm going to get a lunker tonight."

Dan Welman smiled at his son. He was so grateful to be able to spend a long weekend with him. Welman knew his separation from Kevin's mom was hard on the young boy, and he hoped this trip would make up for some of that pain.

It was eight o'clock. The special program was beginning on WDFW-TV. Sheriff King had a monitor nearby, so he could see the special, and his earpiece allowed him to hear what was being said. He almost fell out of his chair.

The announcer was saying, "This special program, The Frogman of Cedar Creek, is the result of a joint investigation by WDFW-TV and the *Cedar Creek Gazette*. Now, here is WDFW Investigative Reporter Mindy Reese."

The sheriff was trying to catch his breath from the "frogman" title of the special as Reese came on camera.

"Good evening. We have breaking news tonight on the investigation into the seven recent apparent drowning deaths on Cedar Creek Lake. *Gazette* reporter Dwayne Murphy and I have confirmed that there is official police suspicion that at least one of the deaths, and perhaps all of them, could be cold-blooded murder."

At the sheriff's office, detective Richardson bounded out of his chair, motioning to sheriff King to pull the plug on the interview. He was too late.

King saw himself on camera in the TV monitor as he heard Mindy Reese in his ear saying, "We have Henderson County Sheriff Buddy King with us live tonight from his office. Sheriff King please fill us in on the new direction that this investigation has taken since you discovered that the last victim, Herbert Alcott, had a broken neck. That apparently someone had violently shoved him into the water before he drowned?"

While sheriff King was trying to recover his composure from this unexpected twist in the TV special, Cody Martin had silently worked his way to just a few yards from the small boat. Dan Welman was reeling in a small bass, and his son was watching him. They had no idea death was lurking less than 10 feet away.

The frogman soundlessly broke the surface and made one last sweep of the area. He saw the man and young son with their backs to him, intent on their fishing. Unlike last night, there was not another boat anywhere nearby, in fact, the boat had ventured into an area of the lake that was filled with small tree branches that were about ten feet high. It was very secluded.

The TV set in the sheriff's office was showing a split screen effect. On one side was Mindy Reese waiting for the sheriff, who was on the other side of the screen, to answer her question.

"Sheriff? Want me to repeat the question?"

"No, that's not necessary Miss Reese. I must say your information is off base, and your question is inappropriate. I cannot comment on the investigation of these unfortunate drowning deaths, as it is still ongoing." The sheriff stopped and stared at the camera.

Reese quickly jumped in, "Are you denying sheriff King that Herbert Alcott sustained a broken neck?"

"Miss Reese, I am not commenting on the specifics of this investigation and will not lend credence to your speculation."

"Well sheriff, what if I told you we have confirmed this information with the Henderson County Medical Examiner Doctor Millinberry, and with Mr. Alcott's widow. Here is what she told us about her husband's death."

158

The color began to drain from sheriff King's face, and he fidgeted in his chair, as the widow's interview began to play.

It was an uncomfortable moment for sheriff King, but less than 20 miles away at Purtis Creek State Park, Dan Welman and his son Kevin were about to become the frogman's eighth and ninth victims.

He grabbed Dan Welman almost effortlessly despite his girth and weight and swept him into the water without a splash. He held the struggling man underwater with his left arm and grabbed the startled seven-year-old boy with his right hand. Kevin Welman was lithe, and light and the killer easily held him below the murky water. The child's lifejacket had not been strapped on tight – and it quickly slipped off of him.

It was over in a minute or so, as father and son gasped desperately for air, but received only water in their lungs instead. Their thrashing in the water did cause some small ripples, but the water muted their screams, and a boom box blaring on shore easily covered any of the noises being made as two more victims fell to a watery grave. The frogman sliced the youth's lifejacket with his knife, and took it with him back to shore, swimming silently, undetected just below the dark water.

Sheriff King was unaware that he would soon have two more victims to contend with, at that moment he was in a death struggle of his own, trying to keep panic from spreading throughout the Cedar Creek Lake area on the eve of one of the three major holidays of the season for area merchants.

Reese was relentless in her questioning, "So sheriff, it seems that Mrs. Alcott believes that you told her that someone broke her husband's neck?"

The sheriff had no choice but to say, "Well, that is true, there was some medical evidence that Mr. Alcott had suffered a broken neck, however we are not sure if it was caused by his fall into the water, or some other means."

Reese bore in further, "And that other means could be a strong person who violently shoved him into the water, and then held him under until he drowned?"

"We have no evidence of that Miss Reese," King quickly and firmly replied.

She did not let up, leaning into the studio camera and asking, "Sheriff King is it not true that you are investigating the possibility that an expert scuba diver could have drowned seven people in Cedar Creek Lake, and is still at large."

King had had enough. He angrily ripped out his earpiece and said, "Miss King I refuse to sit here and give any credence to such unreasonable and unprofessional speculation. I want to assure everyone that Cedar Creek Lake is a safe place to visit this week-end, and we are continuing our investigation and we will tell the public more as soon as we have more information. Good night."

With that, the sheriff roughly pushed back his chair, rose from his desk and stomped out of camera range.

The frogman reached the dark shoreline, and quickly shrugged out of his wet suit and stuffed the gear and the child's life preserver into his carry bag. He slowly walked through the woods to his campsite, and silently entered his tent. He was sure no one noticed him.

Cody Martin felt a sense of accomplishment. He had completed another mission, just like all the others that the United States Navy Seals had taught him to carry out. He was staying in excellent shape, and these missions kept his deadly skills honed for the day they would call and beg him to return to the Seals.

This latest hit, on a different lake, and on the eve of a big holiday weekend, should send the police scurrying in all directions. Martin glanced at his watch. It was just after nine p.m. It had been a long day. He stretched out on the cot in his tent and quickly went to sleep.

It would be a restless night for sheriff King. He quickly huddled with detective Richardson after the TV disaster. The sheriff's department phones began to ring incessantly as the other news media tried to catch up with the stunning story broadcast on the Dallas TV station.

Richardson convinced the sheriff that they had to call a news conference for Friday morning to deal with this situation. In the meantime, they would not talk to any members of the news media.

King's problem was compounded by the many phone calls from Cedar Creek Lake area merchants, demanding how he was going to insure them a successful holiday weekend. A number of resorts and motels were already getting cancellation calls from frightened vacationers.

And worse yet, the national media, and news hungry national cable TV channels jumped on the story. The day before a major holiday weekend was always a slow news day, so The Frogman of Cedar Creek was a moniker being said from coast to coast, around the clock. The network morning programs all did live reports from the lake, and the cable news channels sent correspondents too. Those channels brought in experts and speculated incessantly about the deaths, showing video of the crime scenes over and over again.

As the sun rose Friday morning, there was already a media compound forming in the park along the lake just outside Gun Barrel City. It was near the spot where victim number 7, Herbert Alcott, had been murdered.

Less than fifteen miles away, Cody Martin woke up early on Friday morning, slowly munched on a power bar and drank some orange juice for breakfast. He turned on the radio and was in for a shock of his own.

As he flipped from station to station, he was stunned. They were all excitedly talking about the seven deaths on Cedar Creek Lake, and the theory of The Frogman of Cedar Creek.

Martin forced himself to take a couple of slow, measured breaths to clear his head, just as they had taught him at Seal survival school, his mind already racing through the next scenarios.

Sheriff King, detective Richardson, and the rest of the task force gathered early to determine what was going to be said at the ten o'clock news conference. Once again, they would set up in the Seven Points Library, the only room in the area large enough to accommodate all the media that would attend.

Richardson was up most of the night sketching out a framework for his comments. Once again, sheriff King was relying on the police veteran to be his spokesman.

In the coffee shops around Cedar Creek Lake people gathered to talk about the biggest news to ever hit the area. Many of them were clutching a copy of the *Cedar Creek Gazette's* special edition. It was twice as thick as usual and filled with color pictures and speculation about the Frogman of Cedar Creek. The newspaper was, for the first time in its history, making a second press run as the original batch of papers had disappeared before eight in the morning.

31

Cody Martin unhurriedly broke camp at Purtis Creek State Park. He did not want to arouse attention, but he needed to retreat as quickly as possible to his hideaway on Lake Athens to plot his next move. While he appeared calm on the outside, The Frogman was churning on the inside, with wave after wave of fury grinding through his stomach. How could he have been so stupid and broken that guy's neck? This changed everything. He needed to come up with a new plan of action, and to just lay low for a while until all this attention blows over.

The killer cleaned up his campsite and cast a wary eye at the now deserted site just down the narrow road, where the man and boy had been camping. So far, there was no activity there. Their tent remained as did some cooking gear near the fire pit. Welman's car was parked next to the tent.

Martin climbed into his pickup and slowly drove along the paved road that snaked along the edge of the lake. Campsites on both sides were either already taken, or quickly filling up. There was a lot of incoming traffic.

In Seven Points, the library meeting room was abuzz and packed with media. There seemed to be twice as many as during the sheriff's original news conference a few weeks ago.

Sheriff King walked to the podium. It looked like a microphone farm with dozens of them sticking everywhere, filled with colorful logos from local and national media. This time the pseudo news programs were on hand too, *Inside Edition* and the like.

The room became deathly silent as the sheriff stepped to the podium. King's eyes swept the room as he began, "Ladies and gentlemen we want to give you some information about our investigation into the recent drowning deaths at Cedar Creek Lake. Detective Billy Richardson will be the spokesman. He will not entertain any questions this morning." The media let out an angry murmur after that comment.

As Cody Martin rounded a curve in the road, he could see that a small crowd of people had gathered on the shore of the lake. There were a couple of boats next to the small inflatable boat that had been owned by the father and son.

The killer stopped, rolled down his window, and asked a young man standing along the roadway what all the commotion was about?

The camper, a sandy-haired, freckle-faced boy who seemed to be about 9 years old excitedly told him, "That boat out there was found empty this morning when some guys went out fishing. Some people saw an older guy and a kid, guess it was a father and son, fishing in it last night. They can't find them now."

"Wow," was all Cody Martin said, and then he continued to drive out the exit of the campground. It was time to leave all this excitement. He knew they would not find the bodies for quite a while. The Frogman had seen to that last night.

Detective Richardson, a bit sleepy from his many hours of prep time last night, was ready to go. The world seemed to be focused on this rural part of East Texas, and Richardson was looking into bright TV lights and literally dozens of excited faces. It seemed that close to a hundred politicians, business owners and lake residents also crowded into the room.

Nothing of this magnitude had happened during his long service in Dallas. This story and the catchy name from that TV special – The Frogman of Cedar Creek – had every local and national media outlet crammed elbow to elbow, waiting for Richardson's explanation of seven deaths. Seven apparent unsolved murders.

As he looked around the room, the detective also noticed quite a few area merchants had joined the fray, anxious to hear Richardson's spin on a potential disaster for their tourist trade. Around North and East Texas, hundreds of cars were heading to the Cedar Creek area for the long Memorial Day weekend.

As Richardson began to speak, there was another very interested listener glued to the live radio broadcast. Cody Martin was driving toward his cabin retreat at Lake Athens. He was the only one who knew there were actually nine victims, not the seven that the retired policeman was about to talk about.

Detective Billy Richardson took a breath and cleared his throat. He was now on center stage and needed to give the performance of his life.

"Ladies and gentlemen," he began in a strong, official voice, "I am going to give you information about the deaths in recent months of seven people in Cedar Creek Lake. I want to make it clear that in all cases, except one, the evidence points to accidental drowning." His words were again met with a disapproving murmur from the media audience.

Richardson, undaunted, plunged on, "In the case of the seventh drowning victim, Mr. Herbert Alcott, there is evidence to suggest that he also had a broken neck. Now, there has been some speculation in the media that someone forcefully pushed him into the lake, causing the injury. As of this moment in our investigation, we have no evidence to prove that is actually what happened. We believe such unwarranted speculation is unprofessional and misleading." The media unrest grew a bit as another low murmur went through the room.

"We want to assure every citizen of the Cedar Creek Lake area," the detective's jaw was set, and he was peering with sincerity into the TV cameras, "that a task force of highly skilled law enforcement officials from not only this area, but experts on loan from Dallas County, and the FBI, are working around the clock on this investigation. We ask you to be patient as we follow every lead in these apparent drowning deaths. We also ask the news media to report responsibly on the facts, and only the facts, in these deaths, and not to offer wild speculation that may be far from the truth when all the evidence is pieced together."

Richardson paused, feeling as if his performance was going very well, "We may unearth evidence that points to foul play in Mr. Alcott's death, or those of the other victims. I promise that if we do, we will hold another news conference immediately to fill the public in on what we have found. But in the meantime, we ask the news media to let us go about our jobs without sensational newspaper headlines, or unfounded speculation on the TV and cable channels."

Sheriff King looked at his friend with admiration. He was really doing a terrific job of putting the right spin on the deaths and placing the attempt at hysteria squarely on the shoulders of the news media.

"Finally," Richardson was wrapping up, "Sheriff King and I want all of our Cedar Creek Lake residents, and weekend guests to have a fun and safe Memorial Day holiday. Please drive carefully, and do not drink and drive on our roads or in your boat on our lake."

166

The veteran detective spun on his heels and walked briskly out of the bright lights as shouted questions from the media rained down on him.

Cody Martin drummed his fingers on the steering wheel of his pickup as he turned off the highway into the paved farm-to-market road that led to his cabin. The killer told himself that it was time to lay low for a while. There would be no more missions until the media heat subsided a bit. That may be some time, he knew, because the shock waves would really roll when they found the bodies of his latest victims in a different lake.

32

Martha O'Grady was a strong, muscular woman, with large hands, and a solid build, not really overweight, just bulky. In her mid-40s with wispy strands of gray among the brown hair peeking out from her smoky bear hat, O'Grady was one of the new breed of female Texas Forest Rangers. She was in charge of Purtis Creek State Park. O'Grady was very concerned this morning, standing along the banks of Purtis Creek Lake, beside the small boat apparently owned by the missing father and son.

She had poked around their campsite and found nothing out of the ordinary. Their belongings were undisturbed, their vehicle still parked and locked, and no sign of anything to indicate any foul play.

O'Grady wondered if maybe the boat had floated into the lake overnight. There were two fishing poles in the boat, and one adult life preserver. There was no sign of a youth life jacket on board, and that was a cause for some concern.

The Forest Ranger was hoping that pranksters had maybe pushed the boat into the water. It had happened many times before. Maybe, she thought, the father and son had gone on a long hike this morning.

O'Grady also heard the buzz throughout the campground about the seven drowning deaths in Cedar Creek Lake, and the media speculation about a killer. It seemed far-fetched to her, but she decided to call Sheriff King to let him know about this situation.

Buddy King was feeling pretty good considering the mounting problems he faced. Detective Richardson had put on a masterful performance during the news conference, and as he watched the cable news channels it seemed like things were calming down a little bit. He'd even taken a couple calls from lake merchants who felt better as they swung into the all-important holiday weekend.

The ringing of his cell phone shattered the rookie sheriff's reverie. He warily answered, "Sheriff King here."

The voice on the other end was grave and very concerned. "Hi Buddy, this is Martha O'Grady. We have a situation here."

The phrase brought an immediate frown to King's previously relaxed face. He braced for what was to come next, as O'Grady took an audible breath and continued.

"Buddy, we've got two campers, a father and young son, missing. Their boat was floating in the lake, and there is no sign of them anywhere. They were last seen fishing last night in the dark."

King let out a long breath of his own. He felt the energy and hope drain from every fiber of his body. Some muscles twitched involuntarily in his shoulders. All he could muster was, "You sure they aren't out hiking or something, Martha?"

"Pretty sure sheriff. There's nothing missing from their campsite. It looks untouched, and unslept in. Their car is parked there and locked."

There was silence on the phone as the possible scenarios spun out of control through King's head. Had the killer struck in a different lake? Had he killed a young boy this time? The media was already swarming everywhere. They'd be on this story in no time.

"Martha," King quietly spoke into his cell phone. "Do other campers know about this, ah, disappearance?"

"Of course, it's the talk of the park."

A beaming Dwayne Murphy was holding court during a late breakfast at McDuff's diner. He had the popular Mindy Reese at his side, along with her cameraman, and half the people in the place had stopped by to talk about these strange deaths around Cedar Creek Lake.

Murphy's mouth and brain were in high gear. "Mindy, we stuck it to all those network boys and girls with our scoop during the special last night, now we have to stay ahead of the story." He paused to shovel some egg and biscuit into his mouth.

Their TV special last night had scored high numbers, and the special edition of the *Gazette* today was already on its fourth printing, breaking all records for the weekly newspaper. The two reporters were plotting how to keep their lead on the many news crews and even national print reporters now stalking the story.

Meanwhile, the subject of their fascination sat in his secluded lake cabin using his DVR to watch the news conference for the fifth time. Cody Martin was wrestling with his next move. At first, he had decided to lay low for a few days until things quieted down. It would probably take that long to find the bodies in Purtis Creek Lake.

But then he kept thinking about the sheriff's pretty little girlfriend and the challenge she represented. He was growing more excited by the moment about completing that mission under the noses of the extensive media and police scrutiny. It could be his greatest mission ever.

Meanwhile, the Frogman's potential 10th victim had the morning off. She was helping other SPCA members set up their booth in the large covered shelter at the city park in Mabank, a small town adjacent to Gun Barrel City. The city always had a big classic car show at the park during the holiday weekend, complete with a crawdad boil.

This was one of the biggest fundraisers of the year for the local SPCA, as they held a raffle for donated prizes during the car show. They also would help a lot of needy cats and dogs find homes during the weekend.

As they assembled the booth, SPCA chairwoman Holly Thomas paused for a moment and said in her heavy Texas accent, "Crystal, honey, how is Buddy doin' with these awful murders an all."

Crystal, ever loyal to her man, stopped what she was doing, put her hands on her hips, and said loud enough for everyone nearby to hear, "Holly, these have not been confirmed as murders. You are going on the sloppy work by that Dallas TV reporter, and that snoopy old Dwayne. Don't believe everything you hear."

Holly, a known nosy sort herself, plunged on, "Oh, darlin' y'all know that all those poor folks couldn't of drowned."

Crystal decided to end this debate that she knew could not be won, "I don't know anything Holly, other than what I hear and read. Buddy has been a little busy lately, and I just haven't even seen him for days."

Sheriff King told Ranger O'Grady to try to down play the situation on Purtis Creek Lake as much as possible. He knew sending divers to the lake would only make the story spread quicker to the news media. They decided to do nothing for the next few hours, until King could meet with the task force.

Detective Richardson was slowly stirring a second heaping spoonful of sugar into his coffee cup. He rarely treated himself to real sugar, using the substitutes instead. But Richardson was feeling good about his media performance, and this was his means of a small celebration. The celebration came to a crashing halt when Sheriff King told him about the phone call from Purtis Creek State Park. Unfortunately for both of them, it was about to get worse.

Two local anglers pulled into McDuff's restaurant after a break of dawn fishing trip to Purtis Creek Lake. As they ambled into the place, they caught sight of Reese and Murphy jawing with a number of folks in the center of the restaurant.

One of the fishermen walked up to the gathering. He wanted to get a closer look at the Reese woman, and at the same time give them a scoop.

Detective Richardson and Sheriff King decided to borrow an unmarked personal car from one of the task force members, and stealthily drive to Purtis Creek State Park to personally assess the situation and help Ranger O'Grady keep this situation out of the media.

It took them about 20 minutes to pass through Eustace and arrive at the front entrance of the park. A sign told approaching visitors that the campground was full to capacity; no campsites were available for the rest of the weekend.

The lawmen parked at the Ranger's office and went inside to meet with O'Grady. They had just shaken hands, when a big news van pulled into the park entrance. Through the office window, King saw that Mindy Reese was driving, and Dwayne Murphy was perched right beside her, like a bantam rooster.

Over at Lake Athens, Cody Martin walked out of the refreshing water after completing his daily two-mile swim. It was just after two p.m. He changed into a pair of weather-beaten blue jean shorts, and a tight t-shirt, grabbed his baseball cap and sunglasses and headed out the door. He knew that the marina would be busy on this holiday weekend, so people would pay him little heed as he spent the afternoon devising a plan to make the sheriff's girlfriend his next victim.

Sheriff King quickly walked up to the driver's window of the news van, squinted inside and said, "What's up guys?"

Mindy Reese gave him one of her million megawatt smiles, "Nothin' much sheriff, what are you doing here?"

Sheriff King knew this cat and mouse game was going nowhere, so he decided a confrontational approach might be the best way to attack the media hounds.

His face became very serious, his eyes burrowed into the reporter's eyes, "First off, Miss Reese, that's none of your damn business, and secondly, I did not appreciate the ambush interview last night."

Mindy gave him a sweet smile and with sugar dripping off her tongue said, "That was no ambush sheriff. We had some new information and I simply wanted you to get a chance to respond to it."

King took a deep breath and said in a low growl, "Anyway, what are y'all doing here?"

Mindy smiled again, "Well sheriff, maybe you can help us. We hear that a man and his young son have disappeared after a fishing trip last night. You don't suppose there's been another accidental drowning, do you?"

King was clenching his fists as he angrily replied, "Don't be a smart-ass Reese." He then noticed that there was a camerman in the back of the news van. King pointed his finger at him, "and he better not be taking any video right now either."

Murphy jumped in at this point, "Sheriff we'll just go look around a bit. Can we interview you after a little while?"

King was flummoxed. It was clearly a public campground, so there was no way he could keep them out. He knew that soon the campsite would be on TV, as well as interviews with campers. The story of two missing people would be broadcast everywhere.

Wesley's Marina was packed this afternoon. Cars jammed the parking lot. Nearly all the slips at the boat docks were taken, and three boats were being serviced at the gas dock, while a few other boats circled nearby waiting to replenish their thirsty tanks.

Cody Martin found a spot way at the end of the parking lot for his truck, and slowly climbed the stairs to the bar and restaurant area. The tables were all occupied, and so was every barstool.

The Frogman spotted his prey among the festive scene. Crystal had her usual shorts and tank top outfit on but had added an American Flag do-rag as part of her holiday attire. If she noticed Martin she did not show it as Crystal busily hurried toward a table with a tray full of drinks and food.

A man got up to leave, at the very end of the bar, in the corner. Martin quickly slipped into the vacant spot.

Detective Richardson watched the exchange between the sheriff and the newshounds from a few feet away – and then proposed an idea.

"Sheriff King," the detective said, "We have every right to close this park, and to keep the news media outside the gate, since this is a potential crime scene."

This brought a quick, simultaneous indignant outburst from Reese and Murphy.

Detective Richardson quickly put up both his hands, "Stop," he said, "Let me finish." All eyes turned to the veteran lawman.

"I propose that we make a deal. You have yourselves an exclusive news story you want to protect, and we have, at this point, just a father and son who are unaccounted for. They could have gone on a long hike. They could have gone to a movie in Athens with some friends. Boats break loose, or are sent into the lake as pranks, every day."

Mindy Reese, defiantly jutted her jaw out of the news van window, "So what's your proposal?"

"We'll give you access to the campgrounds, so you can get your video and do some interviews. We'll also give you first call when we find these two missing people. In exchange, you promise that your story will not link this to the drowning deaths at Cedar Creek Lake. If it turns out differently, after we've had a chance to investigate, you're free to report anything you want. Deal?"

Reese glanced over at Murphy, and they both nodded. Sheriff King let out a sigh of relief, and for the hundredth time since these deaths began occurring, he was extremely thankful for the skill and knowledge of his friend the detective.

The din was increasing at Wesley's Marina as a festive Memorial Day Weekend crowd continued to pack into the outdoor bar with its tropical décor. The sun was shining brightly, and the cold beer was flowing. Cody Martin quietly and unobtrusively sipped a cold one of his own and blended into the scene. No one would ever remember he was even at the bar during this busy time.

If anyone did watch him closely, they would have seen his cold killer eyes following Crystal the waitress as she scurried around with trays and trays of drinks and food. Of course, other men in the joint were doing the same thing. Martin's brow was furrowed, his mind working overtime, as he tried mightily to come up with a foolproof plan to make the sheriff's girlfriend his tenth victim.

His months of surveillance had turned up nothing that would allow him to make her death look like an accidental drowning. She was an expert water skier, but that was a daytime sport with lots of friends around her. She never kept a predictable schedule either, sometimes leaving work in her own car, sometimes joining people at the humane shelter, other times getting picked up by Sheriff King and heading to his house for the night. Crystal did not spend any time near the lake at night.

While the sheriff and detective were dealing with the pesky reporters, Crime Scene Specialist Danny Cates was working all the angles on the idea that an expert scuba diver may be killing people at Cedar Creek Lake and making them look like drowning deaths. Cates, on loan from the Dallas County Sheriff's Department, had in recent years, become an expert on using the computer and the Internet to track down crime clues.

He searched databases of all SCUBA instructors, clubs, and classes in East Texas. The list of names was long, but it would be a starting point. He would turn the other detectives loose on the tedious task of interviewing potential suspects from that list.

Cates also tried to get information from the Navy, especially names of former Navy Seals who might be living in East Texas. That task proved more difficult, as Cates was told each time that all information on the Seals was classified. He was slowly working his way up the command chain and getting turned down each step of the way.

At Purtis Creek State Park, the news crew finished their work, and hurried back to Dallas to get the story of the missing father and son on the evening news. With the media out of the way for now, Sheriff King brought in a team of SCUBA divers to search the lake where the father and son had been last seen, and a couple of boats to drag portions of it too. They also questioned a number of the campers but learned nothing new.

No one mentioned the dark blue pickup truck with the silver steel storage case in the bed, or the muscular man who had driven the truck, and used a campsite less than 75 yards from the missing man and boy.

Sheriff King and detective Richardson sat down in the task force war room at six o'clock to watch the local news. They were relieved to see that Mindy Reese had lived up to her word, and not directly connected the story of the missing father and son to the deaths at Cedar Creek Lake.

The TV set was on at Wesley's Marina, but the sound was turned off, and could never have been heard above the noise anyway. Mindy Reese's report caught Cody Martin's eye but he had no idea what she was saying. He'd check his DVR when he got back to the cabin to find out what they were saying about his latest victims.

Martin had been at the bar for almost three hours now, and though he had picked up bits and pieces of conversations between his prey, the bartender, and other customers, he had learned nothing that would help him figure out the foolproof plan for this mission.

Martin drained the last of his beer, left a couple dollars on the bar for a tip, and ambled out of the bar and down the stairs. No one paid him any attention.

Sheriff King and detectives Richardson and Cates huddled in King's office, planning their strategy for tomorrow. The men sipped on stale coffee, as the East Texas sun settled into its nesting place for the night sending orange and white shards of light across the evening sky.

"I need some high up mucky-muck to help me get into the data base of retired Navy Seals," a frustrated Cates said, "These guys are tighter than hell. The farther I go up the command chain the less helpful they become."

Sheriff King scratched his rapidly darkening chin, as his five o'clock shadow grew more prominent, so did the dark rings under his tired eyes. This case was beginning to take its toll on the usually energetic sheriff. He was not only tired, but he felt that he was in over his head.

"How about congressman Pete Dicus, Buddy? He's a friend of yours," Richardson offered.

"Yeah," King muttered, "He should be able to give us a hand." He let out a big sigh, his cheeks puffing out and then back in, and his shoulders slumping down.

Detective Richardson locked eyes with his pal, "Hey, Buddy you really seem down. Lighten up, man, we'll crack this thing real soon."

King sighed again, "You know, I wish I could believe that, but we've got a string of dead bodies, and now maybe a little kid is dead too. Maybe I need to just turn this whole thing over to the FBI?"

Richardson slapped his hand on the table, jarring the coffee mugs, and making a startled Cates nearly jump out of his chair. "Damn it, that's not the kinda talk I'm used to from you. You've never given up in your life, and you sure as hell ain't going to start now," bellowed Richardson.

Cates chimed in, with a more measured tone, "He's right Buddy. We at least have an idea now that maybe some crazy scuba diver or someone who is a really strong swimmer could be involved in these murders."

Sheriff King seemed to gain a bit of new resolve from his friend's admonishments. He slowly rose out of his chair, hitched up his jeans and said with conviction, "Okay, what's the immediate plan? What we gonna do tomorrow to move this damn investigation along at a much quicker pace?"

The killer sat down in front of his television set and worked the DVR remote to get back to the newscast he had seen but had not heard while he was at the bar. He watched WDFW reporter Mindy Reese explain that a father and son were missing at the campgrounds, and no one seemed to know where they were. He leaned forward as she said, "Police say the father and son may have wandered away on a hike and not returned, or they could have fallen into the lake from their small boat while fishing. At this time, police do not suspect foul play."

The image on the TV screen froze as the killer paused the DVR machine. He wondered if that's really what police believed, or if she was now in their back pocket like most of the other media. They'd taught him all about media manipulation during his Navy SEAL training.

He smiled to himself. It looked like his little extra twist was keeping the missing father and son safely hidden under the water at Purtis Creek Lake.

The three lawmen broke up their meeting and headed for the door of the sheriff's office. They'd agreed that Sheriff King would pay a visit to congressman Dicus, who was back in the district for the Memorial Day Weekend and enlist his aid in breaking the secrecy of the Navy SEALS. Detective Richardson would lead a team of scuba divers back to Purtis Creek at the crack of dawn to conduct a thorough search of the lake. Detective Cates was planning on a long night on his laptop computer, cross-referencing accredited SCUBA divers in East Texas with the crime computer to see if he could get any matche

33

It was nearly nine o'clock on Saturday morning of the long Memorial Day Weekend, and the sheriff's department divers, along with a half dozen volunteers had been searching for a couple of hours. They were trying to be as unobtrusive as possible, but a growing number of campers were gazing from the shore as the sun began to beat down from a clear, blue sky. The weatherman had predicted a high of nearly 90 degrees today, about normal for this time of the year.

Purtis Creek Lake is man-made, like almost every other lake in Texas. It was small and had thin tree branches sticking out of the water about six feet in some places. In fact, one section of the lake was dotted with the branches. Many fishermen tied their boats to the branches as they fished.

Sheriff King was about ten miles away as the annual Memorial Day parade slowly wound its way around the Athens town square. Like most small-town parades, it was filled with scout troops, high school marching bands, veterans in uniform, and the usual array of army vehicles and fire trucks. Congressman Dicus was passing by in a convertible, waving to the small crowd lining the downtown streets. King waited at the end of the route, having set up an appointment with Dicus.

King's cell phone started to ring, and the sheriff looked at the caller ID. It was detective Richardson. He flipped open the small device, "What's up?"

Richardson's voice was low and angry, "We just found the father and son."

Sheriff King was hopeful, had they walked out of the woods after being lost, "Where?" he said.

"It's bad Buddy. A couple of volunteer scuba divers found them tied to a small tree that was sticking out of the water. Their hands were tied together, and they were shackled to the base of the tree. The killer wanted to be sure we didn't find them for a while, the son of a bitch."

King saw the car with the smiling congressman approaching from a half block away. He was angrier than ever in his life, but he had to focus on getting the congressman to help them out, "Okay, can we keep a lid on this?"

"I doubt it, Buddy, there had to be 25, 30 people watching from shore. I think it'll get out fast."

King balled his fists, until the veins popped up on the top of his hands. He just wanted to find this sick bastard and strangle him with his own hands.

Congressman Dicus, a dapper middle-aged man, graying at the temples and wearing a dark suit with a red tie was walking toward him now, and had noticed the sheriff's suddenly dark mood. Dicus looked at King with inquisitive eyes.

The sheriff told Richardson he would hook up with him at the park in half an hour. He admonished him to use whatever manpower he had to keep the park visitors away from the crime scene, and to keep this latest information from the news media.

Congressman Dicus, ever the politician, joviality stuck out his hand with a big smile on his face, "Great to see you Buddy." Then he half-whispered so the few people standing nearby couldn't hear him, "Is everything alright?"

"I'm afraid not, congressman. Can we take a little walk?"

As the two men strolled down a deserted side street in Athens, sheriff King laid all the facts out for the congressman, adding the information he had just received a few minutes ago.

King's furrowed brow betrayed his agony, as he said to the congressman, "That's nine murders in just a few weeks. This is a terrible situation, and now a little boy too." The sheriff shook his head and looked at the ground.

"What can I do Buddy?"

"Well," King stopped walking, "This last discovery really clinches it for us. We strongly believe that some expert scuba diver is grabbing people out of boats and holding them under water until they die. He must be very strong, and very good, because he does not leave bruise marks on the bodies. That's why in the beginning we thought we had a puzzling string of drowning deaths. But then he apparently lost control one night and pushed a fisherman into the water and broke his neck. That was our first real clue as to what was happening."

The congressman was staring at the sheriff, drinking in every word. King continued, "Now he's tied a father and son to a tree limb underwater. It looks like they both may have still been alive when he put them there, but we can't be sure. The bottomline is we have to put an end to this right away."

The congressman was shocked and dismayed by this information, especially the news about the youngster. His sad eyes looked into the troubled eyes of Sheriff King as he asked, "What can I do sheriff to help you catch this sick son of a bitch?"

"Well, as I said, we think this guy is a highly expert swimmer, a scuba diver, and maybe someone who is a trained killer, like a

Navy SEAL. The problem is, that is a very secretive organization, and we can't get them to give us a list of any retired SEALS who may be living in East Texas. We need you to twist some arms so we can get that list, and we need it now."

The congressman's jaw was set almost as firmly as the sheriffs. He was clearly disturbed by what he had just heard. There was no hesitation, "I can do that sheriff. I know just what strings to pull. It might be until Tuesday though because of the holiday weekend."

For the first time in days, sheriff King showed a small smile, "That's great. We really appreciate it. It might give us the break we need to catch this bastard."

Sammy Johnson was spending the weekend at campsite 32 at Purtis Creek State Park. He was a big fan of WDFW news reporter Mindy Reese and had been really excited when he got to meet her yesterday while she was talking to some campers about the missing father and son.

She had given him her business card and asked him to call her if there was anything new on the search. Johnson punched the number into his cell phone. This was exciting. He was going to give a scoop to the most beautiful reporter in Dallas.

34

Sheriff King's smile brought on by the congressman's promise of help, disappeared into a tight grimace as he climbed into his car and flipped on the siren and emergency lights for the trip to the state park, and the horrid scene he knew awaited him there.

His mind wandered back to a meeting with a number of local politicians and businessmen and women who urged him to run for sheriff. King remembered one of them, slapping him on the back and saying, "It's the greatest job in the world, sheriff in a rural county in Texas where nothing ever happens except for a couple of drunks on Friday night."

King fervently wished that were the case. These murders overwhelmed him during every waking moment and for half the night as he tried to sleep. He longed for those nights when a fight between a few drunks was his greatest worry.

As he raced down the highway, siren blaring, lights flashing, cars pulling to the side of the road to get out his way, his mind wandered again this time to lovely Crystal. King had seen her for only a few minutes this week and he missed her. Then he remembered that her birthday was on Monday, and he hadn't even bought her a present. Damn, he said to himself, need to take care of that. He also worried about the sick killer somehow going after her to get at him. Crystal was a beautiful woman, and always was the center attention with the dozens of strangers who wandered into the marina bar on a typical busy weekend. Was the killer one of them?

As he slowed down on the outskirts of Euless and turned right onto the two-lane road that led to the park, King remembered a conversation he'd had with a buddy of his who ran a very popular Spy Store in Dallas' West End area. They'd been discussing the killer and King's buddy, a former private investigator, had showed him the ideal gift for Crystal. He made a mental note to call him later today to set up a time to pick up that perfect gift.

Detective Richardson had his officers grab two large blankets from a squad car and form a semi-circle around the divers who were bringing the bodies to the surface. He wanted to block the crowd's view as much as possible. Richardson desperately wanted no one to find out that the bodies had been tied to trees underwater. This could start a panic among the thousands of Memorial Day weekend partiers dotted around the Cedar Creek Lake area.

His detective's mind was also racing. Why had the killer moved his operation to a second lake? Was this crime carried out by a copycat killer? How did the killer commit this crime without anyone seeing anything? This was a very small lake with no place to hide. There were so many questions and not a single answer.

As Richardson watched the sheriff's cruiser speeding toward him, seventy miles away in the WDFW newsroom, Mindy Reese was answering her cell phone. The call was from a very excited fan who had met her at the campground yesterday. Talking as fast as a machine gun, the caller filled her on his scoop about the two dead bodies being found. Fortunately for the lawmen, the tipster had no idea that the victims had been tied to a tree under the water.

Richardson quickly walked over to the sheriff's car. His face was an angry mask as he looked straight ahead, seemingly oblivious to the crowd of 40 or 50 people who walked to the crime scene from their nearby campsites or had dropped their fishing poles and left the pier to get a better look.

He leaned into the car, and his steel blue eyes bore into those of the sheriff. King had never seen his longtime buddy in such a state.

"You okay man?" King asked in a half whisper.

"Yeah," came the half whispered, half grunted reply from Richardson. He dropped his voice another octave as he said, "Listen Buddy, we've got the bodies covered, and loaded into the back of an ambulance. I suggest we drive together to the medical examiner's office and get out of here as quickly and quietly as possible. I'm leaving two detectives here to search the crime scene."

King nodded his head and waited for Richardson to climb into his own police cruiser. He led the small parade out of the park and back toward Athens.

As the caravan sped down the highway, King punched the number of the Purtis Creek State Park superintendent on his cell phone. Martha O'Grady answered on the second ring as her caller ID showed the call was coming from Sheriff King. She was at home getting ready to head to the park having already been notified about the bodies by one of her park officers.

O'Grady spoke into her cell phone, "Hi Buddy. Got the bad news. What kind of sick son'a'bitch would tie a little kid and his father to one of those underwater trees?"

King let out a heavy sigh, "I don't know Martha but we gotta grab his ass pretty quickly. I don't want to have any more dead bodies on my hands. But we've got nothin', except for a crazy theory that maybe he's a specially-trained SCUBA diver."

There was a brief pause as O'Grady was thinking through the situation. The phone line fell silent.

King said, "Martha you still there?'

"Yeah, I'm here Buddy. You know, we might have a great clue for you back at the park."

King sat up a little straighter in his seat as he asked, "Whatcha mean Martha?"

"Well," O'Grady's voice was excited, "A couple months ago, we got approval for a camera that takes still pictures of the license plates of everyone who drives through our gates into the park. We should have the killer's license plate on that system right now."

King was nearly shouting into the phone, "How long will it take you to get those pictures to us?" O'Grady assured him she would get them as quickly as possible and meet him at the Medical Examiner's Office, hopefully in less than 90 minutes.

Mindy Reese hit the speed dial on her office telephone. She needed to quickly confirm this news tip and get the information on the air right away. The sheriff had promised her "first call" when the father and son were found. He had obviously not lived up to his promise and it was time to call him on it.

Sheriff King looked at his cell phone as it began to ring. The caller ID showed it was that Dallas TV reporter. "Damn," he thought to himself, someone must have already tipped her off to the bodies being found.

He decided it was best to answer the call.

He flipped open the phone and said, "Sheriff King here."

The velvety voice on the other end of the phone was all business. "Sheriff King, I guess you forgot to give me a call about the bodies being found in the lake, huh?"

"Now Ms. Reese settle down," he quietly admonished into his phone, "it just happened a few minutes ago. I have just left the scene and was about to give you a call."

The TV reporter was having none of it, "Okay. Sure, sheriff. I've got a deadline here; tell me all the details we've got a newscast coming on soon."

King sighed, "Not much to tell right now Ms. Reese. Looks like a very unfortunate incident of a father fishing with his son, and somehow, they fell out of the boat and apparently drowned. We're on the way to the medical examiner's office in Athens right now."

The sarcasm was dripping through the phone all the way from Dallas, "Sheriff King I was not born yesterday so stop the b.s. right now. We both know there is a serial killer running loose in East Texas and he has now killed nine innocent people. Nine!"

The sheriff forced himself to speak calmly and slowly without anger, "Ms. Reese we both know that there is no proof for your theory, and if you broadcast that information you will create undue panic and ruin your reputation for being a reliable reporter."

There was a pause on the other end of the phone line. Mindy Reese was quickly weighing a number of options in her mind. How could she trip up the sheriff and get him to tell the truth about the investigation?

"You still there Ms. Reese?"

"Sheriff King I just want to be sure that you want me to go on our newscast and say that you actually believe that nine drowning deaths in the past few weeks are all accidental – including the man who died of a broken neck before he drowned? Won't that ruin any reputation you might hold as sheriff?"

Despite his best efforts, her words set off the sheriff, and he angrily replied, "Ms. Reese don't threaten me. My official comment to you is no comment, and if you use anything else in your broadcast, I will sue you and your TV station."

An hour later, the medical examiner had looked at the bodies, and determined the father and young boy had indeed drowned. He also had some more horrific news to relay to the sheriff and his close confidant, detective Richardson. None of the other officers were invited to the meeting.

The elderly doctor took a deep breath, his eyes were sad, as he looked first at the sheriff and then the detective. "Gentleman, I am also quite sure that both of them were still alive when they were tied to the tree stumps." He said the words slowly, with a grave tone in his voice.

Both King and Richardson reacted violently to the medical examiner's words. King slammed his fist on the table in anger, while Richardson spat out a string of expletives as he rose to his feet and paced around the room, not knowing what else to do.

King quietly asked the doctor, "How do you know that?"

The medical examiner looked the sheriff in the eyes and said, "Because of the rope burns on their wrists. If they were already dead, they would not have had the bruises and rope burns because they would not have been struggling to get free as they fought for air."

Park Ranger O'Grady brought the print outs of the campground vehicles and license plates to the sheriff's office. She had not even looked at them in her haste to get the information to the lawmen. All O'Grady knew was that the pictures were from the last three weeks, and there were over 1,000 of them to go through. Would one of them lead the lawmen to the serial killer?

Back in Dallas, detective Cates was trying to find the killer himself by contacting all the SCUBA clubs and businesses in East Texas. He'd driven back to Dallas so he could enlist the help of seven of his buddies in the Dallas County Sheriff's office who had agreed to give up their holiday weekend to help make phone calls and visits to the businesses.

Meanwhile the subject of all this police activity was slowly driving his truck down an old dirt road less than five miles from the lake where the last victims had been found. The back of the pickup was filled with SCUBA gear, nonperishable food supplies packed in waterproof plastic bags, as well as several cases of bottled water. It was all covered by a tarp to keep prying eyes from wondering what he might be doing. But, as he expected, the killer met not one soul during his drive down the dusty five-mile stretch of potholes and ruts.

The truck pulled to a stop in a small grove of trees about a quarter mile off the dirt road. Next to the grove was a large pond, roughly a quarter mile from one end to the other, formed in almost a neat circle.

After a quick check found no one in the area, Martin pulled on his SCUBA gear, filled a mesh bag with gear, and walked into the pond. He quickly disappeared below the surface in a blur of bubbles.

The ex-Navy SEAL's muscled legs expertly drove his fins up and down, quietly and rapidly propelling him through the pond to the other side. This side of the pond ended in a bluff that stretched about 20 feet above the water.

Martin reached an opening in the bluff at the end of the pond, swam inside the cave for 20 more yards and popped to the surface. He was inside a huge cave. It was a cave that anyone going by on the dirt road would have no idea existed. The only entrance was by swimming through the pond.

It was large inside, with a dirt floor that stretched for fifteen yards beyond the end of the water. The ceiling was eight feet above

Martin's head as he walked toward a part of the cave that was already filled with equipment.

Using his flashlight, Martin walked to the portable gas-powered generator and flipped the switch. The machine rumbled to life, and the cave was suddenly bathed in light. The killer had been working on his hideout for months, and it was almost finished.

Back in Athens, sheriff King and detective Richardson were realizing the enormity of tracking down the license plate information from Purtis Creek State Park. The camera basically focused on where the license plates should be on the vehicles, but not all the vehicles followed the exact same path. So, some of the pictures had only partial shots of the license plate, some managed to catch a glimpse of a rear bumper or a taillight, but little else.

Besides those handicaps, King had all of his men already deployed either at the crime scene at the state park, or working the vast expanse of county roads during the Memorial Day weekend. Who was going to start running these license plate numbers?

It was six o'clock Saturday evening and the announcer voice was introducing the WDFW newscast, anchored by Mindy Reese. She looked up at the camera and began telling the story of the father and son, found dead at the state campground, just as thousands of people were gathering in the area for the long holiday weekend.

After a long discussion with the station's news managers it was decided that Reese would not link these latest deaths to the seven victims at Cedar Creek Lake, at least not directly. But her story left little doubt, without saying it, that these now nine suspicious deaths were unexplained, and while the authorities were calling them "accidental," there were some concerns and theories circulating on just what might have happened.

Sheriff King and detective Richardson watched the broadcast and were pleased that it had been less inflammatory than they had feared. Their phones immediately began ringing as other news organizations saw the WDFW newscast and began calling for information of their own. They were told a faxed news release would be on its way soon. The lawmen had decided not to do a formal news conference, as it would only add a larger spotlight to the deaths.

King glanced at his wristwatch. "Damn," he said, "I've got to scoot. It's Crystal's birthday, and I promised to take her to a quiet dinner at Fazio's. She talked her boss into a 90-minute dinner break tonight despite the place being jammed for the holiday."

The police cruiser pulled into the marina, just as Crystal bounded down the stairs. King smiled despite his chaotic situation, thinking to himself how she looked fetching as usual in her cutoff blue jean shorts, and a new t-shirt printed up special for the waitresses for the big holiday weekend. She had it tied tight, with her flat, tanned stomach peeking out below the shirt. Despite his overwhelming problems with the serial killer, King smiled, he was a lucky guy.

As they were having dessert, King pulled the small package with its gold wrapping paper out from under the table and handed it to Crystal, along with a birthday card. She smiled, read the card, and then quickly tore through the paper.

Crystal opened the box and caught her breath. She pulled out a stunning gold bracelet with two small gold hearts dangling off it. It glinted brightly in the small spotlights above their table in the restaurant.

"Oh, Buddy, it's so beautiful," she gushed, suddenly getting up and giving him a big kiss.

"Glad you like it," Buddy said, "And you have to promise me that you will never take it off. Those two hearts are a symbol of our love, and I want you to always keep it with you."

Crystal looked at him oddly for just a second. Buddy was not one to be romantic like this.

"Absolutely," she said, "I'll never take it off. It is just gorgeous."

Buddy smiled, once again silently thanking his spy shop buddy for such a great birthday present idea.

They dashed back to the Marina, just three minutes before Crystal's dinner break was over. The boss was a strict one for being on time, especially on a busy holiday weekend.

She gave Buddy a quick kiss, and scurried into the restaurant, her shiny new bracelet dangling from her wrist. Buddy put his cruiser into gear, and slowly drove away.

At a dark end of the parking lot, the serial killer watched the touching scene in silence. His powerful hands gripped the steering wheel so tight that his knuckles turned white.

35

The rest of the holiday weekend passed uneventfully. Some strong thunderstorms moved into the lake area Sunday afternoon, and the unsettled weather lasted right through Monday night. It ruined some party plans for many holiday revelers but made for a relatively quiet weekend for law enforcement officials.

Activity on the case really picked up on Tuesday. Dan Cates small squad had interviewed in person, or telephoned, most of the SCUBA shops and clubs in East Texas. They turned up little information. They had a long list of names to send through the national police crime computers, but little else. It seems that Navy Seals are a very private bunch, and none of the clubs or shops knew any retired Seals.

Meanwhile, sheriff King had received some assistance from the Athens Police Department in running down the license plates from the campground. Unfortunately, so far, it also turned up nothing. Once the names and addresses were crosschecked with the park's roster of campers, they'd have to contact each person. This could take a long time. So far, they had no hits from the license plates on the National Crime Computer.

In Washington, D.C. East Texas congressman Pete Dicus was meeting with a representative of the Navy Seals. He could not get a meeting with the commandant, but this officer was of a high enough ranking to help him achieve his goal of helping sheriff

King find out if there were any retired Navy Seals living in East Texas.

Commander Justin Levy sat across from the congressman, his back was ramrod straight, not a wrinkle in his uniform, his fingers were steepled in front of his face as he listened to the request. His jaw jutted sharply from a face that held crystal clear blue eyes that seemed to pierce Dicus' soul.

When Dicus finished, the commander leaned forward, his eyes stared right through the elected official. His words had a measured cadence to them, "Congressman, I understand your concern, and I am sorry about this situation, but information on retired Navy Seals is highly classified. These men are trained by your government to carry out some very unpleasant tasks for America, and in return we give them anonymity when they retire. As you can imagine, other governments are looking for some of these men for paybacks."

Dicus knew this was coming, "I understand commander, but this is a desperate situation. We're talking about someone who has killed nine people, including a young boy. We must catch him now." He pounded his fist gently on the desk for emphasis.

The commander's serious, stoic expression never changed, although it seemed his tone became more condescending, "I understand congressman, but there is nothing I can do. We do not reveal identities of retired Seals. Besides, I believe this is a stretch. You really think some former Seal is going around East Texas drowning people for kicks? I have looked into this situation, and none of the victims are connected. People drown all the time. The only one that looks suspicious is that gentleman who had his neck broken."

Before the congressman could reply, the Navy commander arose, brushed off his uniform, quickly shook the representative's hand and strode out of the conference room, without as much as a look back.

Dicus sat back heavily in his chair. Now what was he going to do?

While all these efforts were happening, the man they were seeking arose before dawn, and settled into his usual routine. He was very regimented in his every movement. Each day was planned with precision. That's why the killer was still steamed about his momentary lapse in anger when he broke the quarry's neck. His quick temper had put him in trouble more than once, and eventually led to his discharge from the Seals.

As he quickly did his daily 200 push-ups, and 200 sit ups, muscles taut and gleaming in the low light of his secluded cabin, he once again returned to that night when, in a fit of rage, he had pushed the fisherman into the water with such force that he broke his neck. It also gave the police the only clue that perhaps all these people had not been victims of drowning.

As he moved to his sit-ups, the killer became angrier, snapping them off in a quick precise routine. He thought to himself, it was all that bitches' fault. She was driving him nuts because she never fell into a routine. It made stalking the sheriff's girlfriend dangerous and very difficult.

He sat up for the last time, and effortlessly jumped to his feet without his hands ever touching the wooden floor. He peered out at the sun just rising in the east over Lake Athens. It was then he made his decision. It was time to grab her and move this situation to the end game.

A few hours later, 2,000 miles away in Washington, D.C., Congressman Dicus scurried off to the Capitol Dining Room. As he walked in, the venerable place was abuzz as usual. He strode over to a table, where Senator Bobby Jackson was sitting, looking prim and proper as usual in a dark blue suit, white shirt, and red rep tie.

The senator, in his mid-50's, was trim and fit. His handshake was like being pinched in a vice. He motioned Dicus to sit down.

Jackson was a Navy hero, but one you never read about in the newspapers or history books. The senator from Nebraska was a former Navy Seal with a secret, but storied career that involved many covert operations all over the world. His constituents knew he had won many medals for bravery, but the specifics were disguised in the name of national security.

Dicus and Jackson were elected the same year and met during all the "get to know you" cocktail parties on Capitol Hill. They shared a passion for racquetball and a friendship formed along the way. They weren't pals, but Dicus felt he could count on his friend for some help.

Unlike most Navy Seals, Senator Jackson had a jovial side, although on the racquetball court his other demeanor always surfaced. He was fiery, and nearly impossible to beat. The little blue ball seemed to go supersonic when he sent it smashing to the front wall and buzzing back past the congressman's outstretched racquet. Dicus had won a few games over the past three years, but never a match.

They made small talk for a few minutes, catching up on some bills being considered, and other Capitol Hill gossip and then congressman Dicus leaned forward slightly, and lowered his voice. His expression became very serious. Jackson picked up on the furrowed brow and asked, "What's going on Pete?"

The East Texas congressman filled the senator in on the situation in his district with great detail. He knew this was probably his only shot at getting information on the Navy Seals.

As senator Jackson listened, his face became increasingly tormented. Dicus knew what he was wrestling with in his mind. Jackson desperately wanted to help his friend put an end to this string of deaths, but the code of silence regarding retired Navy

Seals, especially ones who had not assimilated quietly back into society, was like a titanium vault. It was not to be broken.

After Dicus finished, he leaned back in his chair. Senator Jackson stared straight ahead, not looking at his racquetball buddy. It seemed that three or four minutes of silence followed, with Jackson not moving a still finely tuned muscle.

Finally, Jackson in a low, almost guttural whisper told Dicus that he believed this situation demanded his assistance before any more innocent victims turned up in East Texas. But he would have to do so in a covert manner. Jackson asked for a contact, other than Dicus. He did not want the Navy to be able to investigate his actions and trace them back to this conversation with Dicus.

The congressman had prepared for this request and had talked to Sheriff King. Of course, he did not tell him anything about his pending meeting with Senator Jackson. They had decided that King was too high profile, so his chief detective, and trusted friend, Billy Richardson would be Jackson's contact.

Dicus let out a long, grateful breath and profusely thanked the senator for agreeing to help them crack this case.

With little luck in his scouring of SCUBA shops and clubs in East Texas, Danny Cates decided to take his laptop computer to the Athens Police Department. The computer whiz, on loan from the Dallas County Sheriff's Department, loaded all the license plates from the Purtis Creek State Park campground into his laptop, went online, and started running the information using the national crime computer.

Over at the sheriff's office, Buddy King and Billy Richardson were sitting in a corner of the situation room, silently looking at the board filled with information from the investigation and enjoying their second cup of coffee of the morning. Both men were tremendously relieved that one of the busiest tourist weekends of the year was behind them. At the same time, they were concerned when the next shoe would fall from the crazy killer living somewhere in their part of the world.

Sheriff King broke the silence, "When do you think this guy is going to strike again Billy?"

Richardson took another sip of the steaming hot coffee, looked at his best friend, and said with a shrug, "Tough to say, but you can be sure the son of a bitch is going to surface again. He's still out there, and he's still a dangerous menace."

Both men slipped back into their own silent worlds after that, sipping coffee and lost in their own deep thoughts as their eyes took in all the information on their huge crime board.

In Gun Barrel City, sheriff King's girlfriend stepped from a hot shower, and toweled off, preparing to go to work at the marina restaurant. Crystal carefully snapped the safety catch on the gold bracelet with the two dangling hearts. She'd heeded Buddy King's request and only took it off during her daily shower. She cherished the most beautiful keepsake of his love for her.

As the waitress sat at the vanity table in her apartment, she could not see the blue pickup truck parked two floors below, and out of sight on the far side of the parking lot. The killer could not see her either, but he knew she was getting ready for work. It was the only pattern he had been able to count on.

Of course, some nights she stayed with the sheriff, throwing off the routine, but when she was at her own apartment, the stalker could count on her getting into her car about 10:45 to head for her lunch shift at the marina.

The killer sat quietly and waited. He was almost ready. Soon she would be his, and the smart-ass sheriff would be terror-stricken, wondering where his sweetheart had vanished.

Suddenly, a hundred yards away, he could see Crystal coming down the stairs from the second-floor apartment. Cody Martin glanced at his watch. 10:45 right on the nose. He smiled. This was going to be easy.

Martin waited until Crystal's car disappeared in the distance, and then he started his truck and slowly, unobtrusively, drove out of the apartment complex. He drove out in the country to the pond that contained his secret, underground hideout. He parked on the edge of the water.

The ex-Seal walked around for a bit to be sure no snooping eyes were anywhere nearby. Then, he ambled back to the truck, shrugged into his SCUBA gear, grabbed two large waterproof bags from the back of the truck, and disappeared into the murky, green water.

After a short underwater swim, he reached the grotto, climbed out of the water, and lugged the bags onto the dirt floor of the cave. He smiled to himself, a rare occurrence for this very serious, very troubled man. Everything was now in place.

The bags contained canned goods, and more bottled water. He now had enough provisions to last six months. The killer took in the scene with satisfaction. He was set.

To his left, was the chamber that would house the waitress. There was a heavy metal cot for her comfort, blankets, and a small lantern. There was also a large, very strong length of chain to keep her on the cot.

About twenty feet away was his living area. It too had a cot, blankets, several lanterns, and an arsenal of weapons. Through his gun shop connections in Dallas, Martin had secured three AK-47's, pistols, and even some flash grenades that would momentarily blind anyone approaching his underground compound.

A little farther away, in a corner, he had set up a workout room with weights and other equipment to keep his body in great shape. Martin did not want to use a large portable generator, which would be too noisy. So instead, he set up a small, very quiet generator, and had installed a very small vent pipe to get rid of the gases.

He took one last look around, gave a satisfied nod, and headed back into the dark water. All was set for the capture of King's most valued possession in the world.

36

Late the next afternoon, Cody Martin headed to the marina restaurant. He noted with satisfaction that Crystal's car was parked in the lot. The killer climbed the stairs and secured a corner table, with a nice view of the lake. He ordered an early dinner, had some iced tea, and sat in obscurity, watching as Crystal chatted it up with the regulars, and scurried from table to table. The place was pretty busy for the middle of the week, and no one noticed the tanned, well-muscled man sitting quietly at an out of the way table gazing at the boats below as they pulled up to the marina for gas.

It was about five o'clock when the bartender called Crystal's name, and told her the sheriff was on the phone. Martin's ears perked up, but his expression stayed the same as he kept his head down, continuing to work on the crossword puzzle from the newspaper.

He couldn't hear Crystal's end of the phone call, but he did note the disappointment in her face. The bartender, a loud talker, noticed too, and asked her what was the matter.

The waitress shrugged her shoulders and told him that King had to meet with some people tonight, and had to postpone their date until tomorrow. "Oh well," she said, "Looks like I can spend a quiet night at home."

Martin, as was his custom, left a normal tip on the table, along with the fare for his food, and slipped off with no one even taking notice. He was inwardly excited as he headed down the stairs. Tonight, he thought to himself, is the night.

At the sheriff's department, Buddy King and Billy Richardson were excited. Two hours before, Richardson had received a phone call from Senator Jackson. It was a terse conversation but provided a world of information for the stumped law enforcers.

Jackson told the detective there were two recently retired Navy Seals in the area. Both fit the possible profile of their man. They both had been drummed out of the Seals due to some "personality issues," that made them potential killers. Richardson hurriedly scribbled every piece of information Jackson told him.

He had an address for the first man. He was 34 years old, a highly decorated Seal who had a "problem" with his final mission that prompted the Navy to quietly retire him with a large pension. His name was Johnny Barnes, and he lived in an old house on the outskirts of Mabank, a small town just outside Gun Barrel City. Barnes kept to himself, and the Navy had heard nothing from him, or about him, in the past three years. Apparently, he spent his time fishing during the day, and playing Texas Hold'Em poker at the various bars around the lake area at night.

There was little information on the second man. His name was Cody Martin. He'd been one of the top "go to" Seals during his service in the Navy. If there was a dangerous or difficult mission Martin was the man. But last year, the 28-year-old had suddenly gone over the edge. He became needlessly violent on every mission and had to be retired, also with a large pension. Martin had pretty much disappeared. The only thing the Navy knew about him was that he picked up his monthly pension check at the post office in Tool, a little hole in the wall town on the west side of Cedar Creek Lake. They had no idea where he lived. Frankly, the senator said, the Navy was happy they had not heard anything about Martin as they considered him a real risk to do something violent if provoked.

The two lawmen called Dan Cates back from the Athens police department. At first, Cates was irritated because he was smack in the middle of matching the license plates with Texas state vehicle registrations and didn't want to be interrupted. But when they explained that they had two names, Cates quickly slammed his computer closed and hurried to his car, with an excitement in his step.

Now, the three of them were huddled together as Cates fingers flew across his laptop's keyboard. He was plugged into the national crime database, which allowed him to gather every piece of information on the two men. There was quite a bit on Johnny Barnes, but Martin was like a ghost.

Barnes had a checking and savings account at the First Bank of Mabank. Apparently, the Navy was very generous in its settlement with the ex-Seal. He had $48,000 in a savings account, and his checking account received an automated deposit from the Navy of $12,000 a month, tax free. In addition, he had an investment portfolio with Merrill Lynch in Dallas that had a nest egg of $213,000 in it. He had not filed an income tax return in years, apparently with the blessing of the United States Navy.

Barnes flew on American Airlines to Las Vegas once a month, stayed in a room at the Bellagio that was comped by the casino, and played in high stakes no limit Texas Hold'Em poker games day and night. He spent $10,000 last year to pay for an entry in the World Series of Poker at the Rio in Las Vegas but lost in the second round.

The former Seal had a bit of a lead foot. He had been stopped 14 months ago for speeding by the Henderson County Sheriff's patrol and paid a $134 fine for going 14 miles an hour over the speed limit on Highway 175. Just last month, he received another ticket from the Mabank police for going 42 in a 30 mile an hour zone. This time he opted to go to a comedy driving school to have the ticket wiped off his record. He still had to pay a $102 fine.

But, outside of the speeding infractions, Barnes had no run-ins with any law enforcement agencies.

Try as he might, Barnes computer magic was a bust when it came to Cody Martin. Other than the postal box in Tool, there was no record of any bank accounts for him, no investments, and no credit cards. Nothing. While Barnes had a Texas driver's license, and a one-year old Mustang registered in his name, there was nothing on file for Martin. While Barnes had a Visa card and a debit card from the bank, Martin had nothing in his name. There was no record of him living anywhere in the state. He was truly a ghost to the system.

It would take some old-fashioned police leg work to track down anything on Martin. They really had no choice but to head to the post office in Tool, find out his box number, and then stake out the place until he showed up to get his monthly pay. It must arrive in the form of cash from the Navy.

The object of Dan Cates' frustration checked his watch. It was nearly seven o'clock. He eased his truck into the parking lot at the marina restaurant where his quarry was about to finish her shift. His heartbeat was up a bit from its usual 43 beats a minute, the excitement of the chase always got his adrenalin pumping.

This was going to be a bit tricky since it was still going to be light when the waitress came out of the marina and headed for her car. He'd have to be careful.

Meanwhile, Cates, the sheriff and detective homed in on the ex-Seal named Johnny Barnes. Cates retrieved Barnes' license plate,

Texas 634-765, from the state database, and clicked on the program that contained all the license plates from the surveillance camera at Purtis Creek State Park, hoping for a match. The computer was zipping through the hundreds of plates.

Sheriff King had switched from coffee to a Diet Coke. He took a long drink, gulping it down. Detective Richardson smiled at his best friend, "Buddy you are excited aren't yah?"

King, a bit sheepishly put down the can of Coke. "What'ya mean?"

"Every time you're pumped up you grab a Coke and guzzle it down like you've been in the Gobi Desert for a week, that's all."

King rubbed his hands together, "Your damned right I am. This is the first solid lead we've had in this damn case."

Cates jumped in with some bad news, "No match on the plate with the campground vehicles."

Cody Martin looked at his watch again. The shiny, very sophisticated, waterproof to 100 feet timepiece showed it was 7:34. Where was she? She should have been down here a half hour ago?

By now the evening crowd was starting to arrive at the marina on what was turning into one of those big sky nights in east Texas, no clouds overhead just thousands of twinkling stars.

Martin took a deep, controlled breath. It was a calming exercise he learned in the Seals. Keep focused on the mission he told himself, relax and wait as planned.

Sheriff King stood up, "Okay. We need to get over to Mabank and check out this Johnny Barnes. Dan, we'll take your unmarked car, cruise through the neighborhood and scope everything out, nice and quiet. We don't want him to run on us."

"Good idea," Cates said. He rose from the table, and walked over to the printer, returning with an 8x10 color picture of one Johnny Barnes taken from his driver's license.

The men climbed into Cate's car and headed for Mabank, about a ten-minute ride from the sheriff's office.

Martin could feel the demons in his brain starting to wake up. It was now after 8, and still no sign of Crystal. Again, he did some slow breathing exercises, remembering the last time he went off the deep end while stalking the waitress. It caused him to make that stupid mistake, breaking that damn fisherman's neck.

Suddenly there she was, sauntering down the steps of the restaurant and heading to the parking lot. But wait, she was talking to someone and laughing. There were three other people, a man and two women walking with her. They were all having a good time.

Crystal stopped at her car, unlocked the doors with her remote control and hopped in. One of the women slid into the seat on the passenger side. Both cars left the parking lot together.

Martin was seething, "that bitch made me sit here for over an hour, and then she leaves with three people." His hands held the steering wheel of his pickup truck in a steel-like grip, his well-toned muscles bulging under his shirt, causing the veins in his arms to pop up.

"Okay," he told himself, breathing deeply, "calm down. You'll just have to complete the mission tomorrow." He silently weighed the wisdom of following the cars, but his Seal-trained brain shut down that idea very quickly.

The killer slipped his truck into drive, and slowly, so as not to attract any attention from the two new customers walking toward the restaurant, drove back to his cabin just outside Athens.

37

Sheriff King and the two other men drove down Cardinal Lane in Mabank as it started to be enveloped in the growing darkness. It was a typical non-descript neighborhood of modest homes, with less than perfect yards.

They drove past 134 Cardinal Lane and proceeded down two more blocks.

"Looked like no one was home," Richardson said, "But there was a guy next door watering his lawn. How about we have a little chat with him?"

Cates turned the car around and headed back toward the house as Sheriff King nodded his head in agreement. A full moon was rising as the sun set in a radiant red glow in the distance, keeping the darkness at bay for a few more minutes.

They stopped the unmarked car in front of the neighbor's house as he stared uneasily at a car filled with three men pulling up in front of his house. The man held the hose in his hand and weighed his next move.

Sheriff King slowly got out of the passenger door and tried to put the wary man at ease as he shouted, "Good evening sir. I'm Sheriff Buddy King, and these are two of my detectives, hope we didn't startle you?"

The sheriff wasn't in uniform, so the man was not appeased. He said nothing as his eyes followed the sheriff as he walked slowly toward him. The two other detectives stayed in the car.

King had his badge in his hand, and quickly showed it to the man, who started to breathe a little easier. King's voice was soothing, friendly, "Sorry to bother you sir, we'd just like to ask you a few questions about your neighbor Johnny Barnes if that's okay?"

The man, now reassured that this stranger really was a law enforcement official and that he himself had done nothing wrong, relaxed and stuck out a large, calloused hand. "Nice to meet you sheriff. I'm Nick Canter, and I'm proud to say I voted for you in the last election."

King smiled, gave the hand a firm shake, and nodded to the other men to join them. He made the introductions all around.

Canter prided himself on being a gracious host. He had been widowed for three years and spent his retirement days working the numerous flower beds around his little clapboard house. "Come on to the backyard and I'll get us some lemonade," he said turning and heading back toward the house.

The men were stunned as they rounded the corner of the old house and stepped into a gardener's paradise. Those calloused hands had created an oasis of color. The backyard was filled with flower beds. Huge roses were blooming everywhere, along with a myriad of other flowers. The beds were obviously tended very lovingly and tenderly. The men settled into the old lawn furniture that seemed out of place in such an idyllic setting. A myriad of yard lights on automatic timers snapped on, making the colors even brighter in their glow.

After the men made the appropriate compliments to Canter regarding his gardens, the old man asked the first question, "So what'd Johnny do?"

King took a sip of lemonade. It was surprisingly tasty. He looked at Canter, "Nothing that I know of, we just want to have a little chat with him, but it seems he isn't home tonight."

Canter chuckled, clearly happy to have some company in his lonely world, "Hell no boys, he's at Mickey's playing poker. He plays poker somewhere every night."

Richardson jumped in, "Yeah, we heard that about him. Seems to be quite the avid Hold 'Em fan."

"Oh yeah boys. He tells me he's pretty good too. That's all he does – fishin' and poker. Never seen him take a drink, never seen him with a woman. Nothin' but poker and fishin'."

King smiled, "What else you know about him Nick?"

"Not much. Been here for a few years, I guess. Nice enough fella but keeps to himself. Not much of a talker. Friendly enough, yah know, always waves and says hi, but he's not one to talk about himself. I guess he's retired like me, but he's a young fella, so I just don't know. Goes to Vegas a lot, but never seen him work at a job or anything. Just fishes and plays cards."

King glanced at his watch. It was just after 8:30. "How long does that poker last at Mickey's?"

Canter shook his head, the few wisps of grey hair moving in the gentle breeze, "Don't know. Never been there. I hit the sack by 9:43 myself. I'm an early riser."

Cates looked puzzled. He was a man of numbers, and Canter had just thrown out a strange one. "9:43?" he asked, "Why so precise."

"That's what time the weather is over on Fox4. Gotta see what it's going to be like in the morning."

Cates nodded, chuckling to himself, but trying hard not to let the old man see how amused he was at this strange bit of information.

King got up first, "Well, it was great to meet you Nick. I guess we'll head over to Mickey's and see if we can hook up with Barnes. Do us a favor, don't mention this little visit to him in case we don't get to see him tonight?"

Canter lowered his voice and in a conspiratorial tone, almost whispered, "No problem Sheriff. Sure yah can't tell me what he did?"

King smiled in a reassuring way, "Like I said Nick, nothing, we just want to talk to him."

Mickey's Club was like a lot of other drinking establishments around Cedar Creek Lake. It was a long, low steel-sided building with no windows. The parking lot was part gravel, part cement and filled with "Texas Cadillacs," pickup trucks of every style, and description. A very few were shiny and new. Most were a bit dented and rusty with fading paint or with a fender that was a different color than the rest of the truck. A few cars were sprinkled through the parking lot, including Barnes' Mustang.

The three men walked into the bar and were greeted by a cloud of blue smoke that seemed to fill the left side of the large building where a couple dozen players were huddled over three large poker tables, many of them puffing on cigarettes.

A lot of heads swiveled around as the men walked toward the poker tables. Mickey was careful not to break any gambling laws in his four times a week "free" poker tournaments, but some players were still anxious when they recognized Sheriff King and detective Richardson.

Mickey, the owner, was a gregarious guy who was quick with a smile and a quip. He folded his hand and walked toward the lawmen.

"Hey, Buddy. Billy. How y'all doin?" he asked giving them a hearty handshake and a clap on the shoulder.

King returned the smile, "Great Mickey. Looks like business is good."

"I tell you Buddy," Mickey said, "This Hold'em is a big deal. People love the game. We get 30-40 people a night in our little free tournaments."

King lowered his voice and leaned toward Mickey, trying to keep the conversation private, but still talking loud enough to be heard over Johnny Cash's wailing baritone on the jukebox. "Mickey you know a Johnny Barnes? I hear he's quite the poker player."

"That he is," Mickey replied. "He plays in most every one of our games, unless he's in Vegas. Wins his fair share too. He's damn good. What you want with him?"

King was nonchalant, "Oh, nothing special, just want to talk with him. Where's he sitting anyway?"

Mickey discreetly pointed at a man with a baseball cap tugged tight over his brown hair, wearing a sweatshirt and a pair of faded blue jean shorts. He was of medium height and build, but you could see that he was very muscular, and in great shape, just what you would expect from a former Navy Seal. King noticed that the man had the largest pile of chips at the table.

Mickey did too. "Looks like he's going to be playing for a while with that stack. Want me to have him come over here?"

King shook his head, "Naw, we'll just have a beer and play a little pool. When yah think he'll be done?"

Mickey looked at his watch. It was 9:15. "It might be close to midnight if he makes it to the final table and keeps winning."

King had no intention of letting him slip away without them having a conversation. "No problem Mickey, we've got all night. Do me a favor, and don't let him know we're waiting to talk with him, Okay?"

"Sure sheriff. I guess I'll go back and see if I can win some chips then."

The men shook hands again and Mickey walked back over to the poker table, while the lawmen headed to the other side of the building where the bar and pool tables were located.

It happened to be pool tournament night at Mickey's too, and the lawmen soon found themselves involved in some wicked games with the local pool sharks. King and Richardson knew quite a few of the players.

The pool games and the poker games kept going. Sheriff King looked at his watch. It was almost midnight.

The poker room was pretty cleared out except for a small handful of people watching the final two players go at it. King smiled to himself, it was Mickey against Johnny Barnes.

He stuck a few more quarters in the slot and racked the balls for another game of nine ball.

In a very dark parking lot, 15 miles away, Cody Martin sat stone-faced in his pickup truck. He too looked at his watch. The killer was not happy. It was midnight and still no sign of Crystal.

After wrestling with what to do, he had decided to circle back to her apartment complex at 10:30 just in case she returned by herself. But she'd never come back.

Suddenly, her car pulled into the parking lot. Martin noticed two heads in the front seat. They parked in front of her apartment and both women got out talking and laughing loudly. They both went into Crystal's apartment.

Martin, once again seething inside, slowly drove away. He wanted to complete his mission, but this was too risky.

Finally, there was a commotion at the poker table and the two men stood up and shook hands. Mickey and Barnes walked into Mickey's little office and the door was closed.

The three men perked up, but tried to act casual. What was going on? Was Mickey warning Barnes?

In less than a minute the door opened, and Barnes walked out by himself. There were fewer than ten people remaining in the bar.

Barnes and the three lawmen all headed toward the door. Barnes looked up a bit startled.

Sheriff King reached the door first, and spoke in a low, non-threatening voice, "Hi Johnny. I'm sheriff Buddy King. Can we talk to you for a minute?"

Barnes stopped in his tracks. He didn't drink, so he was completely sober, so that couldn't be the problem. How did they know his name? Were they going to bust him for taking the $400 from Mickey for winning the tournament?

He took the hand extended by the sheriff and shook it. King was impressed with the claw-like grip. This was a strong man, certainly capable of overpowering his victims.

Barnes, with a puzzled look on his face asked, "Sure, what's going on?"

Sheriff King smiled, "How about we sit at this table for a minute. Can I buy you a beer?"

Barnes shook his head, "Don't drink."

"Okay," Sheriff King said, and introduced Barnes to the two other lawmen,

The men settled in, and King spoke first looking intently into Barnes' eyes. The sheriff expected that Barnes had a good poker face, so he'd be hard to read.

King decided to try to catch him off guard right away.

He leaned forward, speaking with soft tones, "We're wondering what you know about the string of unusual deaths we've had around here?"

Barnes indeed was a good poker player. King never saw the slightest flicker in his eyes. He could have flopped the nut flush or had terrible cards. He could have killed all those people or know nothing about it. This guy was expressionless.

Barnes voice was also low, and very measured, "No idea what you're asking sheriff. I saw the news about them, but that's it. Why would I know anything?"

Richardson, an expert at the good cop/bad cop routine, jumped in. He smiled at Barnes, and said in a friendly voice, "Mr. Barnes the sheriff is a little edgy with all these deaths. He didn't mean to accuse you. He just is interested in what you might know about them. You know, we all hear things. It's a small town. You hear anything?"

Once again, no recognition from Barnes expressionless face. His Seal training had included many of these role-playing games, and these guys were amateurs in his opinion.

Barnes slowly shook his head. All he said was, "Nope. Sorry. Can't help you."

The sheriff and his trusted deputy slid into the front seat of their vehicle. Both were frustrated to a level neither had experienced before. They finally get just a small break in the most puzzling case of their careers, run down a potential suspect, and get played like rent-a-cops at Wal-Mart.

As the vehicle rumbled over the pebbles that made up the majority of the bar's parking lot, both men stared straight ahead. Neither spoke. They were dog tired and beaten.

38

The sun broke brightly over the horizon as Cody Martin finished his ten-mile run around Lake Athens. Sweat glistened from his chiseled face and torso as he jogged into his cabin. He had spent the entire run thinking about her. She was now an obsession. His mission was taking far too long. Tonight had to be the night. No matter what.

Newspaper reporter Dwayne Murphy was up early too. It was just after seven in the morning as he used a steaming biscuit to sop up the last bit of egg yolk from his breakfast at McDuff's. He was also frustrated. It had been a few weeks since the bodies of the father and young son had been discovered at Purtis Creek State Park and nothing new was happening in the story of the century – the biggest story he had covered in his entire life.

Murphy sipped on his cup of coffee. It was time to bring it back to life. Time to stir the pot, even if that snotty Dallas TV reporter had moved on to other stories. Murphy's editor was clamoring for a big front page spread to once again increase the number of newspapers he sold. The newspaper association that audited circulation was about to check on his paper. Murphy was well aware that the bigger the circulation, the higher price advertisers were charged, and that had a direct effect on his own salary.

Probably the most frustrated people of all had gathered in the sheriff's office on this warm summer morning. It was time for the weekly task force meeting. As Sheriff King looked around the room he could clearly see the set jaws, and stiff postures of his men. These deaths gnawed at them day and night.

King put down his battered coffee cup, "Okay men. Let's get started." They shifted in their chairs, and a number of side conversations quickly came to an end. Fifteen sets of eyes converged on the young sheriff. They saw a man whose face seemed to have more lines than just a few months ago. He looked tired.

King took a deep breath that came off as almost a sigh, "As some of you know we finally have the names of a couple of ex-Navy Seals. They are not suspects, but they certainly fit our profile. Both men were drummed out of the Seals for going over the edge. They are both trained killers. The Navy says they were two of their top men."

The sheriff then related their unsuccessful questioning of one of the men, Johnny Barnes, last night at Mickey's bar. King concluded, "He's a helluva poker player. He gave us nothing at all. But we'll give him more time to crack a little."

King motioned toward a veteran officer, "Ralph I want you to sit outside his house today. Just park across the street and wait. If he leaves, follow him. Not too close but let him get the idea we're watching him closely. We'll relieve you later this afternoon." The officer headed out the door to his marked squad car.

The sheriff then turned his attention to the second suspect. The one named Cody Martin. King shook his head, "The other guy seems to be a ghost. We can't find anything about him. No bank records, no credit cards, no car registration, no insurance, nothin'. All we know is that he picks up his check once a month at the post office in Tool. The Navy is giving us no help, so we don't even know what day of the month it comes. We've got an unmarked car sittin' over there right now. We'll wait for him to show up."

King stopped. Took a deep slug of his coffee, then continued, "Okay Danny what do you have for us this morning?"

Danny Cates, the veteran computer wizard on loan from the Dallas County Sheriff's office hopped up and headed for the front of the room. He brought his ever-present laptop with him.

Cates glanced down at the glowing screen, "Not much I'm sorry to say. I have run Cody Martin's name through every data base known to man with little to show for it. All I know for sure is he went to the same high school here as you did Buddy, in fact graduated in your class, and then headed right to the Navy."

That information caught the sheriff by surprise, "No kidding? Do you have a high school picture of this guy?"

Cates' fingers flew over the keyboard and soon an old yearbook picture of Cody Martin appeared on the screen. The sheriff peered at the picture for a long time, trying to remember anything about the 18-year-old face looking back at him. It was a non-descript, soft face. The young man was not smiling, in fact he looked very serious, and very sad. He also looked like a skinny runt.

Cates broke the silence, "This is the only picture in the yearbook. This guy did not join any clubs or do anything else apparently that required socializing. His grades were mediocre."

King shrugged his strong shoulders, "Nothing rings a bell with this guy. We had a pretty small class, but I don't remember a thing about him. I can't say I ever met him."

Cates stood up, "I found out that he was an only child. His parents divorced when he was a junior in high school. He lived with his Mom until graduation and then headed to the Navy. His father was killed soon after that in a car accident in Houston."

King slapped his hands on the table, "Damn it. So, we just sit and wait until he picks up his check? It could be three weeks from now, and even then, we have no idea if he is tied to this thing? What about the license plates from Purtis Creek? Anything there?"

Cates once again shook his head, "Not really. The Athens PD helped me track down almost every license plate from the campground camera. The vast majority were families camping and fishing with their kids. There was only one plate that didn't match the vehicle in the security camera photo."

You could sense a shift in the room. Was this a clue in a case with far too few clues?

Cates went on, "the plate is Texas GFR-487. It is registered to a Joseph Pigeon in Tyler. I just tracked that all down this morning. We may have something here. Joseph Pigeon is deceased. He was killed in a car accident about seven months ago near Palestine. He apparently had a heart attack while driving down the road just outside of town and ran off the road into a tree. The car was totaled and taken to Smith's Wrecking junkyard in Palestine."

Sheriff King interrupted, "So we could have something here. He was dead long before that picture was taken at the campground."

Cates agreed, "Yes sir, in fact the registration is for a blue Dodge Intrepid. Here is the picture from the campground."

A slightly grainy picture popped onto the computer screen. You could only see a small part of the vehicle, since the camera was set to focus rather tightly on the license plate.

Cates went on, "As you can see, although we don't see much of it, the plate in this picture is clearly on a blue pickup truck. I would guess it is a Ford 150."

There was a murmur in the room. These lawmen were hungry for any clue to these mysterious deaths. Now, for the first time, they could start to look for a blue pickup with Texas license plate GFR-487. It was something at least.

Dwayne Murphy was burning up the phone lines around Cedar Creek Lake, checking with every source he had. The reporter was desperate to uncover something to use for a news peg for a big story on the serial killer. But, after several hours he had come up empty.

Murphy slammed down the phone and headed out of the office. It was coming up on lunch time. He headed to the favorite focal point for gossip around the lake, back to McDuff's restaurant hoping the lunch crowd might have some gossip.

The serial killer closed and locked the door of his secluded cabin near Lake Athens and headed toward his favorite lunch stop. It was the one where his quarry would wait on his table.

Cody Martin had made his decision. This was the day when he would grab her. No matter what. He had been stalking her for weeks. It was an insult to his Seal training that he had not yet devised a way to snatch her.

As the truck zipped along the highway toward the restaurant, Martin knew his frustration was about to end. He might grab her right after the lunch crowd left. He might grab her at the end of her shift. He might grab her at midnight. But she would be his by the end of the day.

Sheriff King sent out an APB on the national crime computer network. It not only went to every law enforcement agency in Texas, but across the country as well. He wanted as many eyeballs as possible to be searching for the license plate and a blue pickup truck, possibly a Ford F150.

Dwayne Murphy pulled into the restaurant parking lot, just as an officer from the Seven Points police department was parking his cruiser. Murphy ambled over to the car and struck up a conversation. As they talked about the latest meth lab bust in a rural part of the county, the cruiser's computer beeped, and caught both men's attention.

Murphy, his newshound ears always perked, leaned further into the police car, "What's up?" he asked. The policeman shrugged as they both peered at the glowing computer screen.

Murphy's heart beat a little faster, the message read – "This is an all-points bulletin. Be on the lookout for a blue, possibly Ford F150 pickup truck with Texas license plate GFR-487. This vehicle may be connected to the death of two campers at Purvis Creek State Park. If you encounter this vehicle, do not attempt to stop it. Keep it under surveillance and notify sheriff Buddy King of the Henderson County sheriff's department."

The policeman tried to quickly shield the newspaper reporter from the screen, but it was too late. Murphy had seen it all.

The reporter quickly backed away from the policeman and hustled back to his own vehicle. The officer shouted something at him, but Murphy pretended not to hear. He climbed into his car and left the parking lot.

The Seven Points policeman was in a quandary. It was against policy for a civilian and damn sure the news media, to see a computer message, especially one like this, in his squad car. If he told anyone he would be reprimanded, and he had already been written up once this month. He decided to tell no one, just forget that it happened.

At that same moment, the pickup truck with that license plate pulled into the Marina restaurant parking lot. There were just a few cars in sight. It was a quiet, mid-week day. The serial killer walked up the dusty wooden steps and took a table far from the bar. Soon, his quarry approached, took his drink and lunch order, and headed to the kitchen to place his request with the cook.

Dwayne Murphy was out of breath as he bounded into the newspaper office. Finally, something new to get the biggest story of his career back on the front page of the newspaper. He sat down at his computer and quickly started writing the story. After a few minutes he sat back, steepled his fingers in front of his face and got lost in deep thought. Murphy realized this was a start, but he needed more information. Who is that license plate assigned to? Where does that person live? Is he the prime suspect?

Cody Martin sipped his iced tea, and slowly picked his way through the grilled chicken Caesar salad. It was a beautiful day on Cedar Creek Lake, not a cloud in the big blue Texas sky, just a gentle breeze out of the west, and the sun had the water shimmering like millions of tiny diamonds. Martin was watching a couple of SeaDoos approach the marina gas dock below.

His ears perked up as he heard Crystal talking to the bartender. Apparently, some emergency had come up, and he had to leave rather quickly. He was asking the waitress if she could handle the bar for an hour or so.

Crystal said, "well you know I've been working on learning the different drinks and all, I can handle it. You go ahead take care of this. Besides, there won't be much business this afternoon, it's the middle of the week."

The killer was getting excited, but you couldn't tell it from his emotionless face as he continued to follow the SeaDoos as they pulled up at the dock, seemingly oblivious to the conversation going on a few feet away.

Martin casually surveyed the open-air restaurant. There was an older couple at one table just finishing up their lunch of burgers and a couple of beers. There was a crusty old fisherman sitting at the bar. He was a regular, who seldom said a word to anyone.

Outside of that the restaurant was empty.

Dwayne Murphy had returned to McDuff's restaurant. He slid into his favorite battered booth and ordered his usual lunch fare, a ham sandwich on wheat with a side of fries, and an unsweetened tea.

The newshound had his ears tuned and his nose was twitching as he strained to overhear any and all conversations. The place was crowded as usual.

Murphy smiled to himself as his eyes locked on an old buddy of his, Johnas Thomas, a longtime veteran of the tiny Tool police department. He was a big man, well over three hundred pounds with a military buzz cut and arms that looked like they could snap a small tree trunk without breaking a sweat. He was working on a small steak accompanied by a couple eggs sunny side up.

Thomas was sitting by himself at a table for two, a table that looked like it was made for a young child in contrast to the policeman's bulk. Murphy shuffled over there.

Thomas was about to chomp into a big piece of steak when he spotted the newspaper pest. He put his fork down and smiled. Murphy was lucky, Thomas was one of the few law enforcement types that hadn't tired of his pesky manners. The reporter also knew he was fortunate because Thomas was not the sharpest knife in the drawer.

Sheriff Buddy King had dispatched his men to comb the area for the blue pickup truck. He, Richardson and Cates then met for another couple of hours to put a plan on paper for moving forward with the investigation.

Cates stomach growled, and he glanced at his watch. It was almost one o'clock, and he was hungry.

Sheriff King heard the gurgling from Cates belly and chuckled, "Guess we better get some grub here pretty quick."

Richardson jumped to his feet, "damn straight, where we going?"

At the marina restaurant, Crystal busied herself behind the bar. She was excited, this was the step up she had been working toward, even though it was only temporary. She quietly hummed to herself as she wiped glasses and put them away.

The killer was slowly sipping another glass of tea. The older couple had gone, and finally the old fisherman started to limp toward the stairway. As he disappeared down the stairs, the phone rang at the bar.

Crystal quickly retrieved it from the cradle and began to smile broadly. Martin knew immediately that the damn sheriff, her boyfriend, must be on the phone. He could only hear snippets of what she was saying.

"Yeah, by myself."

"That'd be great."

"Okay, I'll be here."

A dark expression briefly passed over Cody Martin's face. The sheriff must be on his way over here for lunch. It was time to complete his mission. The killer slowly walked toward the stairs. He said to Crystal, "Need to hit the head, then I'll be back to settle up for lunch."

Crystal gave him a big smile, "sounds good." She was beaming, anxious to show the sheriff that she was in charge of the place.

Martin slowly walked down the stairs to check on who might be lurking around the marina.

Sheriff King hung up the phone, "Okay boys we're headin' to see Crystal. The bad news is she's gonna have to cook for us."

Richardson raised his eyebrows, "Crystal? What happened there?"

King chuckled, "Seems that Harry had some emergency, so she is the cook and bartender right now, and damn proud of it."

"Can she cook?"

Again, King chuckled, "just keep it simple."

The three lawmen jumped into the sheriff's cruiser and headed for the marina restaurant, about 30 minutes away.

Meanwhile, at McDuff's restaurant, Dwayne Murphy was working the Tool policeman hard. The conversation had started generally enough, but then Murphy caught the large lawman off guard when he said, "So, Johnas, you find that blue pickup truck yet with Texas license GFR-847."

Thomas' eyes grew wide as the plate in front of him, "Hush up Murphy, you cain't be sayin' shit like that in a public place like 'gis." A few tiny beads of sweat formed on his brow.

Murphy leaned in, and whispered in a conspiratorial tone, "Hey, relax Johnas, you know I got good sources. I find out this stuff all the time. It's what I do for a living."

The lawmen was not pacified, "Don't give a damn, Murphy, that there is classified information, and y'all ain't supposed to know about it."

Murphy leaned back a little and smiled, "Johnas, I'm telling you to relax, Sheriff King trusts me with this stuff. I know it's linked to the death of the father and son at Purtis Creek State Park."

More sweat began to bead on the rotund policeman's forehead, "Well, fer the record, I ain't said nuthin' to yah, yah hear?"

Murphy switched tactics now that he had the Tool policeman back on his heels. They talked about fishing, the weather and then Murphy slipped in a quick change of pace to the conversation, "I just wish King would tell me his name, but he won't."

"That's 'cause they don't know his name, it ain't his license plate, yah know. It's some dead guy's from Palestine."

"What you saying, Johnas. He killed some guy and took his license plate?"

"Naw, the guy died in a car wreck." Suddenly the cop realized that once again he had fallen into Murphy's trap.

Those beads of sweat had turned into a small stream. The rotund giant flicked some of them off his forehead and leaned toward Murphy, "damn it, you dun it to me agin, Murphy. Yah tricked me into spillin' the beans. Damn it."

Murphy quickly rose from the table, "Johnas don't worry about it, you and I never talked today. He picked up the check from the table, "Lunch is on me."

Martin's eyes quickly swept the perimeter of the marina restaurant. The young kid on the gas dock was filling a bass boat with one fisherman standing next to him. They were in a deep conversation; probably the latest fish tale was being spun. There was no one else in the place. No one in the parking lot either.

Murphy quickly climbed dusty, grey wooden steps to the second-floor restaurant. This had to be quick. This was his window of opportunity.

The killer figured he had about five minutes before the boat was filled, and about twenty minutes before the sheriff showed up.

39

Dwayne Murphy had sped back to the newspaper office. He was already on the computer searching for stories of people from Palestine who had been killed in an auto accident over the past year. He also called a buddy of his at the Burnett police department. It was over a hundred miles from the lake.

Murphy asked his buddy to tell him whose name was on that license plate. He was vague, telling him it was just for a story he was working on, nothing big, but it sure would help. His buddy said he'd ring him back shortly.

Sheriff King and his two buddies were deep in conversation as they entered Gun Barrel City and began the drive on the bridges that crossed the lake. Cates stomach growled loudly once again. He was in pain, "Damn Buddy how much longer?" King smiled and told him about fifteen minutes.

At the Marina restaurant, Martin headed to the bar and asked Crystal for his check. As she rang it up on the computer, he quickly bolted over the bar like a gazelle and was suddenly standing right next to her.

Startled, she reeled back a few feet, but his powerful grip already had her. Martin put a hand over her mouth, and through clenched teeth told her to keep quiet and she wouldn't be hurt.

She was clearly scared to death, her eyes were filled with fear and she said nothing, just stood motionless in Martin's steely clutches.

Over at the newspaper office Murphy's phone jangled. He quickly put it to his ear. It was his buddy from Burnett, "Damn it Murphy how do you find out this stuff?"

Murphy spoke quietly into the phone, "What you mean, just working on a story,"

The voice on the other end was not impressed, "Bullshit Murphy, there is an APB for that license plate…might have to do with those killings at the state park over there, and you damn sure know that."

Murphy pleaded his case, "Yeah, I do know that, but I just need to know the guy who is registered to that plate, the guy who was killed in the car accident."

The Burnett cop proceeded to fill him in.

The killer leaned close to Crystal's neck. He smelled her perfume, and her fear. He tightened his grip to really show he was in total control.

He spoke quietly, but in a menacing tone, "Okay Crystal, we're going to do this nice and easy. We're going to walk downstairs and get into my truck and drive away. I have a knife that I can use to slit your throat in an instant if you don't make it look like we're just strolling out together, like two old friends. Got it?"

She had naturally big eyes, but at this moment they looked huge and filled with unrelenting fear as she stared into his face and nodded her head.

"Good, let's go."

Cates was complaining loudly as the sheriff's cruiser closed in on the marina restaurant. King was clearly amused by his friend's carping.

"Damn it Buddy, we could have gone to some place in Athens and be having desert by now."

"Relax, we'll be there in five or six minutes."

In the newspaper office, Murphy had all the information he needed, and had excitedly stormed into the publisher's office. He now had three sources for his story. They had a scoop, but it was only Wednesday and the paper didn't come out until Thursday. They decided to put it on their web site. That way the Associated Press would pick it up and give them credit all over the state. They could then put a big spread together for tomorrow's paper.

Murphy set to work on the story, his fingers flying across the computer keyboard.

Crystal, in a scared stupor, cooperated fully with Martin. He opened the passenger door of the blue pickup and she slid in. Like a cat, he jumped into the driver's door, quickly started the engine, and drove out of the parking lot.

Crystal was shaking as she asked, "What are you going to do with me? What did I ever do to you? I don't even know your name."

Martin's seal training was now taking over. He knew the most important thing was to keep his quarry calm as they headed for his sanctuary.

Some weeks ago, he had thought of quickly taking her to a remote part of the lake and making her death look like an accident, but those plans changed when he remembered the pond with the hidden cave. Now he was going to take her to his private hideaway and drive that sheriff nuts as he wondered where the hell she had disappeared to.

Sheriff King pulled into the empty parking lot at the marina restaurant. The only car in sight was Crystal's. He smiled; she was so proud to be the bartender/cook. This was going to be fun.

He pulled into a parking space right next to the restaurant. Cates, the famished one, jumped out of the back-seat door and bounded up the steps, two at a time. King and Richardson followed at a more sedate pace.

Murphy finished his exclusive story and filed it on the newspaper's web site. Then he called the Associated Press to alert them to the story. The wire service quickly spread the story across Texas and into Oklahoma.

Cates was puzzled. He saw no sign of Crystal as he reached the top of the stairs. The place was empty. He shouted her name. No response.

By that time, Sheriff King and Richardson had reached the top of the stairs. King shouted at Cates, "What the hell is going on Dan?"

Cates shouted from the kitchen, "Don't know sheriff, but I don't see Crystal anywhere."

Martin glanced at his watch, time for the local news on WBAP. He flipped on the radio, just as the chimes rang to signal the beginning of the news update. The announcer with the deep voice said, "Here's a breaking news story out of Gun Barrel City, about an hour from Dallas, police are looking for a blue pickup truck, possibly a Ford F-150 with Texas license plate GFR-847. They believe this truck may have been involved in the deaths of a father and young son at Purtis Creek State Park…" Martin quickly flipped off the radio as Crystal began to scream at him in terror, "Are you the killer? Oh, my God, please don't kill me."

King and his buddies scoured every inch of the restaurant and the surrounding marina. There was no sign of Crystal. They found her purse and cell phone, undisturbed, tucked behind the bar. It didn't look like there had been a struggle. What the hell happened to her? Cates grabbed his radio and alerted the other deputies to the strange situation.

Martin was surprised by this turn of events. He wasn't even aware that the police had his license plate, and a description of his truck. How the hell had that happened? He turned on the radio again and punched the second button to catch a later news update on another station.

In a minute or so, he found out that the truck had been photographed by an automatic camera at Purtis Creek State Park campground. The radio newsman said the license plate was actually registered to a man from Palestine who died in an auto accident some months ago.

Martin let out a sigh of relief, at least they had no idea they were specifically looking for him, they were just chasing a license plate with no more information. No matter, it was time to get to the pond sanctuary as fast as possible.

The sheriff called for a deputy to rush to the restaurant to secure the potential crime scene, as he and his two buddies scrambled down the stairs. They began to search every section of the marina property.

Martin was hurrying to the secluded pond, but not fast enough to attract any attention. He held the waitress firmly by the wrist with his right hand. She had stopped struggling, realizing it was fruitless to try and escape the steely grip of the man who had kidnapped her. Martin turned up his police scanner, just in time to hear Sheriff King call for a deputy to head to the marina to secure a possible crime scene. He put the gas pedal down just a little farther as he headed down the back road toward his refuge.

40

Sheriff King and the two men systematically scoured every part of the marina property and came up empty. Panic started to gnaw at the sheriff's insides. Where could she be? What happened? Had the serial killer been here? Should he immediately start searching the nearby lake?

In the newspaper office, Murphy's phone was jangling like crazy. He was basking in the glory of still another scoop. He picked up the ringing phone expecting more accolades, and instead his ears were blasted by words from his favorite TV reporter. Mindy Reese was hot. She wanted to know, "how in the hell you could have this information and not share it with me, not give me a heads up, what kind of bullshit is this, we had a partnership." The words spewed out of the phone non-stop for several minutes. Murphy tried to placate her to no avail.

Martin's pickup truck made it to the pond without being spotted. He pulled the truck off the main road and drove down the rutted patch of dirt that led him to the edge of the pond. Crystal was frantic but trying to remain still at the same time. She realized they were all alone with no help in sight. She felt it would be smarter to not cause any problems that might set him off right there and end her life.

County squad cars, as well as cruisers from Gun Barrel City, Seven Points, and Tool were converging on the deserted marina. Sheriff King and Crystal were the favorites of many lawmen in the area and they all wanted to help. Soon the marina was awash with activity. Buddy Richardson knew that King was not in a state of mind to bring things under control, so he stepped up to the plate.

"OK, gather around here everyone," he said, waving his arms at the growing crowd. "As you know by now, Crystal was all alone here today, and when we arrived for lunch the place was empty. We have looked all around the area and there is no sign of Crystal. There is also no sign of a struggle in the restaurant. Crystal's purse and car keys are sitting behind the bar, and as you can see her car is parked right over here. So, we have no idea if something happened to her, but we can't imagine that she would just take off without her keys, or purse."

As Richardson was speaking, Dwayne Murphy's cell phone rang as he sat in the newspaper office working on tomorrow's big story. This time the voice on the other end was Nate Schmidt, an old friend who lived in a small lake house just across the inlet from the marina. Nate was a very trustworthy and valuable source of information for Murphy, as Schmidt was also a Coast Guard Auxiliary volunteer. He was a spry old guy, but too many decades of puffing on unfiltered Camels, had put a distinctive rasp in his 74-year-old voice.

"Murph," he wheezed, "I don't know what the hell's going on at the marina but there must be a dozen cop cars over there, and 20, 25 cops all standing around outside the bar. Thought you'd want to know."

Murphy was already out of his chair and headed for the door, "Thanks Nate. I am on the way. Keep an eye on things and ring me back if anything happens, OK?"

Martin had now handcuffed his left wrist to Crystal's right wrist. He looked her in the eyes, eyes that he could see were bursting with fear. "OK Crystal, I know you're a Scuba diver because I heard you talking about it at the restaurant."

Crystal slowly nodded. The killer continued, "Good, because we're going to go for a little swim together." Crystal began to shake, the fear that he would kill her had become overwhelming.

Martin felt the fear and knew he had to calm her down or they both could drown on the short trip to the underground sanctuary. He rubbed her arm in a non-threatening way, and spoke in a low voice, "Crystal I know you're scared but I'm not going to do anything to you. We're just going to put on a tank and mask and go for a little swim to the other end of this short little pond. I've even got a weight belt just for you. OK?"

Crystal was still shaking, but a little less visibly, "Why, why are we doing that?' she managed to stammer. Martin smiled, "It'll be fine. We need to get going."

He helped her shrug into the Scuba tank, gave her a mask, and helped her put on her fins. He got into his gear with his free hand, and they walked backwards for about 30 feet to the edge of the water, so the fins wouldn't catch on the ground.

Martin checked her out on the standard Scuba diving hand signals and told her to just follow his lead. They'd only be about 10 feet down for the whole trip, which he assured her would only take about five minutes. He admonished her that the water was very cloudy and visibility was limited, so she just needed to relax, and she couldn't drift away from him because they were handcuffed.

With that, they disappeared into the murky brown water of the pond.

Sheriff King stood on the outside of the gathering as Richardson gave orders for the men and women to fan out and give the area one final thorough search. He explained how they had to be sure Crystal was not anywhere on the property before they widened the search. Richardson's words seemed like they were miles away, as King was thinking about Crystal and how important she was to him. He tried to only allow positive thoughts, but that was impossible.

Then it hit him! The ankle bracelet he'd given her for her birthday. Why didn't he remember that sooner, dammit.

King quickly punched the number that was saved in his cell phone. The answer to his call came on the second ring, "Spies Like Us, this is Jerome."

King had moved where none of the multitude of police officers could hear him, "Jerome, Buddy King. Can't explain right now, but I need you to run the GPS and tell me where Crystal is. Quick." Jerome could hear the strong desperation in his voice, "Right away Buddy."

Jerome switched on the tracking gear that was part of the service Buddy bought with the ankle bracelet for Crystal. It had a tiny GPS chip that identified Crystal and her location. King was impatient, "Well what'cha got?"

The Spy store owner typed in the identifier for Crystal's ankle bracelet, and he immediately saw a blip with that number light up on the satellite map. He zoomed it to North Texas.

"Got her Buddy. She's just off Farm-To-Market Road 3276. It's about three miles out of Tool, just off highway 56. Looks like there's some sort of quarry or pond right there."

236

Sheriff King felt the bile rise in his throat. Had the serial killer grabbed her and drowned her in the pond?

At that same time, Martin and Crystal reached the underground cave, sat on the shore, and removed their bulky swim fins and SCUBA gear. Crystal was astonished. Not only could she breathe under the pond, but there were bright lights illuminating all kinds of food items, some cots, radios, air tanks and, frighteningly, weapons.

"Wait a minute Buddy," Jerome's voice rose a bit, "she was moving, but now she disappeared."

King fairly shouted into the phone, causing some lawmen to turn and look at him, "Disappeared? What the hell you mean?"

"I don't know. That's never happened before." Jerome was clearly puzzled.

Murphy, the newshound, was tearing along the narrow road that led to the marina. He rounded the corner of the parking lot, and his tires squealed to a halt as the posse snapped around to see what the commotion was all about. Some drew their weapons, startled by a car careening into the parking lot.

Then many of them recognized Murphy and his car. Never a shrinking violet, Murphy hopped out of his car, slammed the door, and started ambling toward the group. "Hey," he shouted, "what's up fellas?"

Martin handed Crystal a large, fluffy beach towel, and a jumpsuit in her size. He unlocked the handcuffs. "I'm going to turn around, promise I won't look or nothing, but you need to get out of those wet clothes, so you don't catch cold, it's a bit damp in here." Before he turned away, Murphy leveled a tough guy set of eyes at her, "and don't try anything." He turned around.

It was chilly in the cave, so Crystal quickly toweled off, slipped off her soaking wet clothes, and pulled on the jumpsuit.

Martin then clinked the handcuff back on her wrist and guided her to a cot that was on a heavy metal frame. He snapped the other end of the handcuff onto the bed frame.

He grabbed his SCUBA gear, and said, "I'll be right back." Martin quickly slipped into the dark water and soon his bubbles disappeared.

King was trying not to shout into the cell phone, "Jerome, you got her back yet."

"No, sheriff, not a damn thing."

"OK, give me the exact location." King quickly jotted it down, "OK, you get back to me right away if you see her again."

King strode over to Richardson who was dealing with the newsman, as the posse dispersed for their coordinated search of the area. Ever effuse, Murphy gave the sheriff a big smile and a howdy.

The return glare from King was scary, "Shut up Murphy and stand right there."

Murphy was back on his heels a little, he was a little frightened of the sheriff, "Sure just let me know what this gathering is all about."

King took Richardson aside and vaguely said, "Listen, I've got to check something out, I'll be back in a few minutes."

Richardson knew his friend very well, "Buddy where you going? We need to stick together on this."

King shook his head, "No, you stay here and make sure Crystal isn't here, I just need to check out something, I'll be on my cell phone if you need me. And, keep that damn reporter with you."

Before Richardson could protest, King sprinted into his cruiser and sped out of the parking lot.

Martin emerged out of the pond, quickly set his gear on the ground, and ran to his pickup truck. He hopped in, and sending gravel showering everywhere quickly headed back down the dirt road. He stopped about a half mile away at a rundown wooden shed. He quickly opened the battered door and drove the truck into the shed. Martin closed the door and ran at a rapid pace back to the pond. He again donned the SCUBA gear and swam back to the cavern.

This was a very deserted stretch, not a farm or house anywhere in sight. No cars had come down the road either.

King had his lights flashing and siren blaring as he headed to the rural road at a high rate of speed. When he reached the turnoff to the farm road, the sheriff silenced the siren and flipped off the lights and drove slowly forward.

He spotted the pond. It wasn't real large, but it wasn't small either. He guessed it was maybe a hundred yards across. His eyes swept the area.

Not a soul around. Not a vehicle in sight either. He drove a little closer and saw the dirt road that veered off from the paved farm-to-market road.

King's heart was pounding through his chest, as he drove closer to the pond. His mind flashed back to his high school years and he thought this pond looked familiar. What was it?

He put the cruiser in park and jumped out. His breathing and his heart rate were rapid as his eyes darted around every inch of the pond. No sign of Crystal. What was it about this pond? It was so familiar, but why?

He dialed the spy shop again, asking "anything new? Can you see her track?"

The voice on the other hand was puzzled and distressed, "No Buddy, she has just disappeared."

Buddy's frustration was evident in the tone of his voice. "So, that thing doesn't work under water?"

"Oh, sure it does," came the reply over the cell phone, "That's why I can't figure it out. The only thing that would block the signal would be like a thick, steel bank vault, or a cave or something."

The sheriff felt like he'd been struck by a lightning bolt. That was it! This pond had a big underwater cave at the other end. You could even breathe in there. It has been the scene of some great parties during high school.

King muttered his thanks and flipped off the phone.

41

Over at the marina, Richardson and his men had scoured every inch of the property, and nearby lake homes and structures. They found nothing.

Richardson opened his cell phone and hit the speed dialer for Buddy's phone. He did not want any radio traffic on this situation.

Sheriff King was busy in the trunk of his police cruiser and paid no attention to the phone. He needed to move fast and did not want any interference.

King always carried a full scuba gear set-up in the trunk for emergencies. He pulled on the wetsuit and shrugged into the harness with his inflatable vest and air tank. He strapped a knife to his weight belt and stuck his police revolver in a waterproof case attached to the belt.

Detective Richardson slammed his cell phone shut after getting King's recorded voice. He was very upset and worried about his best friend. Buddy King had always been a bit of a rebel, and right now he was off on his own going after a serial killer who probably had grabbed his girlfriend. Where was he?

King made sure he had all his gear in place, pulled on his rubber socks, grabbed his fins, and walked to the edge of the pond. He didn't know if he was searching for Crystal's body in the pond, or about to run into the man who had kidnapped her and taken her to the cave.

To complicate things, this pond was not like the crystal-clear pond near Athens that had been turned into a scuba park. This was a murky, scum filled pond with near zero visibility. The sheriff knew he would be at a huge disadvantage if the killer was a trained Navy Seal.

But, his frenzy to find Crystal shoved those thoughts aside as King spit into the mark to keep it from fogging up, pulled it tight over his face, turned on the air tank, and quietly slipped into the darkness of the pond.

Detective Richardson knew he had to find Buddy quickly. He couldn't let him take on a serial killer by himself, especially when he would be irrational if the killer had captured Crystal, or worse.

Then it hit him. He dialed the cell phone company that serviced all the phones for the sheriff's office. Sensing, the emergency tone in Richardson's voice, they put him right through to a supervisor.

"I need to know the numbers Sheriff King has called in the last hour, and I need them right now," Richardson barked into the phone. The supervisor had talked with Richardson before, and he bent the rules sensing this was a very serious situation.

The phone company supervisor said there was only one call, it was to a place called Spies Like Us in the West End in downtown Dallas. He gave Richardson the phone number.

Richardson slammed the ends of his finger into the phone as he punched out the number to the spy store.

Back at the pond, Buddy King was silently working his way through the darkness of the water. He could barely see his hands when he held them a few inches from his mask. He wanted to make no noise as he headed for the cave, which was now, he guessed, about 75 yards away.

In the cave, Martin was sitting on the edge of the water. Crystal was sitting quietly on the edge of the bed, trying to figure out how to escape from the handcuffs. It seemed impossible, the bed was made of steel, and she was handcuffed to a steel post. She was breathing hard, scared to death of this muscular man who had her trapped underground.

Martin's mind was racing, checking and re-checking things in his mind. He had plenty of food and water to last for months. There was no way that anyone could know where they were. The truck was hidden, and no one had seen them.

Martin smiled to himself. It was a perfect plan. That sheriff would be desperately looking for his girlfriend with no chance of finding her. It would drive them crazy. After a week or so, Martin would take off under the cover of darkness, and disappear. They would never find him or her. There was no way she was leaving here alive.

"Spies Like Us" came the answer on the other end of detective Richardson's cellphone. The owner quickly filled Richardson in on the ankle bracelet with the GPS chip that sheriff King had purchased for Crystal's birthday and told him the last known location for the sheriff's girlfriend.

Richardson quickly turned over a number of scenarios in his mind. He gathered up the police officers and had some of them stay on the scene. He dispatched some others to look for the truck with the license number of the possible killer.

The detective set Murphy free and told him there was no story. Richardson left the newshound sputtering behind him as he walked away. He gave Murphy's car keys to a policeman and told him to keep the newsman at the scene for another 30 minutes before letting him drive away. He asked three of his most trusted deputies to come with him and headed toward the pond.

Buddy King was blindly swimming under the murky pond. He guessed he was about twenty yards away. He stopped. King needed to come up with a plan of attack. If the serial killer had Crystal in the cave, he needed to make sure the man did not kill her when King showed up.

He also had to figure out some kind of a surprise for the killer. King clearly remembered the cave now. The water became very shallow, like a small beach as you neared the cave. It would be far too easy for the killer to see him.

Detective Richardson drove down the farm-to-market road, and spotted King's police cruiser at the end of the pond. He had spent his career in Dallas, so he had no idea there was a cave at the end of the pond.

Richardson stopped his car next to King's. The trunk was still open. The detective knew that the sheriff kept scuba gear in his car. It was not there now. King had been after Richardson for years to get certified, but the detective never did. There was no scuba gear in Richardson's car.

The detective and the other deputies quietly scanned the area. They saw no one. Why was buddy in the pond with scuba gear? Was he searching for Crystal? Was the killer here?

Buddy King was trying to stay calm while every nerve in his body was on fire. He knew it would be stupid to just pop out of the water at the edge of the cave because the killer would have a tremendous advantage. But at the same time he was frantic about the safety of

Crystal. Was she still alive? How much time did he have to save her?

Suddenly Buddy heard a humming sound. What was that? He quietly treaded water and listened as hard as he could. Then it hit him. It was a portable generator. He must be getting close to the cave.

Back above ground, Billy Richardson's police training took over. He gathered the three officers who were with him and told them to search every inch of the area around the pond. It was a desolate, flat stretch of dusty East Texas landscape. There was lots of scrub brush, and dusty soil and little else. Then Richardson spotted an outbuilding about 150 yards away. He dispatched one of the officers to check it out. He instructed them all to be thorough but quiet.

They found some tire tracks around the pond, but they seemed to be from a number of vehicles. Richardson decided to walk to the far end of the pond where there was a bit of a hill.

As the veteran lawman walked around, head down looking for any clues, he heard a faint sound in the still of this barren part of the county. Richardson stood very still and listened intently. It was very faint, but it sounded like a portable generator. Richardson walked in small circles, kicking at the scruffy plants sticking out of the dry soil.

Suddenly his boot kicked a piece of metal. The detective got down on his knees and saw a very small tin vent cover. He put his ear to the cover and clearly heard the whirring of the portable generator.

Richardson stood up, brushed the dirt off his denim jeans, and looked puzzled. What the hell is a portable generator doing near a pond?

Twenty feet below the spot where Richardson stood, Crystal's heart was still pounding as she gazed over at her kidnapper. He was calmly sitting in a chair, reading some sort of manual. Was he the one who killed all those people? What did he want with her?

Crystal decided to ask, "Why are you holding me here? What did I ever do to you anyway?"

Martin raised his head from the manual, gave her an ugly, disdainful look, and said nothing. He went back to reading his manual, knowing that rule one of his Seal training was never talk to prisoners.

King was about 30 yards away, hidden by the murky water, but also aware that his air bubbles could catch the killer's attention if he got much closer. He had been in the water about 15 minutes, giving him maybe about 45 more minutes of air. King had an idea. He started back to shore, away from the cave.

Detective Richardson called the Henderson County Surveyor's office and asked to speak to C.T. Bronson. Bronson had been with the office for nearly four decades and was famous for knowing every inch of the county. His real name was Cyrus Thaddeus, but after getting beat up too many times in junior high for having such a strange moniker, he became C.T. and that was that.

Bronson was past retirement age, but no one wanted to ask him to quit. He had a stern pointy face, thick bushy white eyebrows, and a gravelly voice fueled by his three pack a day habit. He took the phone, "Bronson here, whatcha got?"

Detective Richardson described his location to the crusty old man, and asked him why there would be an underground portable generator there. Bronson did not hesitate for a second, "Well Billy I don't know why a portable generator is out there, but there is an underground cave, so maybe somebody's using that for something."

Richardson quizzed Bronson more about the cave, as he hurriedly walked back toward his police cruiser.

As he got there, Sergeant Davis, out of breath from hurrying back from the old shed, informed Richardson that the truck with the license plate they were looking for was stashed in the building.

42

Twenty miles away, Murphy finally was released by his police captors, and started to drive toward his office. His cell phone buzzed; it was the TV reporter Mindy Reese. She had calmed down a bit but was still angry and let Murphy know it.

"What's going on Scoop?" she asked sarcastically. Murphy decided not to take the bait, knowing they needed to work together because the police were in major lockdown mode.

"Listen Mindy, the cops just let me go. Something big's going on. Sheriff King's girlfriend is missing from the marina restaurant, they still haven't found that truck, and they are saying nothing. They held me for a half hour before they let me go."

"Yeah Murphy, I'll tell you something else, I'm almost to Gun Barrel and have been listening to the scanners all the way, and the cops are saying nothing."

"OK, Mindy, let's meet at the Gun Barrel City PD, maybe we can get somebody to say somethin'."

Suddenly sheriff King popped out of the water, about twenty yards from the circle of lawmen. They all pulled their guns and assumed the shooting position. Richardson yelled, "Holster your guns, its Buddy King."

King was as startled as the deputies. He yanked off his mask, and kicked off his swim fins, as he asked, "what the hell you guys doing out here?"

Richardson quickly explained, and Buddy nodded his head. King looked his friend in the eyes, Billy had never seen him so serious, "I think the killer has Crystal in an underwater cave at the far end of this pond."

This time Richardson quickly nodded, "I figured that. We found his truck in the shed over yonder, and I heard a portable generator on the other end of the pond."

King's look changed dramatically, "I heard that generator underwater, which is why I came back. You heard it too?"

"Oh yeah, I found the little vent he's using to get rid of the exhaust fumes."

King was getting excited, "Great, Billy. I need something to distract him so I can get out of the water. We can use the vent for that."

Billy chimed right in, "Yeah, I got you, we drop a smoke pill in the pipe, he gets distracted and you can jump him."

It was almost five o'clock, time for the local news report on WBAP radio. Martin flipped on the radio in the cave, being careful not to disturb the small wire that went right up the same pipe as the generator exhaust so he could pull in the station.

The lead story was about a double murder at a downtown Dallas convenience store. Then, there was a phone report from that newspaper reporter, Murphy, Martin leaned closer to the radio.

"No, they have not found the truck they are searching for in Henderson County, but I am here to report that police here are searching for a missing waitress from the marina. Her name is Crystal Disborn and she is the girlfriend of Sheriff Buddy King. They are not saying if the two cases are related."

Martin turned off the radio. He had a smug smile on his face. It looked like everyone was clueless, just as he had planned.

King was anxious to get back to the cave, so he and Richardson quickly devised their plan. They synchronized their watches. The sheriff figured it would take him about ten minutes of steady swimming to reach the edge of the underground cave. So, in 12 minutes Richardson would drop a smoke device down the exhaust pipe to distract the killer.

The two friends had argued briefly about sending some help with King, but it was not possible. King had the only scuba tank, and it had about 30 minutes of air left.

The sheriff slipped back into the water, and Richardson headed for the vent where he quietly pulled the lid off of it, so the smoke pill would fit.

The men had talked about the danger to Crystal both from the smoke and the surprise attack, but eventually decided that there was no other alternative to try and save her.

As Murphy and Reese plotted their next move to try and pry some information from the police, the police scanner suddenly crackled, "this is Sergeant Davis, I need two ambulances sent to farm-to-market road 3276. No sirens or lights but tell them to hurry. You will see our cruisers about a mile down the road on the right-hand side."

The two reporters and Mindy's cameraman flew out of the newspaper office, into the TV news truck parked outside, and sped toward the same road.

Buddy King's powerful legs moved the large fins in a smooth rhythm as he sped toward the underground cave. Above ground, his partner looked at his watch once again – four minutes to go.

The TV news truck was careening down the roads that led toward the location where the ambulances were heading. The news hounds listened to the police scanners, but they were once again silent.

The Navy Seal put down his manual, athletically jumped to his feet, and strode toward the steel cot and Crystal. She always prided herself on being able to handle any situation, but she was trembling as he got closer.

She fairly screamed at him, "Leave me alone. What do you want from me? What are you going to do with me?"

The killer stopped a few feet away and looked down at his quarry with an expressionless face. He said nothing. Never talk to your captive.

He walked into a dark corner of the cave and returned with a belt that was about four inches wide. Strapped to the belt were five packets of plastic explosives. Crystal's eyes got wider. They were filled with terror.

Sheriff King could hear the whirring of the generator once again. It was difficult to see anything in the murky water, but he sensed he was getting close to the underground cave. His watch showed him the smoke bomb would be dropped in two minutes.

About fifty feet above King, Buddy Richardson anxiously checked his watch too. He had the smoke pill firmly in his hand. His watch showed 1:45 until he would drop it down the pipe.

Martin still did not talk to his captive. She tried to recoil from him as he got closer with the deadly belt, but her handcuffs kept her tightly in place. He grabbed one of her hands, and spoke in a low voice, almost a growl, "Don't fight, don't move, or you will blow both of us up."

Crystal said nothing. Sweat beads were on her forehead; her eyes looked like she had seen the most unspeakable thing known to man. She sat very still.

The killer wrapped the belt tightly around her waist and secured it with a large padlock. He tripped a switch, and a red light began to blink, both on the belt, and on the remote control he had in his hand.

Sheriff King's watch showed 30 seconds until the drop. He silently stood his ground, his fins touching the bottom of the pond.

Buddy Richardson bent down, moving his hand and the smoke device within inches of the exhaust pipe. 25 seconds to go.

The ambulances, led by a two squad car escort, roared toward the crime scene. They were about two miles away when they came upon the speeding TV truck.

One squad car and the ambulances sped away on their journey after passing the news truck. The other squad car pulled behind the news hounds and signaled them to pull over.

Reluctantly, the cameraman/driver slowed to a stop on the side of the road. The two reporters banged their fists on the seats inside the van. They were about to miss the news story of the decade in these parts.

43

Buddy Richardson counted down as he peered intently at his watch, 5, 4, 3. Sheriff King was in the water below, counting down with him.

"One," Richardson said out loud, activated the smoke pill, and dropped it down the exhaust pipe.

It rattled its way down, pungent smoke rising behind it.

The killer spun around at the sound coming from his exhaust pipe, and then the smoke device hit the ground, spinning around and spewing acrid smoke in a ten-foot circle. Crystal screamed. Martin tightened his grip on the remote control for the explosive belt, and then heard a splash coming from the water.

The Navy Seal spun to his right, just in time to see Buddy King come running out of the water, gun drawn. He was only about twenty yards away.

At first, King couldn't see either Martin or Crystal. His eyes tried to adjust to the darkness of the cave. There was a bare light on the right side of the cave, and the middle was filled with dark, billowing smoke. He could hear Crystal screaming at the top of her lungs. "Thank God," he thought, "she's still alive."

Suddenly Martin popped out of the smoke. He was partially hidden and seemed to have some red light blinking in his right hand.

The killer shouted at the sheriff, "Drop the gun, sheriff, or I'll blow the three of us to little pieces."

King was startled, as his eyes, now watering from the smoke, tried to quickly assess the scene.

Martin, in an icy cold tone, shouted again, "I said drop the gun NOW!"

On top of the hill, above the tense situation in the cave, Buddy Richardson paced back and forth. He had no idea what was going on below his feet. He and the Sheriff had discussed taking a radio along on the dive, but they did not have one that was waterproof.

Richardson saw a squad car and two ambulances quietly approaching, their sirens were off, and just the lights were now in motion on top of the vehicles.

The deputy walked over to his men, who also stood around wondering what was happening, wondering what to do. Richardson had no answer for them. He had never felt so useless and helpless in his life.

Sheriff King's mind raced through all the options available. This man had already killed nine people. There was no reason to believe he wouldn't push the button to blow all three of them away.

The smoke had cleared a bit now, and he could make out Crystal through the haze. She had a large belt wrapped around her waist, and it too had a blinking red light. It looked like she was handcuffed or chained to a steel cot too.

Martin was growing impatient. He growled at the sheriff louder this time, "King drop that gun before I count to three or it's all over. One…"

King reluctantly, carefully set the gun on the ground.

The killer relaxed a little, easing his grip on the remote-control device. He lowered his voice, Seal training taught him to now show superiority over the lawman. The yelling was over. It was time for the firm, low volume voice.

"That's better, King," Martin said in measured, commanding tones, "now lay down flat on the ground on your belly, with your arms wrapped around the top of your head, and don't move a muscle."

Martin cautiously walked near the sheriff, kicked the gun away, and then squatted down to retrieve it. He never took his eyes off the sheriff.

Buddy Richardson, clearly perplexed, and feeling very awkward gathered his squad together on the edge of the pond. The longtime lawman had never been in this position before. He was always the one with the plan; with all the answers. Right now he had none.

There had been no sound from the pond, or underground since he dropped the smoke pill about five minutes ago. He looked into the grim faces of the sheriff's men, and said in a low, pained voice, "any ideas guys? I have none at this point, I am sorry to say."

The only sound was the wind rustling the prairie grass and causing small ripples on the silent pond. Apparently, the detective was not alone in lacking any ideas.

Martin now held the sheriff's gun in his right hand. He stood about five feet away, certainly out of his reach. In his left hand was the blinking bomb activator.

"OK, sheriff, you can sit up and strip off that wet suit and throw it into the water. Do it real slow. You make one move that makes me angry and poof – we're all blown away."

Buddy King looked directly into the coldest, grayest eyes he had ever experienced. The suspect was very muscular, in fact he looked incredibly strong, and in the best shape possible. His demeanor was at once, in charge, mean, confident and he exuded a cold-blooded approach to the situation. This was clearly the worst situation the young sheriff had experienced. He would have to be very careful.

King reasoned that if the demented man was going to kill him, he would have already pulled the trigger.

Crystal was quietly sobbing as she sat as still as possible on the cold, steel cot. The handcuffs were cutting into her wrists, the chain held her tightly to the unyielding bed, and the heavy belt surrounded her with plastic explosives.

Her eyes kept scanning from the blinking light, to the killer, to her hero and lover who was now slowly stripping off the wet suit. She was frantic but trying to keep herself in check. Crystal was afraid if she made a sudden move, she would be blown to bits.

But as she sat motionless, her mind was racing. What could she do? This looked hopeless. The killer had Buddy's gun and his hand on the explosive detonator. She sobbed some more. She was far beyond terrified.

King had removed the wet suit and was now sitting on the damp dirt floor of the cave, wearing only his boxer shorts, and the booties that had protected his feet from the sharp edges of the swim fins. He had placed his hands, fingers locked together on top of his head, as the killer had instructed.

Martin allowed himself a small smile, "I must say lawman, I am impressed that you found us so quickly. How'd you do that? And how many cops you got posted topside?"

Sheriff King took a low, slow breath. He had to be careful here. Maybe he could buy some more time, give himself more time to think, if he could get the killer interested in his story telling.

About five miles away, the radio crackled to life in the news van, "Mindy what the hell's going on? We're getting close to news time."

The call went unanswered, as Mindy Reese and the newspaperman were both sitting in the back of the police cruiser, along with the cameraman. Murphy was getting very tired of being held captive in squad cars. With three of them jammed in the back seat, it was cramped and very hot.

The police officer leaned into the window, "This could take a while. I've called for backup. You were going 87 in a 55 zone. I'm going to have to take all three of you to jail for being that far over the speed limit."

Mindy Reese tried sweetness, "come on officer, we both know we were in pursuit of a news story. Cut us some slack."

The policeman just smiled, pivoted on his heel, and walked toward the news van, leaving them sweltering in the backseat.

The killer was growing impatient, as King took his time to answer the question, "Now sheriff, you will find out very quickly that I am not a patient man. When I ask you a question, you had damn well better answer it right away. We clear on that?"

King nodded his head, "Okay, just relax. What's this all about anyway? Why did you take Crystal? Why are you holed up in this cave?"

Martin walked a few steps closer, his jaw jutted forward, his impressive muscles bulging, along with the big vein in his sculptured neck. "Maybe you got water in your ears, LAWBOY," he roared, voice rising again, "I said ANSWER MY QUESTIONS!" He peered into King's eyes, and said in a lower, even more threatening tone, "I did not say you could ask any questions."

The ambulances parked at the very edge of the pond. Four more squad cars arrived. There were now about 20 officers and EMTs at the scene, all standing looking at each other. No training manual had prepared them for a serial killer holed up in a cave with a female captive, and with the sheriff down there somewhere, his condition unknown. Forty eyes kept glancing at the pond, hoping for Buddy King to surface with the suspect, and Crystal in tow.

The trunks of two of the squad cars were filled with SCUBA gear. Four of the officers were underwater experts.

Detective Richardson was leading a discussion of possible alternatives. "One big problem I see," he spoke slowly glancing at the anxious faces gathered around him, "is that Buddy's air tank is probably empty. I don't know how he and Crystal would get out if he took the suspect?"

Rusty Johnson, a big strapping 6-footer, and the best diver in the sheriff's department spoke up, "Well Buddy, we've got to assume that if the suspect took himself and the waitress to the underground cave, that he had to have SCUBA gear. I'm thinking Buddy could use that, if he took the guy."

Those words rattled around in Richardson's brain, "if he took the guy," that was his biggest fear. What if the suspect got the drop on the sheriff? Then what? Was King already dead? Crystal too? Or was he holding them hostage?

King felt that he had stalled as long as possible. The suspect was clearly very agitated and angry. It was best not to push him any farther right now. It was time to tell him a story, to buy more time.

"Okay, sorry," King spoke slowly, in a defeated, quiet tone, "I got lucky I guess." He paused, pondering how much to tell his captor.

"When you started killing all those people," he started. Martin got even more angry as he took a step toward the sheriff and spat out the words, "What the hell do you think you know about me killing people?"

King smiled to himself, he had struck a nerve again, maybe he could keep the killer off balance, "I just assumed that you are the one who killed those nine people, sorry." Martin refused to take the bait, "Last time, dude, how'd you find us so fast?"

King took another deep breath, trying to keep himself as calm as possible. From across the cave, Crystal leaned a little closer, she wanted to know too.

The sheriff decided it was time to let him know, "When all those people started dying (he stressed the word), I got worried about Crystal, and I have a friend who owns a spy shop in Dallas. So, he set me up with a bracelet that has a GPS device on it. It tracked her to this pond, and then we lost it. When I got out here, I remembered we used to swim in this pond as kids, and we'd found an underground cave that had its own air supply. So, I figured that's where she was."

Crystal was upset as she yelled, "You mean you put a tracking device on me without letting me know about it?"

Martin turned to her, "Shut up, this doesn't concern you."

The killer nodded his head slightly toward the sheriff. He was impressed but said nothing. There was an awkward silence.

Martin broke it about a minute later, "So lawboy how many more of you are there up top, and who the hell dropped the smoke bomb on us?"

44

Topside, on the edge of the pond, Rusty Johnson was now leading the discussion, "I grew up around here, and I've been in this pond, and that cave many times. It's about a 100-yard swim in very murky water, very difficult to see on most days, especially after all the spring rain we've had. The cave is pretty big, it has a sandy floor, and the air is good to breathe. So, if the suspect is using a generator that means he's built himself some kind of a hideout down there, with electricity and lights. I would assume he has a bit of an arsenal too, if he went to the trouble of installing a pipe and a generator."

Richardson nodded his head, "Excellent info, so, any idea, Johnson, on how we can attack this situation, based on your knowledge of the set up?"

Johnson stroked his stubbled jaw, he looked a bit like Buzz Lightyear, "I don't know Billy. This guy is obviously a cold-blooded killer, very strong, maybe a Navy Seal, which would mean he was trained by the best in our government to go into the most difficult situations, quickly kill when necessary, and finish the mission. This isn't like we're after some drugged-up goober from Tool."

Richardson was getting impatient, "Don't tell me the obvious, son. How do we get in there and successfully rescue Buddy and Crystal from this trained killer?"

King took another slow breath, "I really have no idea how many officers are waiting for us up there. There were a few when I dove in, one of them dropped the smoke bomb to distract you. What do you want? How do we end this thing with all three of us getting out of here alive?"

King looked as sincerely as possible at the steely-eyed killer. Martin's expression gave away nothing. His face remained a stony veil, hiding any of his plans. He smirked and shook his head, "Are you trying to work me lawboy?"

King looked taken aback, and said as innocent as possible, "What do you mean? I'm just answering your questions."

Martin smirked again and clammed up. He had to create a new strategy. The killer had not planned on being discovered so quickly. The original mission's outline called for him to wait three or four days, and then send a message to the sheriff to lure him to a remote location. He was to come alone. Once there, Martin would kill King and bring the body back to the cave. It would never be discovered. Crystal would join him in death – forever buried together in the cave. Martin, as he had after so many missions, would then disappear, moving to a new location and his next mission.

The situation was now very complicated, especially with a small army of lawmen waiting him out topside. This would take some clear thinking.

The causes of Martin's concern were topside suggesting and rejecting a number of ideas to end this situation. How about another smoke device, with three or four divers waiting to spring on the suspect? It was rejected as too dangerous because it would most likely result in the deaths of Buddy and Crystal.

How about establishing communication with the suspect? All agreed it was a good idea, but how? They tried shouting down the air vent, but apparently no one could hear them in the cave far below. There was no phone to setup. Someone suggested having a diver swim in with a phone, but that also was rejected as possibly triggering him to kill his captives.

One thing had become painfully clear. An hour had passed since sheriff King had entered the water. It seemed certain he was not going to emerge any second now, with Crystal in tow.

There was one intriguing idea – how about dropping a type of nerve gas into the vent pipe that would knock all three of them out momentarily so some deputies could swoop in and secure the area before they came to? It was a great idea, but no one knew where to get such a gas. And, what if the killer was wearing a gas mask in the wake of the smoke grenade going off?

Richardson and the men suddenly became very quiet. This seemed like a hopeless situation.

While the lawmen fretted, Cody Martin sat cross-legged on the ground, keeping Sheriff King in his clear line of sight, and the waitress in his peripheral vision. He was focusing all his energy on creating a new mission strategy.

Just a few feet away, Buddy King also sat in contemplative silence. There had to be a way out of this mess. But the odds were definitely stacked against him. Crystal was tightly locked up, and the killer had his gun, and a plastic explosives detonator.

Crystal was also thinking as she sat in the suddenly silent cave. Truth was, she was frantic, although she sat as quietly as possible. The plastic explosives encircling her waist scared the hell out of her. How could she help Buddy, especially with her being firmly shackled to the frame of the heavy steel cot?

After 30 minutes of silent contemplation, Cody Martin's new mission strategy was set. He smiled to himself, this was perfect, it would work and once again the best of the best would extricate himself from an impossible situation.

Martin sprang to his feet, startling King with his sudden, cat-like move. The sheriff was clearly impressed, although his face did not show it.

"Alright lawboy," Martin said to King as he pointed the weapon at the sheriff's temple, "keep your hands on top of your head and walk toward that wall over there." King got to his feet, kept his hands up, and walked the few feet to the wall at the rear of the cave.

There were two large steel rings bolted into the wall about four feet off the ground, and another set of steel rings about a foot off the dirt floor of the cave. There were sections of steel chain sitting in the four rings. King's heart sank further.

Martin was motioning at him with the gun, trigger cocked, pointing at the sheriff's head. He threw a length of heavy chain at King's feet and ordered him to wrap the chain around his ankles. Martin then tossed King a lock and told him to tightly lock the chains so he could not move his ankles.

"Turn around lawboy," he ordered, "and put your hands behind your back, locked together." King hobbled in a semi-circle, and Martin quickly slapped a pair of handcuffs on the sheriff's wrists. He backed him against the wall, quickly looped another length of chain through the shackled arms, and secured King's arms to the wall hooks. Once that was secure, he did the same to the chain around King's ankles.

King was now totally helpless. Martin walked to a large metal storage chest in another part of the cave, unlocked the doors, and removed a second large belt with packets of plastic explosives spread around it.

He strapped the belt around sheriff King. Martin got excited when he saw the look of total hopelessness on the face of the sheriff and his girlfriend. He loved being in control.

Detective Richardson had no idea what was transpiring in the cave below, but he had the same hopeless look. He had never been more frustrated during his long, illustrious law career. And now, darkness was setting in.

It had been a long day for Martin, and he needed a quick nap to regain his full energy. He checked the locks on the sheriff, and smiled, they were definitely very snug.

"Alright," the trained killer looked at his two captives, "I'm going to take a quick snooze to get re-energized. I suggest you do the same." His Seal training had taught him how to take a quick catnap – one hour – no more, no less that would put him right back on top of his game.

Martin walked menacingly toward Crystal, stopping when his face was an inch or two from her pretty face. His voice was low, almost a whisper, but very chilling, "while it may look like I am sleeping, I will be fully cognizant of what is going on in this cave, so if you have any ideas, this red button will blow you to hell! Got it?"

Crystal was so frightened; she could hardly nod her head. The killer moved about 200 feet away and curled into a ball on a cot near the edge of the water. He seemed to be quickly asleep, breathing deeply.

Crystal turned her head from the killer to her lover. He looked miserable, the chains had him tightly in their grip. He literally, could not move.

But as she looked into his angry eyes, she did notice a movement. He was looking at her, and then down at his SCUBA booties. King made the movement about ten times in a row.

Crystal was puzzled. What message was he trying to send her? She shrugged her shoulders.

King made the same movement again and again – staring at her, then staring down at his booties. He wiggled his right foot slightly, drawing Crystal's attention to it.

She looked over at the killer, who was still breathing rhythmically, seemingly deeply sleeping.

Crystal again looked at the sheriff and his booties. Then it struck her, when they had been diving in the Bahamas last winter, King had carried a diving knife inside his right boot. Was that the message he was sending to her?

She looked him straight in the eyes, and mouthed the word, "knife?" King immediately nodded his head and looked at the right boot again for emphasis.

45

Darkness had now enveloped the starry East Texas sky. The lawmen had set up a number of portable lights. Richardson had decided to sit it out for a while, to see if the killer would try to send them a message. He felt that was the safest course of action at this time. He looked at his watch, it was nearing midnight.

Crystal's heart was pounding, and her head was spinning. What did Buddy want her to do? It looked like she had enough chain to reach him, but the noise would surely wake the killer. She stared intently at the muscular form that seemed to be in deep sleep. He had been out, she guessed, for about ten minutes.

King was nodding his head and staring intently at her. He mouthed the words, "do it" several times.

Crystal slowly tried moving a short section of the chain. She silently slid it across the mattress, and down the side of the cot, trying hard to avoid the metal frame. It worked.

She estimated that Buddy was about seven feet away from her. The chain seemed to be long enough to reach. Could she do it quickly, and quietly enough not to rouse the sleeping madman who had his hand on the detonator?

Inch by inch, moving in a very stealthy manner, but also as quickly as possible, Crystal laid out the chain on the dirt floor of the cave. She worked to make sure none of the links clinked together. It was hard because her whole body was trembling in fear.

After five minutes of careful work, she had it laid out in a snaking line under the cot. She was ready to move toward Buddy.

Just as Crystal started to move, the killer stirred on the cot. He rolled from his side to his back, and then onto his other side. He was now facing away from them. She sat motionless for another five minutes, making sure he was still asleep before she started her move. By now, the killer had been out for about 50 minutes.

Crystal put one bare foot onto the sand of the cave floor, and in slow motion, brought her second foot around. She stopped. The killer did not move.

Moving a little quicker now, but still very deliberately, Crystal inched her way toward the sheriff. The chain snaked behind her, noiselessly.

With a deep breath, she reached down into the sheriff's right diving boot, and grasped the bone handle of the knife. She stared at the killer, her hand trembling. He did not move, he was still facing away from her.

She looked into Buddy's eyes. Now what?

His eyes went to the lock that held the chain to the iron bracket. He motioned with his head and eyes that she should pry it open. The killer had now been out for about 55 minutes.

Crystal was at a loss. She had never tried to pry open a lock before, especially when she would have to be totally silent. King nodded encouragement.

With another glance at the killer, she slipped the point of the knife into the lock and worked it back and forth, as quietly as possible. Her hands were shaking badly, and her eyes were on the sleeping killer, not the lock.

But amazingly the lock popped open. King smiled at her and motioned with his eyes to leave the lock in place and move to the second lock that held the chains tightly around his wrists. The killer had now been asleep for 57 minutes.

Buoyed by her silent success with the first lock, Crystal worked quickly, and the lock popped in a few seconds. King smiled at her again and motioned with his eyes to pop the locks holding his feet to the steel ring.

Crystal again stared at the sleeping killer, and then got down on her knees and quickly popped the remaining two locks. King again smiled at her and signaled with her eyes to put the knife back in his boot, and then get back to the cot. It had now been an hour.

Crystal carefully put the knife back in the boot, and slowly started moving back toward the cot. Her heart started to pound harder as she saw the killer begin to stir on his cot.

Her heart stopped when he started to roll over. She was still several feet from the cot. Thinking quickly, Crystal veered away from the cot, and headed for the wall as far away from sheriff King as possible. The chain clanked, but she didn't care.

The killer jumped up from the cot at the sound, and shouted, "What the hell's going on over there?"

Like a cat, he sprang off the cot, onto his feet, and was quickly at her side. His eyes bored holes into her skull, "I said what the hell's going on?"

Crystal stammered that she had to go to the bathroom and was trying to find a dark spot in the cave to relieve herself.

The killer's eyes went from her to sheriff King who was standing perfectly still, his chains clearly still in place.

Martin started to laugh, a cold, heartless laugh, "This is no time to worry about modesty. Just do it and get back to the cot."

On top of the cave, detective Richardson was plotting with his men. He had decided to send Deputy Johnson into the cave for some reconnaissance. It had been hours since Buddy King had entered the cave, and there had been no sounds from below. Although it was a risky move, Richardson decided he had to know what was going on, and since Johnson knew the cave well, he should be able to get close without being detected. Richardson looked at his watch, it was 2 a.m.

Johnson shrugged into his SCUBA gear and had one final conversation with Richardson. The veteran reminded Johnson that this was a mission to get information only, "you are not to confront the suspect, in fact, you must not be detected. We need to know what kind of set up he has. Is it just the suspect or are there more of them? What kind of weapons does he have? We need to know the condition of the sheriff and the captive too. Got it?"

Johnson nodded grimly, spit into his mask to keep it from fogging, wiped the glass, and put it tightly over his head. He silently slipped into the murky water and was gone.

Richardson stood on the shore and prepared to wait. There would be no contact with the deputy until he resurfaced.

The killer got Crystal back on the cot and decided that her chain was too long. He unlocked it, moved the lock until there was less than two feet of play in the chain. He told her to sit on the cot and shut up.

Martin again looked at the sheriff and seemed satisfied that he had not moved. King just stared straight ahead, avoiding any kind of eye contact with the killer. It was the same approach he had taken since he was initially shackled.

Deputy Johnson was a strong swimmer, and his bulging calf muscles quickly propelled him across the pond, until he was about 50 feet from the cave, based on his best guess.

He was wearing a black wetsuit, and a black skull cap. Johnson carefully rose toward the surface and raised his head just far enough out of the water, so his mask cleared the surface. He was nearly impossible to see from the shore.

Johnson saw a man taking a drink of bottled water. He was holding something in his right hand with a blinking red light.

The Deputy's eyes scanned to the left, and he could see Sheriff King against the wall of the cave with chains holding him in place. He looked a little farther left and saw Crystal chained to a steel-framed cot. Both of them had belts strapped to their waists with blinking red lights.

Without a ripple, Johnson ducked back under the water, to think about what he had just seen. The good news was they were both still alive, but it looked like a hopeless situation. He treaded water, his mind clicking off alternatives. He kept hearing detective Richardson in his ears – "just look and get back here. Do not let him know you were there."

Topside, a grizzled deputy named Bryson Cogburn, slowly walked over to detective Richardson. Cogburn had just awakened from a short nap, and he rubbed the sleep out of his eyes. He had an unfiltered Camel cigarette clamped in his yellowing teeth.

Richardson glanced up from his own thoughts as Cogburn neared, "What's up Dogman?" It was a nickname that fit Cogburn very well, as he had the sad eyes, and drooping jowls of an old bloodhound. His face was well weathered too.

Cogburn took a big drag on his cigarette, the red glow getting brighter in the evening darkness, "detective, I hear that you sent Johnson down there in that water."

Richardson nodded, wondering where this conversation was heading, "Yup, what of it?"

Cogburn took another deep drag and blew the smoke out his nose and mouth. He coughed a little from the effort, and said, "you work with him much?"

It was almost 4 in the morning, and Richardson had no patience, "Cogburn, what the hell you want to tell me? Spit it out man!"

Several hundred yards away, Johnson was still expertly treading water, as his mind wrestled with what to do. He was supposed to only gather info, but King and the girl were in big trouble. Maybe he could help them out, right now? His mind raced on.

Detective Richardson stepped close to the old deputy, and spat out the words this time, "I have no time for this bullshit Cogburn, what the hell do you want to say?"

The deputy threw the nub of his cigarette on the ground, and mashed it out with his boot, "well I just don't know if you know that Johnson is a bit of a renegade. He's had troubles following orders in the past, always wants to be the hero. He's a publicity hound too, always calling that newspaper reporter."

Richardson's heart caught in his throat, "are you serious? Goddammit why didn't somebody say something before?"

The deputy shrugged his bony shoulders, "don't know man, I just found out about it this minute, thought you'd want to know."

Richardson wearily nodded his head, "OK, thanks Dogman, I appreciate the info."

The killer put down the bottle of water and sat back down on the cot. He bit into a piece of beef jerky and pondered his next move. The quick nap had indeed been rejuvenating, and his head was clear, his body remarkably revived after just an hour of rest.

It was clear that his plan of hiding out in this cave undetected for weeks was not going to happen, not with all the heat waiting for him topside.

That's why he had hatched a new plan in his demented head. At about 7 this morning, in less than 3 hours, he would set the sheriff free from the wall. He'd put a SCUBA tank on him and send him out with instructions to bring an SUV to the shore, so he and the girl could leave.

He would warn them that she, and he would be strapped with explosives, and if they tried to take him the girl would blow up right along with him. He would leave the cave one hour after the sheriff, and every lawman must have put their weapons and car keys on the shore where he could see them and be standing together 200 yards from the shore.

He would tell them that any attempt to follow them and he would set off the explosives. Then he would drive away to his second hideout on Lake Athens. They would never find him there.

Of course, he would take the bracelet with the GPS system off the girl before they left.

While the killer was mulling Plan B, Deputy Johnson had also finished making his plans. He had decided to silently swim to the far-right side of the cave, out of sight of the suspect, and make a rush at him when the timing was right. He had decided he could not take a chance on letting this situation fester much longer, or both the sheriff and Crystal would surely be dead. And besides, after he pulled this off, he would be a big hero in all the media.

The only three media members onto the story were cooling their heels in the Henderson County Jail. They had tried to post bond, but the district attorney, stalling for as much time as possible, had decided to hold them until late morning not only for speeding, but for obstruction of justice for trying to follow the ambulance and the squad cars.

As Martin slowly chewed another bite of jerky, Johnson, as quietly, and as slowly as possible, neared the shore on the right side of the cave. He stuck his mask a few inches out of the water for a quick look. He was about 25 feet away from shore, and it was dark on that side of the cave. The suspect was sitting on a cot eating something.

Johnson moved forward very slowly as the water got shallower, he was pulling himself along using the sandy bottom. He stopped about 10 feet from shore.

Martin looked at his watch. It was nearly 5 in the morning. Two hours until he would send King out with his message.

46

Detective Richardson was even more anxious than before, if that was possible. He felt even more helpless. Now he'd inadvertently sent a loose cannon into the situation, and again he had no way to contact him. Richardson checked his watch, it was 5:15.

Martin checked his captives. It looked like the sheriff had fallen asleep, and that the girl was also asleep. Maybe he should take one more catnap. Another quick hour would set him up for a most exciting day ahead. He closed his eyes, the detonator in his left hand, and the pistol in his right.

Johnson slowly moved his head upward until his mask was barely out of the water. It looked like the suspect was sleeping. He couldn't believe his luck. Emboldened, he slowly swam the last ten feet to shore, and slowly, silently came out of the water. He was totally in the dark and undetected.

Johnson sat down and without a sound popped off his flippers and shrugged out of his tank and inflatable vest.

Sheriff King opened one eye, just a tad, just enough so he could see the killer. He was surprised to see that the man was once again taking a nap. Was this his chance?

King estimated that the suspect was about 50 feet away. That is a lot of ground to cover without being noticed. He wondered just how deep in sleep the suspect was?

Johnson was also plotting various moves in his head. He estimated that he was about 100 feet away from the suspect. Johnson was concerned, that's a lot of ground to cover without alerting the suspect, and Johnson had no weapon.

He could see the gun and detonator in the suspect's hands. Johnson was getting anxious. He knew he was running out of time. Soon detective Richardson would be concerned that this mission was taking too long and might send someone else down to take a look.

As King mulled over what to do, he had to consider the problem of the plastic explosives strapped to his, and Crystal's waists. He assumed that the suspect would have to push the button to set it off. If he did that before King could wrest the detonator away from him, they would all be dead. He couldn't risk using the knife to remove the belt from his waist. If the suspect woke up, he'd see that the sheriff was free from his chains and might shoot him on the spot. Still pondering what to do, something caught his eye, just past the sleeping suspect, in the shadows on the far side of the cave. Who the hell is that?

Detective Richardson was agitated, "Hurry up guys get that gear on, it's time to move in and see what the hell is going on." He had picked two of the best divers from his squad, even though they did not know anything about the cave. He'd had enough of being in the dark. Richardson had to know what was going on.

"I want you to check it out. That is all. Then, one of you stay there out of sight, and the other get your ass back here to me as quick as possible. I need information."

The two divers slipped into the water and disappeared in a sea of tiny bubbles.

Deputy Johnson decided to spring now. The man was sleeping. Johnson was agile and fast. He could get there before the suspect woke up, grab the gun and the detonator and end this standoff.

Sheriff King couldn't believe his eyes. The man was coming out of the shadows, walking very quickly, but silently toward the suspect. The killer did not move.

The man was about 5 feet away now, preparing to spring on the suspect. It looked like the man did not have a weapon. The suspect was sleeping with his head facing the sheriff, away from the approaching man.

The two sheriff's department divers were moving steadily toward the cave. They estimated that they were halfway there, about 50 yards away.

King tensed every muscle in his body, ready to spring at the right moment. Once the man pounced on the suspect, the sheriff would slip out of the chains, grab his knife from the boot and join the fray. Of course, that was if he didn't blow up first.

Deputy Johnson was now within three feet of the suspect. He thought to himself, this will be all over very quickly. He had no idea how quickly.

Suddenly, Martin rolled over and shot Johnson right in the chest. His Seal training had taught him to take these catnaps with his ears attuned to anyone approaching, even as he was sleeping.

Johnson shouted out, clutched his chest and fell backwards as the shot echoed loudly throughout the cave.

King had leaped out of his shackles, grabbed his knife and was in full stride toward the killer, who was faced away from him, looking at the deputy.

276

He was within two feet when Crystal awoke and started screaming, that caused the suspect to swivel around and point the gun right at the sheriff's chest.

But King was already on top of him and using his best old football tackling techniques to swat the gun out of the suspect's hand with his left hand, and to plunge the knife into Martin's shoulder, with his right, just missing his real target, the suspect's neck. With his left foot, King kicked the detonator out of the suspect's other hand, praying it would not set off the explosives.

The suspect clutched his shoulder with his left hand as the detonator slid along the sand-covered floor of the safe. It stopped about twenty feet away. Thankfully, nothing happened.

King was shocked by the strength of the suspect, who easily tossed him aside, and grabbed the knife out of his shoulder. King scrambled to his feet and dove for the gun which had landed about 30 feet away. The suspect let him have the gun and dove for the detonator instead.

They both reached their destinations at the same time.

The sheriff's department divers were startled to hear a gunshot and quickly surfaced. They could see the situation unfolding but were still about 30 yards from the shore. That made them helpless.

The suspect quickly flipped a switch on the detonator and two red lights started blinking. His evil eyes pierced the sheriff, "Nice try lawboy. But now if my hand goes off this detonator, KABOOM!"

King had the gun pointed at the suspect's head; they were less than ten feet apart. Blood was coming out the suspect's shoulder wound, but he seemed oblivious to it.

He kept his eyes on King, "Now put the gun on the ground, and move over to your girlfriend. That way you can blow up together. Drop it NOW!"

King quickly ran through the options in his head. It looked like he had no choice. Could he shoot the detonator and make it ineffective? No. He remembered from his FBI Academy training that such a move would set it off anyway.

With a big sigh, the sheriff slowly bent down and placed the gun on the ground. He slowly walked over to Crystal who was cowering on the cot, sobbing and trembling.

The killer kept his eye on both of them as he moved to a different section of the cave and opened a first aid kit with one hand. He flipped the "ready" switch off on the detonator so he could take his finger off the button. But he kept the detonator in his hand as he managed to wrap a bandage over his shoulder wound to stop the bleeding.

King held Crystal in his arms, trying to calm her down.

The two divers quickly swam back to shore and reported what they had seen to detective Richardson, "Johnson is dead, the sheriff and Crystal both have plastic explosives around their waists, and the suspect has the detonator." Richardson could only shake his head.

Martin was beyond angry, "Ain't that a touching scene. Listen to me. This is over. King you are going to put on this SCUBA tank and swim out of here. You will also keep the plastic explosives strapped on. You will park an SUV at the end of the pond and move all the cops back 200 yards from shore, but where I can see them. You will leave the SUV running, and it better be full of gas. I want you in the rear of the SUV with your hands handcuffed behind your back. I will give you one hour to set this up, then your honey and I will swim out of here, get into that car and drive away, with no one following us. Got it?"

Sheriff King's mind was whirling. He really had no choice. He liked the fact that he had an hour to come up with a counter plan. He also knew it would be hard for the suspect to swim with that deep knife wound in his shoulder.

Crystal was now trembling so hard, he thought she was going to pass out, or worse yet, have a heart attack. He took her face in both his hands, and stared into her eyes, "I am going to do what he says, it is the only way we're going to get out of here alive. Okay?"

Crystal's lips were trembling, as she muttered, "Okay."

Sheriff King strapped on the air tank and inflatable vest, a difficult task with the plastic explosives also wrapped around his waist. The suspect gave him another evil look, "One hour and we're coming out. You better have everything set up or the girl blows up."

The sheriff pulled on his swim fins, glanced back at Crystal one last time, pulled on his mask and disappeared into the dark, very murky water.

Detective Richardson was startled as sheriff King suddenly popped to the surface, just offshore. The dozen deputies who had pulled their guns put them away as they recognized King.

They helped him out of the water. The sheriff looked at his watch, he had 41 minutes before the killer was coming out with Crystal.

King pulled Richardson aside, and quickly filled him in on the situation. He also took Richardson's cell phone and dialed the cell phone number for his instructor at the national FBI Training Academy in Quantico, Virginia.

Meanwhile, detective Richardson started moving the lawmen, squad cars and ambulances back the requested 200 yards. He found an SUV with a full gas tank and parked it on the shore. They now had 24 minutes.

The killer was trying to calm Crystal down. They had to swim several hundred yards, and he could not risk having her panic and drown both of them. His Seal training was hard at work, as he used all the tricks to calm down a captive and prepare her for their journey to freedom.

Sheriff King strapped on a new air tank. He had a spear gun in his right hand. Detective Richardson had argued with him for several minutes, but finally gave up, "this is a crazy idea that will result in you blowing up all three of you." But the sheriff was adamant, "this is the only chance we have. If we let him go, Crystal is dead anyway, and we'll never find her."

The killer checked his watch. It was time. Crystal had calmed down a bit, and he helped her put on the inflatable vest and gave her fins. He'd already cut the bracelet and tossed into a dark part of the cave. He told her, in a most soothing voice, how they would swim out handcuffed together. They would inflate the vest a bit to stay on top of the water so the detonator would not get wet. He had to keep it dry and had wrapped it in plastic to give him time to make it to the surface. But he did not want to take any chances, so he wanted it to get it in the air above the water as quickly as possible. If she tried anything, he would use the gun in his other hand to shoot her.

Sheriff King glanced at his watch, less than ten minutes to go. He dove under the water and disappeared.

It was much more difficult to swim on the surface, than under the water, but Crystal was a strong swimmer, and she had little difficulty as they moved slowly forward. After a few minutes, they were halfway to the opposite shore. The killer could see the SUV sitting there, and no sign of any police anywhere. He allowed himself a small smile, a rarity, but he was pleased that his clear thinking, coupled with his Seal training, would allow him to complete still another mission.

47

Sheriff King was treading water about ten feet below the surface. He held his breath as much as possible, limiting the air bubbles popping to the surface. Suddenly he could hear the thrashing of feet in the water, but it was so dark and murky that he could not see the swimmers.

He inched slowly upward and now he could see the splashing of their feet, although it was still nearly impossible to see both of the swimmers. This was going to make the task very difficult.

King had found out, as he suspected, from his trainer at the FBI Academy, that the detonator would become harmless if he could get it very wet, very quickly.

While the murky water caused problems for the sheriff, it also worked in his favor, as the killer and Crystal could not see him either, as he inched closer and closer, his spear gun cocked and ready.

King guessed that Crystal would be on the right side, as the killer was right-handed and that would allow him to keep his gun ready to use on her, if need be.

Suddenly they were right on top of him, King saw the killer and fired the silent spear gun right toward the startled killer's heart. The sheriff quickly broke the surface and grabbed the detonator.

The suspect fired his gun and grazed Crystal's left arm. King dove as far down as fast as he could, ripping the plastic covering off the detonator. He took it to the bottom of the pond, and held it there, as water seeped into the guts of the device.

On the surface, the killer still had a grip on the gun, as he floated next to her, blood gushing from his spear gun wound that had missed his heart by inches. He was still handcuffed to Crystal.

She put her self-defense training to work as the killer gave her a wicked, cooked grin, and slowly raised the gun toward her, struggling against the pain from the spear. Crystal used her free hand to quickly snatch the bone-handled Scuba divers knife from the startled killer's belt.

In one motion, Crystal raised the knife and plunged it deep into the side of Martin's neck, directly into his carotid artery. His grin turned to a look of shock, anger and pain, as Martin realized his death was seconds away.

Crystal was still moving fast. She yanked the knife out of Martin's neck and slashed his wrist. The killer quickly dropped the gun as pain shot through his arm. It floated away in the murky water.

King used a small rope to tie his weight belt around the detonator so it would stay on the bottom of the pond as the water rushed in, making it harmless.

He quickly swam back to the surface and grabbed Crystal. He could see the blood streaming out of her wounded arm. The killer was floating face down in the water. He was dead.

The sheriff noticed the gaping wound in Martin's neck. Is that where the spear had gone? It looked more like a knife wound. The killer also appeared to have a deep slash on his wrist.

Other divers from the sheriff's department quickly swam to their aid. They grabbed the dead suspect, while King used his handcuff keys to free her from Martin's side.

Sheriff King and another deputy helped Crystal swim to shore. Her eyes were wide, she was clearly out of breath, but King noticed a satisfied look on her face.

He looked deep into her eyes, his own heart racing from the exertion of the attack, and with fear that Crystal might have been easily killed by the mad man, "You okay, honey?"

Crystal had caught her breath by this time, and gave him a small grin, "Yeah no thanks to you. You're not much of a shot with that spear gun Buddy."

"Huh?"

"You just grazed him, I had to grab his knife and stab him in the neck before he shot me!"

At that point they reached shallow water so they could stand up. King grabbed Crystal by the arms, his eyes seemed terrified, "What? Are you telling me while I was getting rid of that bomb, you're the one who killed that bastard?"

"That's right," Crystal said, "I guess those self-defense classes really paid off for me."

King shook his head again, "What self-defense classes?"

Crystal smiled at Buddy, "Lover there is a lot about me that you haven't found out yet."

He smiled back and held her tight as they walked out of the pond arm in arm to a standing ovation from the other law enforcement officers gathered on shore.

ABOUT THE AUTHOR

Jim Willi is a retired longtime partner in a media consulting company, and advisor to dozens of TV stations, as well as CNN and MSNBC. Prior to becoming a consultant, he won two EMMYs and numerous other awards as a radio and TV anchor/reporter, news director and TV general manager. He's enjoyed the Cedar Creek Lake lifestyle for over two decades.

Made in the USA
Middletown, DE
06 November 2020